P9-BIT-575

Dear Reader,

I am so thrilled to be launching my Special Investigations Group series with HQN. The series follows a group of special agents working for the California Department of Justice. Considered the "best of the best," they investigate challenging or high-profile cases all over the state, lending support to other law enforcement agencies. I'm particularly excited that this series found a home with HQN, a line dedicated to bringing a deeply emotional and sexy romance to its readership. I love exploring the darker aspects of humanity but only as a contrast to romantic elements that shed light on our capacity for hope, redemption and love.

Writing about a blind heroine obviously presented its challenges but enabled me to stretch my understanding of those with disabilities, both physical and emotional. I enjoyed bringing together Mac and Natalie, two courageous characters who are larger than life but ultimately incomplete without each other. I hope you enjoy their story!

Wishing you much love and happiness always,

Virna DePaul

VIRNA DePAUL

SHADES OF DESIRE

HQN™

Recycling programs
for this product may
not exist in your area.

ISBN-13: 978-0-373-77635-1

SHADES OF DESIRE

Copyright © 2012 by Virna DePaul

This edition published by arrangement with Harlequin Books S.A.

For questions and comments about the quality of this book
please contact us at Customer_eCare@Harlequin.ca.

www.Harlequin.com

Printed in U.S.A.

Acknowledgments

In the past few years I've grown as a writer and a person. Neither would have been possible without the support of my agent, Holly Root, and my editor, Margo Lipschultz. Thank you for believing in me and for making my work better. I appreciate all the hard work of Harlequin's superb art, sales and editorial staff, and all the insight I've received from various law enforcement officials and friends. To all my readers, you'll never know how much your support means—thank you! Finally, as always, much love to my boys!

SHADES OF DESIRE

CHAPTER ONE

PLAINVILLE WAS A QUAINT picturesque town. Northern California's version of Andy Griffith's Mayberry. Bucolic enough to provide cinematic contrast for any low-budget stalk-and-slash film. Juxtaposition played just as important a role in still photography as it did in cinematography. Maybe that's why Natalie Jones had picked Plainville for her final descent into darkness.

The climactic scene in a comedic tragedy. Cast of one. Audience of one.

Curtain closed.

For now, however, she enjoyed one last intermission.

She could pretend she'd never heard the words *retinal degeneration*. Pretend the darkness wasn't coming for her. Pretend she was just a normal woman whiling away a morning at the local farmers' market, perusing the organic fruit and vegetables and enjoying a sense of community.

When she spotted one of the horse cops that occasionally circled the market, she resolutely lifted her camera and snapped its picture. Doing so, however, made pretending impossible.

She wasn't normal. In truth, she never had been.

She could appreciate the imposing size of the animal,

see its general shape and movements, knew it was a typical chestnut brown. But even with a super-magnified lens, she couldn't see the bunching muscles moving underneath the horse's skin, distinguish the leather saddle that had been placed on its back from the blanket that was likely underneath it, or say with certainty that its rider was a man as opposed to a large woman.

Pressing her lips together, she lowered the camera and blinked back the threat of tears.

The saying's true, she thought. Bigger wasn't always better—not if she couldn't see the details on a twelve-hundred pound equine. Still, it was better than nothing.

With a snort of disgust, she started walking again, making sure to keep her head up and her strides slow. But not too slow.

She passed a grove of redwood trees to her right, then paused again when the bright rays of the sun unexpectedly shone through them, momentarily blinding her. Her mouth curled with irony just before she closed her eyes and lifted her face toward the sky, relishing the subtle warmth that spread across her skin. She'd have to recall this moment in darker times. Store it along with her memories of other places that had brought her peace.

The Seine in France.

The winding mountain trails in Switzerland.

The dirt roads in Malaysia that were bordered on either side by the lush green of the tropical jungle.

The memories would help hide her grief.

Hide.

It was a term she'd become quite familiar with. A skill she'd honed to near perfection.

She'd spent so many years dreading what might be coming that, no matter how much fear and panic she felt inside, her outward appearance rarely reflected it. Now that the disease was no longer possibility but reality, her ability to hide her feelings would give her something precious. Control, yes, but even more important than that—dignity. Unlike her mother, she'd face her fate with grace and wouldn't allow her situation to defeat or destroy her. And it wouldn't matter that she faced her future alone, either. Alone was better, even if she'd forgotten that for a while.

Her thoughts automatically turned to Duncan Oliver. Despite the rays of light still shining on her face, she shivered and pulled her sweater closer to her body.

Why, in addition to everything else, did she have to feel so cold all the time?

Nothing—not coffee, not the warmth of a fire, not even an electric blanket—could quite cut through the chill that had settled inside her ever since Duncan had come to her two weeks ago, his expression tense yet resolute, saying they needed to talk.

"I'm sorry, Natalie. I love you, but—but I can't handle this. I can't bear to see you go through this," he'd said.

At the time, Natalie had barely stopped herself from crying. "But you *can* bear for me to go through it alone? When going through it alone will make it a hundred times worse?" Forget a hundred. Try a thousand. A hun-

dred thousand. But of course she hadn't said the words
out loud. Instead, she'd moved on. And that's exactly
what she'd keep doing.

With a sigh, she opened her eyes, blinked until her
vision went from fuzzy to less fuzzy, then started walking again. In the background, she could hear Pete, a
local who'd served in several wars, only to return home
and lose his wife to cancer, calling out his doomsday
predictions and political rhetoric. The cops would tol-
erate it only until it got more crowded, then they'd start
to gently nudge him along.

She moved toward him with deliberation, taking
care to avoid stepping in anyone's path. The market had
just opened, so there weren't the throngs of people that
would descend upon the park in a little more than two
hours. By then, she'd be long gone, editing her photos
on her computer with the help of a magnified screen,
trying not to judge them too harshly or dwell on the fact
they were going to be some of the last she ever took.

She stumbled when something brushed against her
lower legs, and she automatically reached down, her
hands sinking in a soft thatch of fur. She laughed, the
husky sound surprising her. "Hey there, sweetie," she
crooned and patted the dog until its owner whistled
and it loped away.

Her smile didn't fade for several minutes, and she
savored the unexpected feeling of contentment. When
she reached Pete, he stopped addressing the crowd to
greet her. "Hello, pretty Natalie."

She smiled again at the familiar greeting. Pete was

unfailingly polite to her whenever they met. He always recognized her, and it amazed her how his mind could flip from delusional to rational in the blink of an eye. "Hi, Pete. How are you feeling today?"

"Right as rain. Don't be afraid. Things are going to work out just fine."

"Thanks, Pete. I appreciate that." She dropped a five-dollar bill into his basket and kept moving, oddly moved by his words of good tiding. They were the same he always said to her, easily dismissed most of the time. But today, she clung to them.

Despite the progression of the disease, she could still see. Still work. Perhaps Pete was right and things really would work out fine.

She'd already provided *Plainville* magazine hundreds of photos for its feature on the renovation of its downtown district. The unusually sunny day, however, would make the farmers' market shots a nice touch. Although far from crowded, there were still several people wandering about. Some of them moved so quickly that their bodies were a kaleidoscope of blurred colors. When they slowed down and she got close enough, however, she could classify them—businesspeople, couples, families.

She circled the park several times, framing shots and repeating them until she got them just right. Several times, when objects or individuals gave her a particular feeling, heightened by setting or, where she could see it, facial expression, she mentally gave the shots a title to go along with the image. It was a habit she'd adopted in Dubai, and it had stuck ever since.

The shot of the petite dark-haired woman tilting her head as she laughed with the silver-haired man beside her, her hand on his arm, was "Joy."

The one of the three women walking together, two of them huddled closer than the third, who walked with her arms crossed, was "Left Out."

And the one of a man leaning against a tree, his head turned toward a nearby playground, something that looked like a video camera in his hand, she dubbed "Watcher."

An older woman walked by, her expression solemn, but she immediately smiled when the baby in her arms blew raspberries on her neck. The distinctive scents of baby shampoo and formula were a faint tickle on the breeze as they passed. Unable to resist, Natalie turned to keep the baby in her vision, hazy as it was, for as long as possible. It wasn't very long.

In the bustle of the now-growing crowd, Pete's chatter drifted toward her again. "Not what you think…he's blinded you…"

Frowning, she turned her head, then gasped when she ran into something hard.

Strong fingers grasped her arms to steady her. "Whoa there, little lady. You should watch where you're going."

Natalie's brows shot up in automatic annoyance. *Little lady?* He'd sounded sincere if a little distracted. Tilting her head up, she squinted her eyes, but because he was backlit by the sun, she saw even less of him than she normally would. He was tall and smelled of tobacco, but there was another scent competing with it, as if he'd doused himself with cologne in an attempt to hide his vice. He was wearing some kind of hat. Given his words and the faintest hint of a Texan accent, she'd guess a cowboy hat, but there was some kind of colorful design on it, a blur of gold that looked like a diamond.

Forcing her mingled embarrassment and annoyance down, she said, "I apologize," and walked around him. Pete was shouting now, and she winced when he accused someone of being a hypocrite. A charlatan. It was when Pete started addressing individuals that the police finally cracked down on him. This time she stopped before turning. Pete was pointing at a couple, and several people had stopped to watch.

"Don't give him what he wants," Pete shrieked. "Go home! Go home. Go—"

A figure approached him. "All right, Pete. That's enough. Come along now." The voice was kind but also held the ring of authority. Definitely a cop. Sure enough, Pete's voice quieted, then disappeared altogether as the cop led him away. The crowd dispersed.

She wondered whether the cop would simply escort Pete to the edge of the park or drop him off at his mobile home several blocks away. She'd been there once, to offer her help. She knew the cops had offered their help, as well. Pete graciously shunned all such attempts.

She started walking again, but Pete and his accusations played through her mind. When she heard children laughing and the sound of water, she shook off her distraction. She was approaching the park fountain. Since it would make a nice final shot, she quickened her pace.

With no warning, she felt pain explode behind her eyes. She saw an intense flash of light before her remaining vision tunneled.

Her hands, which had been lightly gripping her camera, jerked violently, snapping the strap around her neck. Vaguely, she heard the camera hit the ground in front of her. Then her other senses seemed to go haywire. Her hearing faded. Her fingers went numb. Her already cool skin seemed to ice over with realization. But there was none of the detachment she'd hoped for. None of the calm acceptance she'd been slowly hoarding for almost twenty years.

Nowhere to hide.

"No," she whispered. "Not now. Please, not now."

Just like that, Natalie's world had gone completely dark.

CHAPTER TWO

Eight weeks later...

A THERAPIST ONCE TOLD Liam "Mac" McKenzie to distract himself when images of death plagued him. For a homicide detective and recovering alcoholic, that had been about as helpful as her advice to schedule a regular date night with his wife, which was why he was now divorced. Interestingly, the end of his marriage hadn't tempted him to drink any more than it had made him consider giving up his job, something his wife had demanded. He supposed both were telling—about how little Nancy had known him and how little his marriage had truly mattered.

In the end, there would be no distracting death. It was in his blood, just as being a cop was in his blood—he couldn't have one without the other. Whether it was due to talent or sheer stubbornness, Mac had an uncanny knack for tracking down killers who almost got away with their crimes.

The same had been true for his father. And his father's father. In fact, almost every male McKenzie in the past five generations had been cops. Divorced ones. Yeah, on one hand it sucked, but it seemed a small price to pay for bringing justice to victims who couldn't seek it out themselves.

He'd spent a decade in homicide investigation at the city level before joining the California Department of Justice's elite Special Investigations Group, aka the SIG Unit. Now, he basically did the same job, just with a different title, broader authority, better pay and more flexible hours.

"Hey, McKenzie. How's it going?"

Mac glanced up, grinning when he saw Greg Hilbourn, a buddy of his from the San Francisco Police Department's Homicide Division. Standing, Mac extended his hand. "Working, which is what you should be doing. What brings you to DOJ?"

Hilbourn shook his hand and took a moment to look around Mac's office. "You've really moved up, Mac. Your own office. Your own team of hotshots. What's next? Upper management?"

Mac snorted. "You're kidding, right? The brass would laugh their asses off if they ever saw my name on the interview list. Besides, someone's gotta make them look good on the streets."

"They'd laugh because they wouldn't believe it. They know you'd be bored out of your mind if you had to sit behind that desk too long."

"There is that. I've gotta check in with my commander in a few, but have a seat." Mac waved to the small sofa in front of his desk. When Hilbourn complied, Mac asked, "So what brings you by?"

"I was wondering if you have any openings on your team."

Leaning back in his chair, Mac lightly pressed the fingers of one hand against those of the other to form a steeple. "Everything okay at SFPD? Kilpatrick still busting your ass?"

"Never fails. You know I can handle it but—" A shadow came over Hilbourn's face. "Lately, even the streets are starting to feel confining. I need some breathing room. Your team works all over the state and with different agencies. It's exactly what I need right now."

Mac frowned. Though SIG was headquartered in San Francisco, it was rare for his special agents to be in the office more than a few days a week. The inherent variety and constant travel kept things interesting. But last he knew, Hilbourn loved working for the SFPD and wouldn't want to travel far from his wife and children. Something had changed, and since Hilbourn was still with SFPD, that meant—

"Something going on with you and Sandy?" he asked.

Sure enough, Hilbourn's mouth twisted. "She moved out. Took the kids with her. Said she's fed up with all the long nights and moody silences."

"I'm sorry, man. I really am," Mac said. And he was. If any cop could've made his marriage work, Mac would have put odds on Hilbourn.

Hilbourn shrugged. "You and Nancy still…?"

Mac shook his head. "The divorce has been final for a while." If Hilbourn's wounds weren't so fresh, Mac might have said splitting with Sandy was for the best. It had been that way for Mac but not for completely selfish reasons. Nancy was a good woman. She'd find someone else, someone who'd be able to put her first. Chances were, Sandy would, too.

"Do you miss her?" Hilbourn asked, unable to hide his grief.

Mac hesitated before answering, but it was a hesitation born out of guilt rather than indecision. His instinctive response seemed unfair to the woman he'd once loved enough to marry, but he answered truthfully anyway. "I miss someone being there when I get home sometimes, but I don't miss her."

"So you think it's worth what we do?" Hilbourn asked. "Being alone? Sacrificing what comes to others so naturally?"

Mac shifted in his seat. It wasn't as if he and Hilbourn were best buds who'd swapped personal war stories over the years. But he knew the guy was hurting, so he tried to give him an encouraging answer. "I don't know."

He knew the job, inside and out. He knew what it took to satisfy it. And he knew he was capable of giving it. No false expectations or disappointments. Just follow the clues. Close the case. Move on to the next. Made life less complicated, but was that worth the isolation? "Maybe it's just a matter of finding someone strong enough to handle what we do. A woman who can take care of herself." Since Mac had never met such a woman, he really didn't believe what he was saying; from the expression on Hilbourn's face, he knew it.

"Right." Hilbourn cleared his throat. "So about that opening?"

Wincing, Mac said, "I'm sorry. We're filled up right now, but I'll let you know if I hear anything."

The other man closed his eyes briefly before standing. "Yeah, I figured. Thanks, Mac. You working anything fun right now?"

Mac picked up a stack of files and stood, as well. He clapped Hilbourn on the shoulder as he walked beside him. "Never a dull moment."

Taking the stairs to the commander's office, which was several floors up, Mac considered the truth of those words. The cases his team handled were some of the most complicated, which made the job interesting and challenging. But Hilbourn's question about what they were giving up gave him pause. He couldn't do the job forever—none of them could. What would happen once he was handed his retirement papers? Would he still think the absence of complications had been worth it?

Mac gave a mental shrug. Worth it or not, he'd have solved a lot of cases. Helped a lot of people.

Just as he was going to help the Monroe family. First, however, he had to notify Commander Stevens that the missing persons investigation was now a homicide case.

A few minutes later, he was in the commander's office. "We've got a positive ID on those skeletal remains," he said, handing Stevens the medical examiner's report. "And the news isn't what her father was hoping for."

Stevens grunted as he flipped through the report. "He wanted to rule out his daughter as the vic, and instead he got scientific proof she was buried like a piece of trash two hours away from where they lived. Sixteen years old. At least now he knows. A lot of parents don't get that closure."

Last month, when two fishermen had found a skeleton near the edge of a river in Redding, the chances of finding out the victim's identity, at least without significant time and cost to the state, had been slim. That had been before the governor's former college roommate had asked him to rush the tests.

Too bad Monroe's relationship with the governor wasn't going to get him his daughter back.

"Anything else?" Stevens asked.

"Trace DNA on a patch of orange fabric found with the vic. There was the victim's blood, but there were also a couple of hair fibers. We got a hit on an Arizona parolee named Alex Hanes who absconded from parole almost a year ago."

"Did you call the FBI about getting a UFAP warrant?"

"Sure did," Mac confirmed. Now any non-Arizona cop, including any member of SIG, could arrest Hanes for unlawful flight. "I'm not counting on an arrest happening anytime soon, though."

"So what *are* you counting on?"

"I've talked to Monroe and the rest of Lindsay's family. We've got her computer in forensics, and I'm going through the items we collected from her room. Her journal reveals she met a 'new friend' shortly before she ran away, one she referred to only as 'M.'"

"Nothing on her computer so far?"

"It's going to take a few days." Maybe even more, Mac thought. As a state agency, the Department of Justice had well-trained staff and state-of-the-art forensics equipment, but it experienced just as much backlog as the county departments. No matter how hard they worked, the good guys always scrambled to keep up with the bad ones.

"So what was Hanes in for?"

"Everything from drug use and sales to rape and attempted murder. He's spent fifteen of the last sixteen years in prison." It wasn't the worst rap sheet Mac had seen during his career, but it gave them ample reason to view Hanes as their number one suspect.

"Anything with underage girls?" Stevens asked absently as he continued to read the medical examiner's report.

Mac swiped one hand over his face, trying to remember when talking about pedophilia and murder would have last fazed him. Five years ago? Ten? "No minors on his sheet," he said. "He raped a twenty-four-year-old. Doesn't mean he's not good for Lindsay Monroe."

Stevens looked up and grunted. "At least it's a start. You've racked up an impressive success rate over the past six months, Mac. Let's hope your winning streak holds true on this one."

Mac knew Stevens's words weren't meant as a challenge, but Mac still viewed them as one. Every case he took on was a challenge. And Mac never lost a challenge.

Not without one helluva fight.

"Don't worry, sir. I've got a great team, and I won't hesitate to ask for help from any of them if I need it. We'll find Hanes. And if he's not Lindsay Monroe's killer, we'll find the person who is."

CHAPTER THREE

NATALIE PUNCHED IN THE KEYPAD CODE to her home's front entrance, pushed the door slightly open, and turned to Joanna. She forced herself to smile again. "Thanks for the ride. I'll see you in two weeks."

"Take care, Natalie."

She stepped inside, shut the door, then leaned back against it, sighing with relief. Although she always took a cab to her appointment, Joanna often gave her a ride home after therapy. Today, however, she'd suggested they stop at a nearby restaurant for dinner. It was the last thing Natalie had wanted to do, but had she said so? Of course not. Instead, she'd pasted a smile on her face, endured the small talk and pretended to enjoy the "treat" out.

Now, as she absorbed the comfort of being inside her own home, the tightness in her chest loosened. The air felt as it should. She knew exactly where she was and how everything was supposed to look. Everything was in its place. There were no surprises lurking around every corner. Most of all, she could move freely, without having to wonder how she appeared to others or what they were thinking about her.

Freedom to be exactly who she was rather than what her disability made her.

She took in several deep breaths, wondering what Joanna would suggest next in her attempt to encourage Natalie's return to civilized society. For a long time, Joanna and Bonnie, Natalie's adaptive coach, had agreed that Natalie should stay home and take ample time to adjust, but lately Joanna—

She frowned.

Something, she wasn't sure what, smelled…different. She turned her head to the left, toward the hallway that led to the kitchen and office, but all she heard was the faint hum of the refrigerator. All she saw were the hazy gray blobs that amounted to what was left of her vision now.

After that day at the farmers' market when her vision had shorted out completely, she'd assumed it was permanent. But afterward, hints of light had started to break through her lids again. Her blindness had seemed to reverse itself, but only to the degree that she could see shadows and sometimes even shapes. It was barely anything, nothing like the blurry but still precious colorized vision she'd had days before. She wasn't sure if it was a small reprieve to be thankful for or a cruel trick meant to prolong her suffering.

Turning, she took several steps to the right, then paused. She'd meant to make more iced tea before leaving for her therapy appointment. She retraced her steps to the front door, then proceeded past it toward the kitchen.

That's when she heard it. A faint dragging sound from down the hall. Coming from the direction of her office. What the—

She moved forward to investigate. Was past the kitchen and halfway to the office when a flicker of movement disturbed the shadows in front of her. An instant later, she heard the breathing.

Someone was inside the house with her.

There was fear, yes. Plenty of it. But to her surprise, what she felt most of all was anger.

"Who's there?" she called.

"Don't be afraid," a low, husky male voice replied. Shadows flickered again as he stepped closer.

She took several steps back, but he followed, his shadow getting bigger. More ominous. Another burst of fear penetrated her anger, but she raised her chin, keeping her gaze steadily in his direction. "Get out," she whispered.

He didn't move.

"Get out!" She screamed it this time. "Get—"

"Shut up," he hissed.

She turned and lunged in the direction of her front door. She heard his heavy footsteps careening after her.

"Damn it, stop. Where do you think you're going?"

Pain exploded in her temple, knocking her off her feet. She landed on her stomach, hit her face against the hardwood floor, and felt warmth trickling out of her nose. She shook her head, trying to clear it.

"I'm sorry, but I have to protect God's kingdom. I have to know for sure."

Jerkily, she picked herself up, swayed to her feet and tried once again to get to the door. "Bastard, get out of my—"

He hit her again, then again.

Sucking in a breath, she fought the pain in her skull. When he wrapped his hands around her throat, fear—no longer a trickle, but a tidal wave—washed away everything else.

He dragged her up and shoved her against the wall until her toes barely touched the ground. Mercilessly, he squeezed the breath out of her. She fought anyway, kicking out at him, but she was unable to put any real strength behind it. Her fingers clawed at his, but she couldn't get enough air.

She felt his breath on her face, hot and desperate. He kept talking to her, kept saying he was sorry even as his fingers tightened.

The eyes, she told herself. The eyes are the most vulnerable part of the body.

With an image of the Three Stooges flashing in her mind, she reached out with her pointer and middle fingers separated and stiffened, and aimed for his face. Somehow she managed to hit her mark. He howled.

He released her and she swayed, disoriented by the sudden relief of pressure. He was in front of her, blocking the front door, so she scrambled in the opposite direction, toward her bedroom. Anywhere that she could get away from him.

He grabbed her arm and she screamed. He hit her once. Twice. She staggered back and slammed into the wall. Heard glass break. Kicked out at him and connected. She heard him grunt and fall hard. Managed to keep moving.

She made it into her bedroom, slammed the door shut and locked it. Then, before she could even reach the phone, she shouted, "The police are coming. I'm calling 911."

She shouted the warning again and again while she managed to dial 911. The operator came on, asking what the emergency was. She croaked out, "Help me. Someone—someone's in my house."

The woman's voice came again, prodding her for more information, and she tried to answer. But her voice faltered, and she could barely keep her grip on the receiver.

The pain in her head and throat was fading.

Pure blackness was closing in.

She heard another voice in the distance.

Heard thumps against her bedroom door.

Renewed terror battled for dominance in her waning consciousness.

And then, once more, she surrendered to the dark.

CHAPTER FOUR

KILLING THE ENGINE to his car, Mac studied the large mission-style home located in one of Plainville's most prestigious neighborhoods, about an hour south of where Lindsay Monroe's remains had been found. Natalie Jones, the house's owner, was a victim herself, but unlike Lindsay, she'd somehow managed to escape her attacker.

"Nice place." Beside him, Jase Tyler, the tall, lanky Texan with sandy-brown hair, a slow drawl and a steely mind for details and faces, whistled. He was the newest member of SIG, the only one besides Mac who hadn't served in the military. Of the five of them, Mac mused, he was also the most easygoing and charming—not to mention the most fashion-forward man Mac knew who wasn't actually a full-blown metrosexual. But that was only until he was crossed. Then Jase was as focused and lethal as the rest of the team. Screw his expensive suit and tie—he'd be the first to jump into the fray and get his hands dirty.

Right now, however, he looked completely impressed and not a little envious of the house's owner. "Taking pictures must pay a lot more than I thought it did."

"Natalie Jones can afford to buy a dozen houses like

this," Mac said. "Celebs paid her the big bucks to photograph everything from their houses to their dogs. Her
photos were regularly in *Architectural Digest*."

"Well, thanks in advance for asking me to come
along. Can we get a tour before we pull out the old
spotlight and bamboo shoots?"

Mac snorted. Despite the fact SIG members were
based in San Francisco and normally worked their cases
alone, Mac had asked Jase to take the two-hour drive
up with him. Given evidence found in Natalie Jones's
home last night, it looked like Lindsay Monroe's killer
and Natalie's attacker might be the same person. Even
so, it always helped to have a second set of eyes scour-
ing the evidence. More important, Jase would create
a buffer between Mac and the woman he was far too
anxious to meet.

After getting the call from Plainville PD about the attack on Natalie Jones, Jase hadn't researched the woman
or her website the way Mac had. Thankfully, Jase also
had no idea how unsettled Mac had been by what he'd
found, or that his odd reaction had prompted him to
bring Jase along in the first place.

Of course, Mac would go to his grave before admit-
ting that.

As SIG's lead special agent, Mac prided himself on
maintaining a reputation for unshakable calm and ruthless focus. He never let his emotions get the better of
him, not even when Nancy had walked. That a stranger,
one he hadn't even met in person, had such an impact
on him was disconcerting, to say the least. He'd been

curious about how Jase would react to her. Even better, he had no doubt Natalie Jones would quickly spill whatever information she had about Lindsay, if any, as soon as she fell under Jase's spell.

Not that Mac wouldn't be able to ferret the information out or was incapable of putting on the charm to do so. But, while Mac was hardly ugly, he knew his limitations. Serious, intense and impatient usually held little appeal next to Jase's suave charm and "aw-shucks-ma'am," golden-boy looks. And right now, he just wanted to get in, do his duty, while at the same time satisfying his curiosity about Natalie Jones, and get out. "Simple, uncomplicated and unfettered" was his new motto for his personal life, and nothing about the photographer's photos or face even hinted at any of those things.

Unaware of Mac's thoughts, Jase focused on Mac's use of the past tense. "Her photos are no longer in *A.D.* or she just doesn't get the big bucks anymore?"

"Neither, as far as I can tell," Mac murmured. He flipped through the pages he'd printed from the internet. "Her career was skyrocketing when she suddenly vanished from the public eye. She completely stopped taking pictures around the same time Lindsay was murdered."

"Coincidences are rare, but they do exist."

"They do." But Mac would reserve judgment.

"So you're thinking Lindsay and Natalie's sabbatical are related? And what about the guy that tried to kill her?"

Mac stared at a grainy picture of Natalie Jones and recalled the details he'd read in Plainville Police Officer Munoz's report. Yesterday, she'd walked in on a burglary in progress, and, after a brief struggle, the man had tried to strangle her. Somehow she'd managed to escape long enough to call 911. When they'd searched her place, officers had found a broken chain and cross pendant on the ground. Natalie Jones had denied ownership, and it had been logged into evidence.

At least now they had reason to believe Alex Hanes, the source of trace DNA on Lindsay Monroe's remains, was still in California. That was assuming three things, of course. First, that the cross pendant had actually belonged to Lindsay. Second, that the pendant had been taken by Hanes. Third, that Hanes had kept the pendant with him until he'd burglarized the house in front of them.

Assumptions weren't ideal, but they were a starting point, and he'd take anything he could get. Moreover, given the unique inscription on the pendant, which had immediately registered a hit on DOJ's Automated Stolen Property system, the first assumption was more like a sure thing. Time would tell whether the pendant contained any trace DNA by Hanes or anyone else besides Lindsay.

After the patrol officers had secured the scene, detectives had arrived within the hour and canvassed the neighborhood, but no one had seen or heard anything. Mac had immediately made plans to drive the two hours north from San Francisco to Plainville. In the meantime, he'd gotten up to speed on Natalie Jones. What he'd learned was far too much and far too little.

He'd barely started to explore the portfolio on her website before concluding she deserved the big bucks she'd been paid. It didn't seem to matter what she was photographing. How unimportant the person or place seemed to be. Each of her photographs exuded a feeling, whether it was joy or fear, passion or grief. She clearly didn't shy away from emotion, and consequently she made sure that anyone viewing her photographs couldn't shy away either.

The press had raved about her work, as well as her travels, which had taken her from one side of the world to the other. From that alone, he'd expected her to be unique. Then he'd clicked on her bio page.

While the person who'd taken the photo hadn't been as talented as her, the picture still managed to transmit Natalie Jones's essence. What should have been a two-dimensional image of an attractive woman with light eyes, honey brown hair and a clear, olive complexion seemed instead to be a deliberate tease, a small sample of an edgy passion almost too strong to be contained, yet one that hinted at even more beneath the surface. Staring at her image was almost as painful as staring at her work, except in a completely different way.

Her image had electrified him. It still did.

No shock there.

He'd dated since his divorce. Slept with women. Even cared for them. But it was the intensity of his reaction to Natalie Jones's picture that was so mind-blowing. Especially because he wanted to feel it again and again, even as he dreaded doing so.

Still, Jase was right. Despite the correlation between her becoming a hermit and the timing of Lindsay's death, the most likely answer was coincidence. That she'd just been in the wrong place at the wrong time when their perp decided to commit a burg.

It was his job to find out for sure.

Unfortunately, something was making him hang back. A feeling that if he got out of this car, he was going to walk head-on into the very complications he wanted to avoid.

He glanced at Jase, who was staring at him with an odd look on his face. "Sorry. You asked whether I think Natalie Jones's disappearing act is connected to the timing of Lindsay's murder? Not in the sense that she had anything to do with it, but I've little to nothing to back that up. Plus I've been wrong a time or two." He grinned. "Barely. But it wasn't a random burglary. Nothing was disturbed. The guy was after something specific, which means he picked her for some reason— the question is why. Come on." Mac swung open his car door and stepped out. He strode up the walkway, Jase close behind.

"You get in touch with Hanes's parole officer to tell her about the pendant?"

"I'm going to try her again later today."

"And what about the results of the neighborhood sweep?"

"The detective in charge, Samuel Carillo, said he

faxed me all the reports. They talked to all the neighbors, and no one saw or heard anything unusual. Most residents are working age. Few retirees or families."

"Well, SIG's all about taking on the tough cases. Good thing you brought me along."

Mac snorted.

"You said no more than an hour," Jase reminded Mac. "I want to get back to the office before dinnertime. I've got a date and don't want to be late."

Mac didn't blink at Jase's words, but he couldn't help wondering who Jase's latest flame was. The last woman he'd dated had been an NFL cheerleader. The one before that, a model. He liked them gorgeous, feminine and high-maintenance. The kind of women that deferred to men so often they pretty much forgot how to think for themselves. It was no surprise when, inevitably, Jase started to grumble about the demands his ladies made.

At some point, the piper came calling, demanding payment.

Mac, while he enjoyed an occasional splurge now and then, had gotten used to single life, unencumbered and debt-free. No mood swings to deal with. No neediness or anger when he couldn't drop everything at work and rush home to be at another person's beck and call.

Even so, by the time they reached the house porch, Mac's muscles were tight with anticipation.

He couldn't deny it. He was curious to see if he felt the same punch in the gut when he met Natalie Jones in person. Most of all, however, he was charged up, feeling that same rush of adrenaline through his veins that hit him whenever he worked a case and knew he was on the verge of an important discovery.

Lifting his hand to knock, he paused and frowned. Loud music with a deep, rock bass drifted through the solid front door, but he heard something else, as well. Thumps. An occasional low moan, as if someone was in pain. It made his eyes narrow. His pulse pick up speed. His breaths escalate.

Even so, he remained cool. Calm. His knuckles rapped the wood, and he called out, "Hello? Ms. Jones?"

MOST PEOPLE HATED exercising, but to Natalie, running on her treadmill in the privacy of her own home while listening to the music on her iPod speakers was as close to heaven as she'd been in over three months. Given her blindness, heaven was motion and speed and power without fear of repercussions, like running smack-dab into anything from a tree to a brick wall to a Mack truck. Moreover, given what had happened yesterday, heaven was repetition and rhythm and exertion that diluted the sheer terror she'd experienced when she'd realized someone was inside her house.

Her sanctuary. Her haven from prying eyes.

Anger flashed through her at the memory, but it competed with her lingering fear. The fear was winning. Story of her life, but she supposed, in this case, who could blame her?

She still smelled him: sweat, coffee and desperation edged with something else.

She still felt his fingers, tightening around her throat, too strong to escape.

And she still heard his voice, measured at first, then more ragged as she'd continued to fight him.

She was going to die, she'd thought, and it was going to happen without her ever seeing her killer's face.

Only she hadn't died. She'd fought back.

She'd felt no sense of victory then, and she didn't now.

"Stop it," she muttered, clenching her fists. Her anger was now directed at herself. He hadn't broken into her house and mind again; she'd just willingly let him in.

When her breath began to hitch, she told herself to calm down. Her fingers found the small pieces of wood—children's puzzle pieces in a variety of simple shapes—that she'd glued to the flat treadmill buttons in order to distinguish one from the other. Her speed increased. She willed herself to *become* her movements and barely heard the knock on her door. When the noise finally caught her attention, her stride faltered, but she quickly compensated. It didn't matter who it was. She didn't answer her door unless she'd scheduled time for someone's visit.

Several more thuds followed the first. She upped the speed on the treadmill again, hoping to drown out her visitor's knocks completely.

Bonnie had assured Natalie her need for isolation was only temporary. That it would give her the time she needed to adjust before taking life by the horns again. Her therapist, Joanna O'Neil, said it made sense, as well.

Bulbs, after all, were entitled to their time underground.

Joanna, however, seemed to think Natalie's time for hiding had come to an end. Bonnie didn't agree, and Natalie was fine with giving her the benefit of the doubt.

Sweat dampened her hair and soaked through her thin T-shirt and shorts. She concentrated on the music. The strength of her breaths, pumping air in and out of her body. The strength of her legs and feet as they pounded out a steady rhythm. It didn't matter. The knocks on the door kept coming, beating steadily, getting louder and louder with every second that passed. Vaguely, she heard a male voice.

Go away, she thought crossly even as she strained to make out his words. The voice came again, this time louder, and she finally heard what he was saying.

Police.

The police again. Maybe with an update. She should—

Her distraction made her gait falter.

Her foot twisted. She felt herself fall even as the conveyor beneath her feet continued at high speed. Quickly, she thrust out her arms, knowing from experience that it would limit the number of bruises and cuts she suffered, but that was assuming her head missed the treadmill console. The last time she'd fallen, she'd knocked her head so hard she'd had to get stitches. Worse, being inside a hospital again had thrown her into a full-blown panic attack.

As her body hit the conveyor belt and was dragged backward, she screamed in pain. Something sharp scraped along her bare legs, then her cheeks. She hit the safety of her living room carpet and lay there stunned.

Until a huge crash exploded behind her. Rolling to her back, Natalie shoved herself up on her arms and strained to see. Nothing. She saw nothing. But she could hear them. Heard them identify themselves. Heard the footsteps pounding swiftly across the tile of her entry-way and then growing quiet as they stepped onto the living room carpet.

She saw two large shadows. Hated the idea that strangers were in her house again. "No, stop—" she tried to call out, but her voice got stuck in her throat, only small gasps for air coming out. "Please," she managed to say. "I'm—"

"Check the bedrooms," a male voice snapped. A second later, the room became quiet as the treadmill stopped. Natalie jerked her head around. Strong fingers wrapped around her arm, and she flinched away, his touch burning through her skin like fire.

The shadow at her side took shape but remained blurry.

And then she heard his voice again.

Rich. Smooth. Gravelly.

Like dark chocolate with just enough toffee to tease and make you crave more.

"I'm Special Agent Liam McKenzie, California DOJ. Are you all right?"

"ARE YOU ALL RIGHT?" Mac repeated. Natalie Jones just continued to stare at him, eyes wide and unblinking, chest heaving underneath her thin T-shirt. His own heart was still knocking against his ribs, and his muscles were tensed in preparation for an attack. His eyes swept over her, noting both physical traits and bodily condition. Tawny, brown hair pulled back in a ponytail. A lean, lightly muscled frame that signaled strength even as her pinched expression indicated she was in pain. She had red marks on her legs and cheek, but they were nothing compared to the fresh bruises on her neck, or the numerous bruises on her arm that looked older.

Frowning, he readjusted his hold so that his fingers barely brushed her soft skin, but he didn't let go completely. He felt the same irrational wave of protectiveness he'd experienced when he'd heard her scream. He hadn't hesitated or stopped to confer with Jase before breaking through her door. He'd acted instinctively, drawing his weapon, sparing no thought for procedure or exigent circumstances or even his own safety. He'd acted like a man whose woman or child was in danger when she was a total stranger to him.

For a split second, a wave of something unfamiliar but frighteningly good shot through him. Before he could identify it, she trembled and pulled back. In-

stinctively, he tried to hang on, but then deliberately
let his hand drop. As soon as he broke contact, he felt
normal again.

Had she felt it? Had she felt the loss of it? Maybe,
because her eyes looked panicky. "Easy," he soothed.
Or at least that was his intent, but she flinched. "I need
you to answer me. Are you okay?"

She opened her mouth, but nothing came out. With
absolutely no makeup and her hair plastered away from
her face, she was all eyes and lips. Big caramel-colored
eyes with a green ring around the iris, the color still
compelling despite the ocular blood hemorrhages that
were common in victims of attempted strangulation.
Long lashes much darker than her hair. Bare, pouty,
swollen lips, slightly parted to reinforce the impression
of confusion and vulnerability.

And bruises. Cuts and bruises scattered across her
face, fresh and old.

He saw other things, too. Subtler things. He saw the
small creases beside her mouth, which hinted that she
liked to smile, and the deep, impenetrable wall of sadness in her eyes that told him she no longer knew how.
Everything about the woman was a contradiction, as
mysterious and uncomfortable as the intense desire
throbbing through him. For a crazy second, he wondered what she tasted like.

Maybe she'd hit her head when she'd fallen, but what
was his excuse? Good thing he had the best poker face
of anyone he knew.

He tried to stand, but something wouldn't let him.

It was as if an invisible chord linked them together. It forced his gaze to yet another part of her body, this time her damp T-shirt, which clung to her full breasts. "If you don't answer me, I'm going to call a cab."

Her brows crinkled in confusion.

"An ambulance," he clarified. "We call them cabs."

Whoa. He saw her muscles tense. She looked ready to bolt.

"Ch-chair…" she whispered, trying to push herself up. Mac shifted his grip so he cupped her elbow and easily helped her to her feet. Mindful of her slow, stiff gait, he led her to the green sofa set back several feet from the treadmill. "Water. Please," she croaked out as she sat down.

"The bedrooms are clear," Jase said as he walked into the room. From behind her, Jase shot him a questioning look.

"I'll be right back. Stay with her." Mac went into the kitchen, rifled through a couple of cabinets that were sparsely and immaculately ordered, but couldn't find any glasses. He crouched down to check drawers. "Where are your glasses?" he called.

He barely heard her soft reply. "Paper cups on the counter two steps from the microwave."

He grabbed one and filled it with filtered water from her refrigerator. She lifted her hand as he walked into the room and took the cup he offered. She took one long gulp, then several smaller ones.

She lowered the cup, keeping it clasped lightly between her palms, and stared at it. "Why are you here?"

"We're with the California Department of—"

She lifted her face and looked at a point over his shoulder. "You said you're a police officer."

"Technically, yes. A detective, but for the state, which is why I'm called a special agent."

"Whatever your title is, I already gave my report to Officer Munoz yesterday. Did you catch the man who attacked me? Is that why you're here?"

The woman had been as wobbly as a wet noodle, covered in sweat, struggling for breath. In a manner of seconds, she'd gotten herself together. It was as if drinking a cup of water had filled her with a cool, calm composure—and a hint of animosity toward them. Why?

He chalked it up to some people just not liking cops, even though those same cops were actually trying to help them most of the time.

Jase cleared his throat and raised his eyebrows as if to ask, "Are we going to stand here all day?"

Mac's eyes returned to the Jones woman. She stared unblinking, almost as if she was playing a game of chicken with him. She'd trembled beneath his touch. What would she do, what would Jase do—hell, what would *he* do—if he reached out and touched her again? As he'd predicted, as he'd hoped wouldn't be the case, his reaction to meeting her in person was twice as intense as his reaction to researching her on the web. He didn't like it. Not one damn bit.

Shaking his head in an attempt to clear it, he said, "I'm here to talk to you about the man who attacked you last night. But first…do you know Lindsay Monroe?"

She frowned. He wondered if she could fake confusion as easily as she faked calm. "Who?"

Her voice was stronger now, with a hoarseness that again evidenced the violence she'd suffered the day before. Somehow he knew, however, her voice would be naturally low. Sultry. But he needed to get back on track here.

"The name doesn't sound familiar to you? Not at all?" he asked, testing her.

She scowled and crossed her arms over her chest even though one hand still held the cup of water. Her arms plumped her breasts up, and he vaguely wondered if she'd done it on purpose.

"Why don't you stop playing games and tell me what this is about, Officer?"

"Special Agent. Or Detective," Mac replied absently, his eyes still focused on her chest. Realizing that, he switched his gaze immediately to hers, but she kept her own eyes averted. "Patrol officers usually wear uniforms." For some reason, that brought a flood of color to her cheeks.

"Listen," he said. "I apologize for breaking in, but I heard you scream. I'll send someone over to fix the door. But right now, I want to ask you some questions. We can go to the local police station if you prefer...."

If possible, her face closed up even more. "I'm not going anywhere with you."

Her vehement response made Mac pause. And instantly made him more suspicious. Why the hell was she being so prickly? "Is there something about me that troubles you, Ms. Jones?"

She licked her lips. "Other than you forcing your way into my home and scaring me half to death? Of course not. I already told you, I don't know a Lindsay Monroe. And even if I did, what does she have to do with a burglar trying to kill me?"

"Quite a lot, considering your burglar might actually have killed Lindsay." His voice was more gruff than he'd intended.

Her face drained of color.

"He already killed someone?" she repeated hoarsely. She touched her throat, as if remembering the feel of the intruder's fingers trying to squeeze the life out of her.

Mac mentally cursed. Damn it, he shouldn't have blurted it out like that. This woman had almost died at her attacker's hands, and now she had to imagine another woman who hadn't been able to escape the way she had. "Listen," Mac said. "Let's backtrack for a bit. You don't remember meeting Lindsay, but how about Alex Hanes? Does that name sound familiar?"

"No. Should it?"

"Not necessarily. But I have some pictures I'd like you to look at." He pulled the eight-by-ten glossies out of a folder and dangled both of them, side by side, in front of her face. She blinked, stared at the pictures impassively, then glanced away.

"I—I don't recognize them and I don't know what this is about. Now, will you both please leave?"

She sure was in a rush to get him out the door. "Why

won't you look at me, Ms. Jones?" Her refusal to do so ate at him, making him edgy—edgier—in a way it shouldn't.

"Mac—"

Mac shot Jase a quelling look.

"Do you know the first thing they teach us at the academy? That refusal to make eye contact is a sign a person is hiding something. Are you hiding something, Ms. Jones?"

"Hey, Mac—"

Jase stopped when Mac glared at him again. Eyes narrowing, Jase crossed his arms, leaned back against the wall and motioned for him to continue.

The woman's chin rose defiantly. "I know my rights. Unless you arrest me, I don't have to go anywhere with you. And I don't have to talk to you, either."

"What makes you think I won't arrest you?" he murmured, then immediately wished he could recall the words. Jesus, what was wrong with him? The woman wasn't a suspect, but a victim of attempted murder. She was also a possible source of information in another murder investigation, and he was acting like an ass because she wouldn't look at him? He ran a hand through his hair and struggled to regain his composure. "Look, you're not under arrest and I don't know how we got off to such a bad start. Again, I'm sorry we broke in. I was concerned when I heard you—"

A mechanical voice interrupted. "The time is 11:00 a.m."

Silently she reached down and pressed a button on her watch.

Without looking down. And not before touching her hand first and trailing her fingers up to her wrist.

Mac stared at her for several long seconds. "Cool watch." He took another look around, searching the sparsely decorated, dimly lit room through new eyes. Wide walkways. Everything pushed out of the way. Nothing to trip over. Cabinets precisely organized with everything in its place. A large swath cut around the treadmill as if anticipating the very thing that had happened earlier.

That's when he spotted it. Tucked into the corner next to an upright piano. The white of the cane almost blended into the stark white of her walls.

A walking cane.

For someone who was blind.

Mac's gaze bounced to her, then to Jase, who still leaned against the wall with his arms crossed. The other man's expression said it all.

No shit, Sherlock.

CHAPTER FIVE

THE SILENCE STRETCHED ON for so long, Natalie wondered if the detectives had dematerialized. Like Captain Kirk and Spock in the old *Star Trek* shows her mother had watched incessantly. But no, a slight shifting of light indicated one of the detectives—Detective McKenzie, the one who'd touched her earlier—had moved closer to her.

"Did you lose your sight in some kind of accident?" he asked, his voice softened by what sounded like pity. Natalie's spine immediately stiffened.

"What? No."

"Your watch. Your walking cane. How long have you been blind?"

"What makes you think I wasn't born blind?"

"You're a photographer—"

"There are blind photographers," she said, hating how waspish and defensive she sounded. "Evgen Bavcar for one. And Alice Wingwall, from the East Bay."

"Somehow I don't think NASCAR would have let you behind the wheel of one of their cars if you were blind, even if it was just to do one lap on opening day. That was what, about two years ago?"

She tried to keep the surprise off her face but knew she failed. Just as she probably failed to mask her regret. Driving a stock car had been an intense rush, and she'd enjoyed every minute of it, but she'd gladly trade the experience for the chance to see again. A little better. A little longer.

"You've made quite a name for yourself with the press. I didn't have to look very hard to find out a whole lot about you. But there's been absolutely no coverage about you being blind." His voice lowered again. "When did it happen?"

His soft voice, tinged with a gentleness that suggested he actually cared, was like a needle stabbing at a raw wound. "That's none of your business."

She could practically hear him grind a layer of porcelain off his teeth. She saw a blur of movement and heard the rustling of clothes as he squatted in front of her. She strained to see his individual features but could only get an impression. First, of body heat, warm and intense. Then of scent, citrus and sandalwood. Then, for just a few seconds, her visions focused and gave her a hint of him. Stark. Angular. Dark brows that framed his eyes. A square, aggressive jaw.

Her fingers itched and her pulse sped up. It was a feeling she'd experienced often in her life, but one that took her by surprise now. After the farmers' market, even when her vision had improved, not for one moment had she ever thought she'd take a picture again.

Now, she had the desperate urge to reach for her camera. To capture the pure aesthetic beauty that made up his face. His body. Unfortunately, her camera was out of reach. More importantly, it wasn't as if she could ask

the detective to strike a pose. Still, the rush of adrenaline she'd felt so many times in the past, the one that
sped the creative muse through her system, prodding
at her to take picture after picture, had made a rare and
unexpected appearance. And with good reason.

For the first time in weeks, Natalie saw color outside
her dreams. Well, not *really*. In reality, his countenance
and everything around him were still shades of gray, but
as she stared at him, her mind conjured up swatches of
dark mocha, burnished gold and deep passionate reds
and plums. Not soothing, by any means; not the cool
blues and greens of the Greek Islands or the Cascade
Mountains, but the deep fall colors of New England
or the Italian countryside. Aged and weathered by the
years to a sensual patina of decadence that made her
all the more desperate to capture it on film.

She wasn't sure how to handle it. Her comment about
blind photographers to the contrary, she'd thought that
was all behind her. That her passion *needed* to be put
behind her. Exorcised. Excised. Ruthlessly cut off like
an atrophied limb threatening to take blood the rest of
her body needed to survive. Color was a memory to be
gorged upon in sleep, just like feelings of peace and contentment, both stemming from the fact she had 20/20 vision in her dreams. Those weren't things she could ever
hope to experience again during her waking moments.

Now, she wasn't so sure. Now, she didn't know if
she'd embraced Bonnie's isolation theory out of pragmatism or fear. The notion that she could once again
experience life as more than a monochromatic exis-

tence loosened something inside her that immediately unfurled and attempted to stretch its wings.

"I know what happened to you last night," the detective said softly. "How scared you must be. Please, let's start over. I'm not here to make things harder for you. I just need to ask you some questions about a case I'm working on. Can I do that?"

The movement inside her halted. Now he sounded as if he was trying to gentle a horse. Was her fear showing that much? Had she gotten that bad at maintaining her cool? Tremors ripped through her and she struggled to concentrate. To answer him. "I'm sor—"

The subtle contrast of light and dark in front of her blurred as he waved his hand in front of her face. Outraged, she threw up her hand to knock his away but ended up entangling their fingers instead. Before she could draw away, his fingers curled, trapping hers in a gentle but inescapable grip. Her body stiffened the way it had when he'd touched her earlier.

She yanked away and tucked both hands protectively underneath her thighs. "I'm legally blind, not completely blind. Not yet. I see hints of light and dark. Can often distinguish shapes."

"You didn't tell Officer Munoz any of this. At least, it's not in his report. Why?"

She swallowed hard. Why? Because it was *her* business, not a stranger's. Because she didn't want anyone, not Officer Munoz, not *this* man, to know her weakness.

Weaknesses could be exploited.

"As you said, I've been in the public eye a lot. The

press doesn't know about my...condition. I want to keep it that way."

He paused, then blew out a breath. She felt it disturb the air in front of her seconds before it caressed her face. Instinctively, she turned her head slightly, as if to maintain contact with it.

"Okay. So, in Officer Munoz's report, the reason your identification of your attacker was so...vague... is because—"

"It was dark," she whispered. "I—I was in the dark."

Instead of blowing out his breath this time, he held it. The small reaction drew her figuratively closer. A rush of unexpected intimacy swirled around them, as if her words had suddenly transported them into the very darkness she'd spoken of.

It wasn't a darkness that scared her. Instead, it was erotic. Heady. *Heavenly.* In her mind, it pressed her against him. Prompted him to put his arms around her. Made her nipples harden and her breath hitch and the spot between her legs ache. Heat fluttered its fingers across her entire body, not just warm but *hot*, banishing the coldness that had continued to cling to her over the past month. In the intimate space of the enclosure, she greedily reached for more, pressing harder against him, wanting to get inside him, wanting him inside her, big and thick and hard and ruthless, refusing to let her turn away or hide for one second longer—

"Ms. Jones?"

His fingers were wrapped around her arms, and he gave her a slight shake. Almost immediately, he re-

leased her, as if her heated skin had burned him. And
not in a good way.

She blinked rapidly, willing herself out of her disori-
enting fantasy. Dear God, what had happened to her?
Sex hadn't interested her much when she'd been at her
most sighted and adventurous. She tried to erect the
mental barrier that would keep her calm. Protected.
She couldn't find it.

Desperately, she cleared her throat. "Per-perhaps you
can tell me a bit more. Was Lindsay Monroe's home
burglarized, too? Does she live close by?"

After a beat or two, he spoke, but not to answer her
question. In a deceptively mild voice, he asked, "Photography might not be your business anymore, but you
still *take* pictures, don't you?"

She bit her lip, wondering if he was purposely being
cruel. "Why would you think that?"

"You talked about blind photographers. You've got
a lot of fancy equipment here."

He'd obviously spotted the massive console against
the wall, the one she'd seen in the Philippines and immediately fallen in love with. Carved out of mahogany
and accented with pewter handles and scrolled carvings,
it now stored boxes of meticulously filed photographs,
each group separated by dividers with embossed labels
that had cost her a small fortune to have custom-made.
A computer system rested on top of the console, including the oversize monitor with the attached magni-
fying screen. It mirrored the setup in her office. If she
bent down and pressed her nose against it, she could

sometimes discern the contrasting edges of images in her photographs, but only if she darkened the edges in Photoshop first. She'd had a short reprieve, but she knew someday she'd lose even that.

"I figured you still use it to—" he continued, jerking her from her thoughts. His incorrect assumption threatened to shatter what little composure she was clinging to.

"You don't know me. You don't know anything about me." She struggled to breathe, wanting to cover her ears to block his clumsy questioning. Her fingers automatically climbed to her throat, brushing skin left tender from last night's attack.

She dropped her hand. Suddenly all she could think about was getting them out. Out of her house.

Don't fear your need for isolation, Bonnie often said. *Embrace it. Go at your own speed. Take time to adjust before putting yourself out into the world again. That way, when you do, you'll stay there. Happily.*

Once more, she asked herself, pragmatism or fear? Right now, it didn't matter.

"You're right, I don't know you. But I do know one thing. We have reason to believe the man who killed Lindsay Monroe may be the same man who attacked you last night."

She felt the color drain from her face. She'd been expecting something bad, but not quite…that. "He killed her?" she repeated hoarsely, sinking back into her chair. Her fingers jumped to her throat again. Pressed against her fluttering pulse. "Did he—?"

"He killed her, a sixteen-year-old girl, and dumped her body for some fishermen to find."

She sucked in a breath. Her gaze strained to distinguish the shadows of both men—she'd almost but not quite forgotten about the other one, but he'd stepped closer when Agent McKenzie had talked of the fishermen finding Lindsay.

They were both big. Agent McKenzie was a few inches shorter, but broader in the shoulders, with a hint of attitude that made him more intimidating than the taller man beside him. She imagined people gave them wide berth, both on the job and off. She felt their eyes laser into her, their curiosity keen.

"I'm Special Agent Jase Tyler, ma'am. You didn't know Lindsay was murdered?" Despite his probing question, he sounded relaxed, his accent very much a drawl. She immediately pictured a cowboy, but one equally as comfortable in a Ferrari as he was on a horse. The image reminded her of something.... A horse? A car? Her brow furrowed before she forced it to relax. It didn't matter.

A teenage girl had been murdered. Possibly by the same man whose fingers she could still feel staining her skin. She shook her head.

"No—no. Of course not. I don't even know who Lindsay is—was. When—?"

"Her body was found about a month ago. Estimated time of death is anywhere from four to eight weeks before that. We have some leads, but after what happened to you last night, we were hoping for something more."

"We were hoping you might have seen something that could help us catch Lindsay's killer." That came from Agent McKenzie.

He probably hadn't meant to sound accusatory. Disappointed. But he did.

Helpless. Useless. That's what she was without her sight. He might as well have come right out and said it.

"Is there anyone who might want to hurt you? A boyfriend? A former coworker? Someone you got into a fight with at the grocery store?"

"No! No one."

His partner shifted position, then Agent McKenzie did the same. Her head swiveled back and forth between them, and her breath caught. It was difficult trying to keep a sense of both of them, which was adding to her unease. Her feeling of being out of control. She wished she knew something that could help, but—

"The cross pendant," she suddenly remembered. "The one the officers found. It must belong to him—"

"We're looking into that, but we need more. Maybe you remember other things. You guessed he was about five feet eight inches, muscular build. So you touched him?"

"I did more than touch him. We wrestled. Or maybe grappled is a better term."

"Did he have long hair? Short?"

"Very short. Almost a crew cut. Nothing I could grab on to."

"See, that's good. We didn't know that. How about words? Smells? When he spoke, did he sound familiar to you? Did he seem to know much about you? Did he say whether he was looking for something or was waiting for you specifically?"

Her anxiety increased as he continued to pepper her with questions. "No. He didn't say anything like that. He said he was sorry a couple times. I didn't really believe him, given he was still trying to kill me." She heard the rising hysteria in her voice and bit her lip.

Stop, stop, stop. Hold it together, Natalie.

"It's okay. I know this is hard for you, Ms. Jones." She heard a swiping sound. Imagined him running his hand over his hair. What color was it? What did it feel like? What made her think that instead of being short and rough, like her attacker's, it was thick and cool and would likely bring her the comfort he himself had been seeking? She twisted her hands together to keep herself from reaching out for him.

"We've already established you're a celebrity in your own right, but you recently took a sudden hiatus from your career. Because you went blind?"

The sudden change in subject matter surprised her. Instantly made her suspicious. "Why is that relevant?" she asked automatically. Then, realizing how defensive she sounded even to herself, she held up her hand. "Never mind. I'm not trying to be difficult, honest. Just give me a second."

He waited, impatiently it seemed by the tense lines of his body.

She struggled for a way to make him understand that she wasn't a quitter. That even though she'd known it was coming, she'd still been taken off guard. "I was told when I was seventeen I had a fifty percent chance of suffering retinal degeneration the same way my mother had. That in all likelihood I'd go blind before I was thirty. It could happen suddenly. At any time. Or it could happen slowly, not reaching its height until I was sixty. For me, it was triggered almost two months ago. It was slow at first, then started speeding up. Every day I lost more and more vision. Even then I thought I had some time to adjust, to…" To get used to the idea that she'd soon lose the ability to do the things she'd loved most.

Even *love* was too weak a word for how she'd felt about her career. For her, taking pictures satisfied a deep need. It filled her up and gave her energy the way caffeine or alcohol or even drugs did for other people. She was still going through withdrawals without it. "But one day it was just gone. Thankfully, it improved a few days later. Not by much. I still barely see anything. But something…"

She lifted a shaky hand to her forehead. Why was she telling him all that? Why, when it didn't matter? All that mattered was letting him do his job and then returning to what relative peace she had left. "I'm—I'm not feeling well. If you need to ask me anything else, please do it, but then I'd really like you—you both to leave. Please."

This time, Agent McKenzie didn't answer her. "We're sorry to have bothered you, ma'am," the other man, Jase Tyler, drawled, the pity she'd wanted so desperately to avoid clear in his voice. "Any more questions, Mac?"

The man's question had a definite air of sarcasm to it. She waited, her shoulders stiff but her chin still held high.

"You live alone here?"

"Yes."

"Are you going to ask someone to stay with you?"

"Why would I do that? I thought criminals rarely return to the scene of a crime."

"Rarity isn't impossibility. I'd think you'd at least be a little scared. Are you?"

Of course she was scared, but she refused to show it. "If I wasn't blind, would you be asking me that question?"

His hesitation was her answer, and she wasn't surprised.

"We'll leave our business cards with our cell numbers on the dining room table if you need to reach us. I'm assuming someone can help you—um, that is, I know you can't read, but—"

"I can get in touch with you. If necessary, dialing 411 shouldn't strain me too much." Now it was her sarcasm that laced the air.

He hesitated for several seconds, just enough time for her to feel cranky and childish. "Then I think we're done here," Agent McKenzie finally said. "For now."

JASE BROKE THE SILENCE as soon as they stepped out onto the porch. He shook his head and laughed softly. Almost mockingly. "I tried to tell you."

Mac froze and struggled to hide his embarrassment. "So you figured out she was blind before I did. And?"

"And nothing. Officer Munoz obviously missed it, too. Plus, my sister's best friend is blind, so I spot it more easily. But you were too rough on her, Mac."

Mac's brows shot up. He'd sensed Jase's protective demeanor the longer he'd questioned Natalie, but the fact that the other man chastised him about his interviewing technique was out of line, not to mention uncharacteristic. Jase was well aware that cops had different methods for questioning witnesses, and while Mac might have been aggressive, he hadn't been inappropriate—not outside his own mind, anyway.

It didn't take a genius to figure out why Jase had suddenly donned his coat of armor. "Would you be saying that if she wasn't blind? Or was it her rack that made the biggest impression on you?"

Jase opened his mouth, then shut it. He shifted uncomfortably.

Mac bit back a retort. Hell, he couldn't blame him. The guy had a pulse, after all. Of course he'd been attracted to her. *He,* however, hadn't let it affect the job. Mac had.

Had he been too rough on her? Because of the attraction he'd been fighting? Because he'd been shocked to learn about her blindness? He didn't want to accept he'd made her uncomfortable because of his ego or libido but... For a moment there, when he'd squatted in front of her, he'd stared into her eyes and sworn she could see him. Every. Single. Part. Of. Him.

And the curious thing was that he hadn't cared. Hadn't wanted to run or hide.

Instead, he'd had the crazy urge to take off his clothes and let her see more. And he'd wanted to strip her naked, as well. Make her show him who *she* was. Make her open up to him. Literally.

One second he'd been interviewing a witness in a murder investigation and the next he'd pinned his sights on her, not as his prey, but still as his target. He'd felt a primitive hunger infuse him. A sense of possession. He'd wanted to throw her over his shoulder, away from Jase and the entire world, and carry her into the bedroom, lock the door, and spread her out on a bed. Then he'd wanted to explore every inch of her from top to bottom, figuring out exactly where she liked to be touched, for how hard and for how long.

Muffling a curse, he sensed Jase staring at him and bit out, "Sorry you didn't like my technique, but I'm through coddling needy women. Blind or not, whether she knows it or not, she might know something that can help us. So I'll be back. And if you don't like how I do things, you can damn well stay behind."

He stalked to the car and hesitated before he got in. A quiver of sensation ruffled his neck, causing him to take a quick glance around. The neighborhood was well kept but quiet. Officer Munoz and Detective Carillo had assured him that the neighbors had been interviewed and shown both Lindsay's and Alex's pictures. Even though no one had seen anything yesterday, he wondered if the neighbors ever thought to check in on

Natalie. Whether they'd tried to befriend her and she'd rejected their attempts.

From what little he knew about her, she'd likely view a well-meaning gesture as pity, and in many cases she'd probably be right. It was difficult not to feel pity based solely on her situation. Still, she was overlooking one thing. Once someone stood in front of her, talked to her, spent any time with her at all, it was equally difficult not to realize that the woman was extraordinary. Probably the only person that needed to be reminded of that was her.

With a final glance around, he climbed into the car, barely giving Jase time to do the same before he sped away. Their conversation during the two-hour drive back to SIG Headquarters, located within a separate city building next to the San Francisco Police Department, was nonexistent. They immediately went their separate ways once they arrived.

Mac didn't verbalize his snide thoughts by telling Jase to have a good time on his date. When he got to his office, he shut the door. That was a benefit of being a supervisor—he didn't have to share a cubicle with the rest of the agents in the detective pit. His computer monitor was still logged on to Natalie's website. He navigated to her bio page and the professional photograph posted there.

It was strange seeing her all made up, her hair curled, her lashes layered with makeup so they looked smoky and even longer than they had in person. It was also hard to believe those eyes were nothing but window dressing.

What he'd felt when he'd taken her arm, what he'd felt as he talked to her, was unlike anything he'd ever felt with a woman before, not to mention a woman he was supposed to be interviewing for a case. He'd never met someone—not even his wife—who could distract him from the job. Of course, that was the reason he'd never truly been able to meet a woman's expectations out of bed, never been able to meet her emotional needs. Sure, it was a common failing among men, especially cops, but Mac's failure rate in that regard was definitely noteworthy. It was also the reason he'd sworn to keep his relationships with women brief, uncomplicated and emotionally uninvolved.

Frankly, he hated failing. At anything.

Natalie's needs obviously exceeded those of the average woman. Had his dick cared? No. Quite the opposite. She'd hardly tried to draw his attention, but her prickly demeanor and the body underneath her sweat-stained gym clothes had still made him ache. And that had been *before* he'd found out she was blind.

Her vision or lack of it shouldn't have made a bit of difference—it should have been a major turn-off actually—but the minute he'd realized she was blind he'd been hit by compassion, admiration and—as much as he wanted to deny it—a spike in lust that had made him dizzy.

Her blindness wasn't the reason he wanted her, but it added another dimension, a pinch of intensity to the arousal he'd felt the moment he'd seen her picture on her website.

Need saw need.

She was clearly in need of human contact, of human connection, of a man's touch to make her remember that she was a passionate, attractive woman. His primal urges howled to be that man.

To compensate for them, he forced himself to rerun their conversation in his mind. What she'd told him about taking a professional break due to her vision loss made sense. That didn't change the fact she'd lied to Officer Munoz about her blindness. Granted, it had been a lie of omission, one understandable given her need for privacy, but she'd still lied. Hell, she would have let Mac walk out of her house without telling him about her blindness, either. If he was going to stop the man who'd left those bruises and finger marks on her skin, he needed to know *everything* she knew.

He also had to consider something else.

As ludicrous as it seemed, as much as it went against his instincts, could Natalie have had anything to do with Lindsay's murder? Had she worked with someone? Perhaps even Alex Hanes?

A man who'd then turned on her?

Mac didn't know the answer to any of those questions, but he wasn't going to rest until he did. Natalie was merely a piece in a puzzle, not a prize to be won, not a woman to rescue and certainly not a female to fuck.

With a scowl and an abrupt click of his mouse, he

wiped her photo off his computer screen. In the back of his mind, however, he knew getting her out of his head wasn't going to be quite so easy.

CHAPTER SIX

ALEX HANES HAD GIVEN himself to God.

After almost three decades of fucking up and being fucked over, he'd left prison a changed man. He'd thought the church would keep him far from temptation, or at least help guide him away from it, but instead it was his very past the church needed. He had sinned, but for a grander purpose. All those years of misery, for himself and his victims, had been designed to train him, like a boy being molded into a warrior, so that he could do what was needed to spread God's word.

Outwardly, he'd never hesitated—doing so would have made him appear weak, and the weak were quickly preyed on—but inwardly he'd never been sure if he'd been doing the right thing. Taking the path in life that he really was meant to.

He'd thought Lauren—although now he knew from the news reports that her real name had been Lindsay—had been an accident. At least, that's what He'd told him. But now Alex knew there were no accidents. God was everywhere, in everything. In his children, no matter how small. The church, however, was the only way God could reach his disciples, and, as such, it was the church, much like the gates of heaven themselves, that needed to be protected and guarded, barricaded and secured and fortified, both from the human heathens and unholy demons that sought to tear them down. When he'd seen the photographs in the paper, a threat to everything He stood for, and confirmed there were more, he'd known what he had to do.

He was part of Him. His conscience and protector. His Savior. He'd spoken to Alex throughout his life, even before he'd exited his mother's womb, but Alex had ignored Him. Pushed Him away. But no longer. Now he would trust and do what he needed to be granted passage through the very gates he now guarded. He had to be watchful. Smart but bold.

From his position across the street from Natalie Jones's home, Alex studied the two men standing on her porch.

Things had just taken a major turn for the worse.

Even though he tried not to dwell on that or think about his chances of failure, it was hard not to. After all, he'd never been able to outsmart the police in the past. Eventually, they'd always caught up with him, and these men in particular seemed ruthlessly efficient. Especially the less pretty of the two. He moved with a restless energy, his eyes ever watchful and drifting more than once down the street in Alex's general direction.

Of course, the cop had no idea he was there, but the man's sheer intensity was enough to cause a frisson of doubt to play up his spine. This one wouldn't be as easily evaded as the local police. He had experience. Higher training. Hell, maybe he was even FBI or CIA.

The kind of cop that wouldn't be called in to handle a simple residential burglary, even one where the victim had been assaulted.

That meant they were investigating something bigger. Something like Lindsay's murder. A whimper of fear escaped him. Fear for himself, but also for Him. His brother. His church. His family.

But Alex reminded himself he was part of a far more powerful organization, one that grew every day and one whose purpose was not just ensuring the domestic safety of the nation, but the eternal salvation of every soul on earth. Given His support, Alex would outsmart the police, and he'd start by staying close to the woman until he had his chance to get to her.

Lucky for him, Plainville's real estate market, just like most cities in the United States, had been hit hard by the spiraling economy. After failing to subdue the woman yesterday, he'd managed to find a house that was being foreclosed on just down the street and across from hers. Its owners had abandoned the property, and although it had looked respectable from the outside, the inside was trashed.

There were still dirty dishes in the sink. Stains on the carpets. Crap everywhere. It was disgusting to see how people lived or, even if they lived well, how they chose to leave a former residence. Even when he'd been in prison, Alex had kept his cell clean. Respectable. And he'd left it that way on the day he'd been released. No F-you to the guards by smearing his own feces on the wall or pissing on the sheets. Even if he wasn't afraid it would delay his release, he had more pride than that. More hope. He wasn't an animal. Not anymore. Not now that he'd given his life over to Him.

Alex stared at the paper on which he'd written His missive days before.

Natalie Jones.

Her name shot up at him like the flames of hell.

All he was supposed to do was get copies of the pictures she'd taken at the farmers' market that day. Make sure none of them showed Lindsay or the man she'd been walking with. It was obvious from the sequence of photos he *had* copied, however, that she'd been trailing right behind them, closing in on them, increasing the chances she'd actually caught them on camera. She might even remember seeing them. Assuming they'd asked her the right questions, she might already have described what she'd seen to the police or shown them one of the photos he hadn't managed to copy.

But he didn't know. Didn't know her or what she knew. Didn't know what the police knew either. He needed to find out.

And besides…he had to admit, he was curious about her. About the woman who'd managed to fight him off when so many before her hadn't been able to.

Her house wasn't what he'd pictured for an artist. He'd expected her décor to be more…well, just *more*. Her walls were a bland white rather than colorful. They were also mostly blank, not peppered with her photographs, enlarged and custom framed in thick wood or sleek metal.

It's what he'd have done if the place was his.

He'd have made it into a showcase for his talent so the whole world would be forced to see the beauty inside him. The beauty that no one ever seemed to see. But he'd never had the luxury of living someplace so grand, and he'd accepted long ago that his value to others wasn't in his inner beauty or deepest longings, but in what he was willing to do for them. Even his brother Clemmons had proven that to be true.

Alex had been raised in the projects of Los Angeles by his old man. Initiated early into the gang life. The tattered, hollow-eyed youths who'd made up the gang had become his family but always with a price. He was accepted only after being jumped in. Praised only when he defeated others. Stealing and raping and poisoning his body with chemicals became the standard method for proving his loyalty and gaining approval. He protected them and they protected him the only way they knew how to. With brutal force. He who was the most ruthless ruled the streets and lived to tell about it.

Ironically, it was only in prison that he'd learned there was another way. Only when he was incarcerated that his father told him he had a brother, one his mother had decided to take with her, leaving Alex behind with seemingly no thought or regret. More than anything, that had haunted him. He'd felt slighted by his mother, who was long dead, but held on to hope that once he got out, he'd have a real family at last. So he'd prepared.

He'd gotten educated. Learned to read despite the fact all they'd given him at first was a Bible that talked about a God and His son that Alex had never believed in. But he'd started to believe before too long, and that belief had only magnified tenfold after he learned his brother's name. It had been his old man's final gift to him—one grudgingly given after Alex had threatened to tell the police about his illicit side-dealings if he didn't.

From there, things had just gotten better and better, as if God was enthusiastically answering Alex's prayers and then some. He'd learned his brother was a man of God. He'd written to him, not really expecting to hear back. A week before his release from prison, his brother had contacted him, offering him support during his transition.

Strangers yet not. Blood bound to a man of God before Alex had ever believed God existed. Everything had seemed to fit together perfectly, as if it was always meant to be.

Alex believed now, and he believed in the power of knowledge to raise not just one's earthly existence, but one's eternal soul. Luckily, he not only had his brother to rely on, but a whole church of followers, as well. They'd welcomed him in and that act would not go unrewarded.

Yesterday, when he'd found the woman's house dark during the middle of the day, he'd used everything he'd learned before prison to get inside. Then, he'd used everything he'd learned *inside* prison about computers to get what he needed.

It had taken him less than five minutes to find the

pictures he was looking for and begin copying them onto his flash drive. While he'd waited, he'd browsed through them, searching for familiar faces, noting the sequencing that suggested she might have seen Lindsay after all.… But then she'd come in.

A faint noise nearby caused him to jerk in surprise. He glanced at the screen, which indicated only half of the pictures had been copied.

Come on, come on, he urged. Faster.

He heard the front door opening. Muted voices as a hint of light disturbed the cool darkness around him.

He pressed his lips together to silence his breathing, which suddenly sounded too fast and too harsh.

Copying was sixty-five percent complete.

"Thanks for the ride. I'll see you in two weeks."

Another feminine voice answered the first, but it was too low for Alex to decipher what she was saying.

Copying was seventy-five percent complete.

The door closed, and a moment later, a car engine started and the sound of the motor faded as it was driven away.

Inside, the woman sighed. She walked away from Alex, down the hall, toward the other side of the house.

Copying was eighty-five percent complete.

His muscles went limp, and he barely kept himself from blowing out a sigh of relief. Those very same muscles tightened to stone when he heard her muttering to herself and retracing her steps.

Damn it. No!

Copying was ninety percent complete.

She was getting closer. Closer.

Alex yanked the flash drive out of her computer and swiftly turned the power button on the monitor off so the whole room went dark. He lunged toward the doorway, the only doorway to her office, and stood just inside it, praying she'd bypass the room and move instead into the kitchen. Then he could just slip out and she'd never even know he was here.

But this time, God didn't answer his prayers.

He deliberately stopped his thoughts. Didn't want to relive the way he'd hurt her. Instinctively, Alex's hand rose to the pendant hanging around his neck, but then he remembered it was gone.

He'd cursed himself upon finding Lauren's pendant missing. He knew it had been foolish, carrying it around with him, but it had also given him much-needed resolve. Given him certainty that what he did served a higher purpose. Even now, despite the fact it could lead police to Lauren and then to him, its absence was a sign that the woman needed him just as much as He needed her. That she'd lost her way.

So he tried to focus on the importance of his mission, instead. Because he hadn't gotten all the pictures off her computer, he couldn't rule out what she knew and what she didn't.

He needed to know more, to question her, to be absolutely sure. He needed to know what the police had wanted and what she'd told them. Yes, heathens and demons would forever be a threat, but it was in assumptions and carelessness that God's kingdom could be most easily toppled.

He'd take her. Kindly. Softly. It was his duty to show her the light of God and teach her the comfort of eternal salvation.

Just as He'd led Alex onto the holy path, so would Alex lead Natalie Jones.

CHAPTER SEVEN

"DUMB ASS," Jase murmured as he strode toward SIG's break room. He wasn't sure if he was berating Mac or himself. Mac's lustful reaction to Natalie Jones had been obvious, but his comment about Natalie's blindness affecting Jase's reasoning had been spot-on. The woman had guts, which he respected, but he'd let her disability make him feel pity more than anything else, when he knew perfectly well it didn't rule out the possibility that she was a murderer or might have been in cahoots with one.

His cell phone buzzed, and he checked the screen. Marcia, the movie actress he had plans to meet for dinner, had just texted him: On my way to restaurant!! Can't wait!!!

Wincing at the number of exclamation points she'd used, Jase shoved the phone back in his pocket. Hands on hips, he stared at the worn linoleum floor.

Marcia was a horrible actress but a nice woman. As enthusiastic as she was over text messages, she was equally enthusiastic about life, and that included sex. She was fun—or at least she'd been fun for a while. Right now, she seemed like a whole lot of effort. Even the thought of her unique brand of sexual gymnastics

wasn't doing it for him. And that was just damn de-
pressing.

When he reached for the coffeepot, he cursed at the
black sludge pooled at the bottom. Exactly what he'd
found in the detective pen. Closing his eyes, he rubbed
his stomach. *Be grateful. Any more of that crap and
you'll develop that ulcer the doc warned you about.*
Digging out his antacids, he popped two in his mouth,
then stalked to the vending machines. He didn't want to
take the time to brew another cup. He needed caffeine
now, even if it came in the form of chocolate.

His hand retrieved thirty-five measly cents from his
pocket. "Shit." He glanced around. Frowned when he
caught a glimpse of curly red hair slipping out of a
tight bun.

Carrie Ward.

He groaned when the blood rushed straight to his
dick.

Instinctively, he glanced down. *Jesus,* he wanted to
yell at it. *Don't you recognize a man-eater when you
see one?*

"See something interesting, Tyler?"

He closed his eyes at the amused tone in Ward's
voice. Caught checking out the goods. Nice.

He glanced up, ready with a quick retort, only to
find that her eyes were still on his lower half. Her gaze
jumped to his. To his amazement, she actually blushed.
Well. Wasn't that interesting? He'd always thought she
had a thing for Mac. Most of the time, she acted as if

Jase was an annoying little brother. Maybe there was more to her antagonism than he'd realized.

She narrowed her eyes. "What? You think I'm interested in what you have to offer? Think again."

"Now why would I think that, darlin'?"

Ward looked as if she wanted to say more, but she turned away. She hadn't gone more than five feet before Jase called out to her, using her given name for the very first time.

"Hey, Carrie."

She halted, shoulders tense, her muscles fairly vibrating through her simple Dockers and tailored button-up shirt. Although her clothes always hugged her figure, she never showed skin or cleavage, and rarely wore makeup to work. If she ever really pulled out all the stops, he suspected he'd have to drag his tongue off the floor.

"Hey, Jase," she mocked, turning around.

He advanced on her slowly, liking the way her eyes widened. Liking the color that climbed up her neck until it tinged her cheeks a gorgeous pale pink. Unlike Natalie Jones, Carrie Ward was a tough-ass cop who could, with expert precision, literally cut the balls off any man who got too close.

He leaned down until his breath fluttered the hair next to her ear. "Can I borrow some change? I've got a date with an actress who likes to put me through my paces. I need my energy."

He didn't know why he said it and half regretted he had when she stiffened and pulled away. She smiled thinly, reached into her Dockers, and held out some change. He took three quarters. "Thanks."

"Anytime. And don't worry." This time it was her breath against his ear as she raised on tiptoe. "Maybe she won't notice."

"Notice what?" He closed his eyes when she pressed her hand against his chest.

"Notice she got the short—" she paused for effect "—end of the deal."

He grabbed her elbow when she tried to step back. "Anytime you want to see how I measure up, just let me know."

"If you don't let go of my arm, you're going to measure even smaller than normal." She smiled nastily and deliberately looked at the front of his pants, this time with mal intent in her expression. But her eyes widened again at what she saw there.

Slowly, he released her arm. "Maybe you should get your eyesight checked."

She licked her lips and shook her head. "You know, maybe you should transfer out of SIG now rather than in a few months. Given your history, you like to jump ship fairly frequently, right?"

"And you'll do what? Pretend like you don't care?"

Hands on hips, her face tightened. "What does that mean?"

He didn't know exactly, but he ran with it. "It means me and the other guys aren't blind to how you look at Mac. You've convinced yourself you want him, but he's not the one who's got you scared now."

She practically thrust her face in his. "I'm not scared. I'm never scared. And you don't know what you're talking about."

"He doesn't see you that way, Carrie. He never will. Try focusing on what's available."

As her mouth hung open in surprise, Jase loaded the coins into the vending machine. He wasn't sure what he was saying to her—that *he* was available? All he knew was he didn't want to see her wasting her time over a man who clearly had the hots for the witness he'd just interviewed. Not when Jase was still quivering from the effects of feeling her breath in his ear. When he glanced back, Carrie was walking away.

Telling himself to forget about her and enjoy his date with Marcia, Jase turned back to the vending machine—then watched with disbelief as the chocolate bar caught on the silver ring halfway through release.

CHAPTER EIGHT

THE DAY AFTER Agent McKenzie had busted down her door, Natalie did something she'd never done before—with her walking cane in hand, she went for a walk outside, by herself, heading toward a nearby Starbucks. The walk had nothing to do with wanting to prove anything, she told herself, but rather with satisfying a craving.

She loved coffee. Adored coffee. Nowadays she preferred the flavored kind, enjoying a variety of different brews. She could make her own with her single cup machine, but she hadn't found one that hit the spot like a Starbucks Caramel Macchiato. It would be a nice outing to take her mind off what had happened over the past two days. An uncomplicated treat.

Unfortunately, this treat was turning out to be as pleasurable as going out to dinner with Joanna had been.

As she stood outside the coffee shop, she'd never felt as conspicuous or as insignificant.

A steady stream of customers entered and exited the shop's front door—the same door she'd been unable to pass through when the sounds and energy from inside had blasted her. Instead, arms crossed over her chest, head bowed, she leaned against the building and tried to disappear, tensing when footsteps approached from either direction. Each time, she waited for the inevitable pause in conversation or break in stride that told her someone had seen her cane. Waited for a child to ask, "Mommy, why's that lady holding that stick?" only to be quickly hushed away. Waited to be ignored altogether.

Within five minutes, all three had occurred, some more than once, and every mental hatch mark brought a sliver of pain. Interestingly enough, the most common reaction, and the one that brought the most pain, was the silence.

Apparently, she'd rather be noticed as an oddity or annoyance than outright disregarded. The thought almost made her smile. Pride had always been, and it seemed would always be, her downfall.

Placing her fingertips on her watch, which in addition to the voice function had raised symbols denoting the time, she confirmed Melissa would be at her house soon. Sure, she could ask Melissa to go on her regular coffee run, but that would be weak. Needy.

I'm through coddling needy women.

Even though Agent McKenzie's words had been less than complimentary, Natalie's abdomen tightened as she recalled his darkly intense voice. Her hands shook slightly even as her body warmed, bombarded by mixed instincts for flight, fight and fucking.

She deliberately thought the *f*-word to describe what she wanted from the man. From *any* man. That's all it was and all it would be. Physical relief for a libido that hadn't had any in a good long time. It was the reason she'd reacted so strongly to Agent McKenzie. The only reason she continued to react to his memory.

Right now, she had bigger problems. Like trying to decide whether to go inside and order her coffee, or simply head home with her tail between her legs. In the end, her pride would allow only one answer.

You've come this far, Natalie. Don't chicken out now.

Bracing herself, she straightened and stepped toward the front door, then through it. She tried to block out the stimuli that suddenly overloaded her senses, but it was impossible. They rained down on her with the strength of a tsunami. The noise. The press of bodies bumping into her, then the awkward, heavy silence as those same people stepped away. The prickling of her skin as they stared at her. The fear that she was going to fall or crash into a wall. Or worse, that someone would recognize her from the press about her photos. Connect the blind woman with the strong, vibrant person she used to be.

The process of ordering and waiting for her drink was tortuous, and by the time she held the warm cup of coffee, she was struggling for breath. The walk home was only slightly better, and by the time she'd calmed down, she'd lost her desire for the caffeinated beverage altogether. She left it on her kitchen counter and practiced some meditative and breathing exercises until she was sufficiently calm. In control.

It was only minutes later that Melissa arrived. And although she initially answered the door with more dread than excitement, that eventually passed, too. She began to enjoy her friend's company. And she was especially proud of her composed demeanor while she told Melissa what had happened the day before.

"So they just left?"

Natalie shrugged, trying to keep her expression cool even as she "pictured" the "they" to whom Melissa referred. Tall. Broad. Tough. "I'd already told them everything I knew. There wasn't much more they could get from me, at least not without a warrant."

"How do you know so much about the law?"

"I did a stint as a crime beat reporter right after college."

Her friend laughed. "What haven't you done?"

The air crackled with awkward silence as they both thought of all the things she'd never do again.

"I haven't replaced a door," Natalie volunteered. "At least they sent someone over to do that." After they had left, Natalie had sat stunned for approximately twenty minutes, running over everything that had happened. She hadn't even thought about the door or the fact that someone—anyone—could walk right into her home, until a vehicle had pulled up and someone called out that "Mac" had sent him to repair it. She'd murmured, "Fine," walked to her bedroom and locked herself in until the man called out that he was done. She hadn't come out until she'd heard the truck driving away.

Melissa cleared her throat. "So it took him that long to figure out you were blind? Some detective."

"Make that Detective Special Agent. He probably knew the whole time and was baiting me, seeing if I'd crack and give something up about this Lindsay Mon-

roe." Or maybe he'd been just as thrown by the attraction she'd felt. Before he'd learned of her affliction, of
course.

"The poor girl," Melissa breathed. "Murdered and
dumped by some psychopath." At Natalie's automatic
wince, Melissa said, "Shit. Sorry. How are you feeling?"

"A little sore, but okay, thanks." Carefully, she
palmed her favorite camera. "Are you sure you don't
mind me taking a few shots of you, Melissa? You've
already set up the background and light for me. I know
you have better things to do...."

Her friend laughed. "Who else are you going to photograph? I can't exactly see Coach Bonnie standing still
long enough to pose for you, so you might as well get a
few shots while I'm here."

At the image of short, stout, "all about business"
Bonnie saying "cheese" for the camera, Natalie giggled, even if doing so felt rusty. Her adaptive coach was
wonderful at teaching her ways to deal with her blindness, but she was militant about everything having its
time and place. Although she tried to understand Natalie's passion for photography, Bonnie didn't quite get
it. Natalie shrugged. It didn't matter. Bonnie was patient. Kind. Realistic and encouraging. Heck, she even
supported Natalie's need to take risks every once in a
while. *When* she was ready. Bonnie was exactly what
Natalie needed in an adaptive coach.

"You sounded so much like yourself just then, Natalie. It's good to hear you laugh."

I laugh, Natalie almost protested. But then she tried

to remember the last time she had and couldn't. So she simply smiled and said, "It felt good to laugh. You ready?"

"Ready."

Taking a deep breath, Natalie held her camera up to her eye. This morning, she'd called Melissa and asked whether she'd pose for her. To her surprise, even the fiasco at the coffee shop earlier hadn't squelched her desire to take pictures. In fact, in some ways her trip to Starbucks just made her more determined to experiment with the camera she hadn't touched in over two months.

In the back of her mind, she knew it was Agent McKenzie's unexpected visit and his hurtful words that had her suddenly wanting to push herself. She'd heard him and his partner talking on her porch after they'd left. Heard him refer to her as a *needy* woman he didn't want to coddle. Humiliation had almost made her knees buckle. There she'd been, lusting after him while he'd obviously been seeing her as a helpless, pathetic pain in the ass.

Despite yesterday's hurt, however, something was different now. Once again, some part of her felt as if it had been awakened from a deep slumber and was trying to stretch its wings. What would happen if she gave it the freedom to do so? Would she take flight or crash and burn?

With the bright lights Melissa had set up, she could just make out Melissa's shape as she lowered herself into a small chair. Hesitantly, she took one shot. Then another. Each time she did, it got easier.

No, she couldn't see details or colors, not even what color Melissa had decided to dye her hair this week. The last time Natalie had "seen" her friend, she'd had magenta streaks in her blond hair that had perfectly matched her favorite lipstick. But Melissa's fuzzy shadow, combined with the clear mental image Natalie had in her head, gave her the instant illusion of vision. Of competence. Of artistry.

For once, she didn't see what was missing, only what was in front of her.

She focused on the framing of her shots and the lines Melissa's body made against the white screen behind her. Before she knew it, she was instructing Melissa to shift her body in order to maximize the results.

"Raise your hips and slide forward a bit more. Good. Now, turn a little to the left and lean toward me, but don't put very much weight on your elbow. No, that's too much. Ease up a little. Good, that's good."

Natalie snapped one shot after another, losing herself in the motions that had always felt so natural to her. Soon, she even fell into the easy dialogue she'd always shared with her clients.

"So, how are things going with Mark?" Natalie asked despite already knowing the answer. It rarely changed.

Sure enough, her friend sighed. "Same as always."

She didn't expand and Natalie dropped the subject. "The same" meant the man was still jobless and depressed. Do not give her advice, she told herself. She doesn't want to hear it.

"How about your job with the new photographer? How's that going?"

"He's cool. Not nearly as talented as you."

Natalie laughed. Again. The sound was so deep, it actually startled her. "You're just saying that because you're afraid I'll post these pictures later today. I guarantee it won't be my best work."

Melissa laughed, too, and leaned back, her shoulders loosening and her head tilting to the side. "His best work can't match your worst, Nat."

"Hmm." *That's it,* Natalie thought with excitement. *That's the look I want.* She took several more pictures.

"Like this?" Melissa asked, sensing Natalie's mood. Proving once again why they'd always made a great team.

"That's it. No, wait." Knowing there was nothing standing between her and Melissa, Natalie walked forward and reached out, her hand hovering near Melissa's waist. "May I?" she asked

"Of—of course."

Natalie placed a gentle hand on Melissa's lower back, smiling encouragingly. "Arch your back. See how it brings the shoulders up? Good. Stay like that. Just like that."

Natalie stepped back until she was several feet away, the shot already captured in her mind. She pressed the button once. Twice. "Perfect," she murmured. "That's perfect."

Her blood was buzzing with joy. With victory.

She'd hesitated before asking Melissa to set up the

equipment. She'd started taking pictures cautiously and had tried to control her excitement, afraid where it might take her. Yet it had all come back to her, feeling more natural than breathing. And she knew she'd gotten the shots she wanted. Depending on how she framed them, the gray blobs she saw could be changed into something more. Something richer, with a deeper meaning that others might see, too. Something almost... colorful.

"Oh, Natalie."

Natalie froze at the sadness in Melissa's voice. She lowered her camera and straightened.

"What is it?"

"You look just like you used to when taking pictures. You look happy."

Her friend's voice cracked with emotion. Slowly, the euphoria that had swept through her body faded, and she pictured Melissa, frozen forever in her mind as she'd looked just months ago, the magenta streaks in her hair suddenly reminding her of blood staining a pristine white sheet.

Frowning, Natalie shook her head, and the image vanished. "Things are getting better. I'm as tough as I used to be. I mean, I held my own with Agent McKenzie, after all. You would have been proud of me." How would Special Agent McKenzie react if she wanted to photograph him? If she wanted to touch his waist and adjust his posture so she could capture his strong, masculine body to its best advantage?

"You bet I would have been proud," Melissa said

a little too loudly, her words sounding a bit forced, as well. "Anyway, don't mind me. I've just missed you so much. When I saw—" She cried out. "That's right! I didn't even tell you. The Plainville Post ran a couple of your photographs last week. Did you see—"

Natalie ignored her friend's moan of embarrassment at her poor choice of words. "Really? Which ones?"

"They were taken at the farmers' market."

Natalie nodded but instantly remembered the crack of her camera hitting pavement. The feeling of being trapped in a menacing darkness, so different from the kind she'd imagined sharing with Agent McKenzie. Other than that moment, she had very little memory of attending the farmers' market that day. She remembered arriving and starting to walk. Taking a couple of pictures. But then things were a blank until she'd felt the pain behind her eyes, experienced her vision shorting out, and then felt pain again when she'd tried to move.

She'd bumped into one person after another, their surprised exclamations and questions of concern sounding like alarm bells, virtually deafening her, and she'd ended up falling and knocking her head against the pavement, causing her to lose consciousness. When she'd woken up, she'd been in a hospital emergency room, even more disoriented by the medicinal scents and the moans of pain from others around her. Her head had filled with memories of her mother. Drugs. Restraints. The nurses and doctors had been strangers with no idea that she couldn't see, and she hadn't told them at first, which had merely complicated things, and her panic had grown into pure hysteria that had—

Whoa. Freeze frame. Rewind. Don't go there.

She was acutely aware of her chilled skin, sweaty brow and hitching breaths. Curling her fingers so she felt the pinch of her nails digging into her skin, she forced herself to calm.

"The renovation layout for *Plainville* magazine," she said, marveling at how composed she sounded even to her own ears. "It must have been a follow-up piece. How'd they look?" She asked the question to distract herself but found she was actually curious about Melissa's answer. The farmers' market pictures weren't anything exciting, but even an innocuous subject could be photographed well. Or badly. "I wasn't seeing too clearly at the time and then—"

"No, no. It was great, Nat. In fact, I was wondering if I could see some of the other pictures you took that day."

Her brows crinkled. "Well, sure, but why…"

"I'm thinking of setting up a stand there. To sell some of my own photographs. Things are getting pretty tight, and I figured if I could see what other people are hawking, it might give me an advantage."

Natalie cleared her throat. "Mark hasn't gotten a job yet?" she asked gently.

"Not yet. But soon."

Right. Soon. Why did Melissa put up with the guy's crap?

Not your business, Natalie.

At her friend's continued silence, Natalie waved her

hand. "On my computer in the office. The photos are organized by date and location. You remember."

"Thanks, Natalie."

Melissa rose. She stepped out of the room, and Natalie could hear her fiddling with the computer. "You've got such a cool setup here. But— Hey, what's this?"

"What?" Natalie called.

"The farmers' market pictures are already up. So you were looking at them already?"

A small laugh escaped her. "No. Of course not. I haven't been on my computer since..." Icy fingers trailed up her spine to grip her by the throat.

She hadn't been on her computer since before the burglary, and she certainly hadn't been looking at those photos. But someone had.

The man who'd tried to kill her.

CHAPTER NINE

NATALIE'S THROAT SEIZED as fear and confusion shot through her in equal measure. Unaware of her predicament, Melissa continued to chatter from the other room.

"Well, the monitor was off, and when I turned it on, there was a 'job interrupted' message on the screen. There's also a flash drive removal error notification."

"The guy who attacked me," she whispered, her heart thumping against her chest. "Do you think that's what he was after? Do you think he copied them before I came in? But why—"

Her friend was suddenly kneeling beside her chair. "Great. And I just got my prints all over the mouse and keyboard. The police are going to freak."

Reaching out, Natalie laid a hand on Melissa's arm. Her thoughts raced along with her pulse. The man had wanted copies of her photos? "You couldn't know. Besides, they'll probably just be happy to have another clue. Only…" Only why would someone want to steal her photos? *Those* photos? It seemed ludicrous. Maybe she was jumping to conclusions.

But she knew she wasn't. No one should have been on her computer except her, and it was too much of a coincidence. First, her pictures run in the local newspaper. Just days after, a man attacks her in her home for no apparent reason. And then she finds out her computer's been messed with? No, it had to be connected. Maybe she'd captured something incriminating in the photos and hadn't even realized it.

Not too far a stretch. Not only had her vision been poor, but she'd been distracted. "Can you help me look through them?"

Her friend hissed in a breath. "There's hundreds of them, Natalie. That could take hours. I can't stay that long. I'm sorry."

"It's okay," she said. But Melissa was right, and she didn't want to put off telling the police about her theory if the missing photos were somehow important to their investigation. On the other hand, she didn't want to get anyone's hopes up without good reason.

Agent McKenzie thought poorly of her as it was. She wasn't about to give him additional ammunition—reason to think she was physically needy but also needy enough to imagine a significance to her photos that didn't really exist—until she knew more. Next, he might call her an egotist, a cocky artist who actually believed all the press written about her and thought her photos were worth stealing. Even killing for.

"What are you going to do?" Melissa asked.

Natalie considered her options. "I'll blow them up. See if there's anything incriminating in them. Maybe I'll see something, maybe not. Either way, I'll get Agent McKenzie the photographs, so he can look at them himself. In any case, I probably shouldn't give you copies until I've told Agent McKenzie what's happened."

"Um. Hmm."

Her assistant's hum of agreement was edged with something that made Natalie narrow her eyes with displeasure. "What's that mean?"

"What?" Melissa's voice dripped with honey.

"Don't play innocent. I can still read you like a book."

"You just seem a little…I don't know…different when you talk about him."

"It's annoyance. He broke through my door!"

"He thought you were in trouble."

"He *waved* his hand in front of my face." That, probably more than his questions, had pissed her off.

"You don't accept your blindness. Why would anyone else?"

She didn't know how to respond to that. What the hell was Melissa talking about? Natalie more than accepted her blindness. She was just trying to do the best she could. To move on, rather than cling to the past.

The silence hung awkwardly between them until Melissa cleared her throat. "Sorry. Will you tell him to meet you here?"

She resisted the idea immediately. She didn't want him back here. It had already become too much of a distraction, remembering that he'd been in her house, marking it with his words and scent.

But then a thought struck her. Envisioning him in her

space was far preferable to envisioning the man who'd attacked her, wasn't it?

But the fact was, she didn't want *anyone* intruding on the peace her house had always brought her.

"No," she said. "I'll—I'll go see them."

"I'll go with you."

Natalie's denial was swift. Automatic. "No. Thank you. I'll go alone."

Melissa snorted. "You do alone better than anyone I know. But I'm your friend. Let me help you. Please."

Melissa's entreaty took her by surprise. So did her apparent need to help her. She forced herself to lower her barriers a bit. Melissa wasn't Duncan. Plus, Melissa's insistence brought her too much relief to turn her down.

Walking to the local Starbucks had been bad enough. The very idea of having to enter a public building like a police department made her feel dizzy. She didn't want to walk into Agent McKenzie's turf and be subject to everyone's scrutiny except her own.

She didn't even want to contemplate it.

And she knew exactly what that made her.

A coward.

Being a coward might be acceptable, but not when it could mean allowing a young woman's murderer to go free....

She inhaled sharply when Melissa covered her hand with her own.

Sure, she'd laid her own hand on Melissa's arm just moments before. But people, Melissa included, had

stopped touching her months ago. She knew why—
that they hadn't wanted to startle her or intrude—but
in her mind, it somehow always turned into not wanting to be infected or feel embarrassed. She hadn't realized how much the lack of physical contact had affected
her until now. No wonder Agent McKenzie's touch had
thrown her.

Hell, who was she kidding? His sheer presence had
thrown her, and that included any kindness he'd shown.

He'd been arrogant and pushy, but she couldn't deny
he'd also been kind. He'd been genuinely concerned for
her well-being. He'd also smelled good. Looked—from
what very little she could see of him—solid. Like he
could easily take on the world's problems, which he obviously did quite often, given his career.

*And he doesn't need to take on any more, Natalie, let
alone a blind woman with the hots for him, so let it go.*

Pressing her trembling lips together, she covered Melissa's hand with her own. Her friend spoke again before she could.

"I *am* your friend, Natalie. And I wish you'd rely on
me more. You can count on me. I'd never abandon you
the way Duncan did. He was a fool—"

Natalie felt her mental walls slam back into place.
She couldn't believe Melissa was criticizing Duncan,
no matter how well-deserved the criticism was, when
her choice of men was so bad. Yet she knew her friend
meant well and was, in her own way, reaching out. With
a forced chuckle, she pulled away and shook her head.
"He's human," she said lightly. "Most men fear commit-

ment anyway. Can you imagine how they'd deal with commitment to a blind woman?"

Melissa didn't have much to say to that. Natalie asked her to program Agent McKenzie's and Agent Tyler's numbers into her home phone and cell.

"Four-one-five area code. He's in the bay area. You love it there."

Natalie ignored Melissa's words and her teasing tone. "I'll call you later. If you really want to drive me to the station, that is."

"Yes! Thanks, Nat. You've always been here for me. You deserve so much more than Duncan would have given you. Someday, I'll prove that to you."

After Melissa left, Natalie went to her office. It felt like a violation, knowing her attacker had sat at her desk, going through her things and getting insight into who she was and all the places she'd been. She supposed she shouldn't mess with anything else, even if her fingerprints were already over everything. But that didn't mean she couldn't access the pictures the man had been after. Just like the computer in the living room, the contents of her desk computer were mirrored on her laptop, and that included the internet, all her pictures, and all the special programs she needed to access each of them.

Going back to the living room, she removed her laptop from its place inside the large mahogany console and sat down on the couch. Technology made it easy for the blind to navigate the web. Thanks to programs that not only converted text to speech but also described in minute detail everything on one's screen, including the position of a mouse cursor, Natalie could "read" the newspaper online, upload songs to her iPod, and pretty much do anything else a sighted person could do. What she wanted to do now was enlarge and print out copies of the farmers' market photos.

But first… First she wanted to know as much about Agent Liam "Mac" McKenzie as she could.

M

The single initial was all over the pages—witness interviews, copies of Lindsay's diary, printouts of her MySpace, Facebook and Twitter messages—that Mac was reviewing. Unfortunately, the combined total told him jack shit about the person Lindsay had befriended before she'd run away from home last fall. Even when talking to friends about him, Lindsay had used the initial, being very careful never to reveal his identity, where they met, or anything significant about their relationship other than she loved him, he loved her, and everything was going to work out.

He'd been tracking down clues to M's identity for weeks but had found nothing, and that hadn't changed simply because Plainville PD had found Lindsay's pendant in Natalie's home three nights ago. Still, even though their main objective was tracking down Alex Hanes, Mac needed to keep looking into other possibilities. Other potential suspects. Investigation wasn't about focusing on one person but the weight of the evidence as a whole.

He was distracted, however, by thoughts of Natalie Jones.

He supposed that wasn't such a bad thing. She was just as much a clue as Lindsay's diary or pendant. But she was equally unrevealing, teasing him with hints of information that didn't lead anywhere. So far, all his phone calls and interviews with Lindsay's friends and family, trying to determine whether there was any connection between the young girl and Natalie Jones, had yielded squat.

No matter. Persistence and patience were a detective's best tools.

As exciting as TV made police work out to be, most of it involved painfully dull legwork rather than back-alley chases. But it was always worth it when he got to see the relief on a victim's or loved one's face.

That was why he hated when things got away from him. When he couldn't take seemingly unrelated pieces of evidence and work them into a complete picture.

Like the way he'd failed to discern Natalie's blindness.

Like his inability to find Lindsay's killer.

Like his indecision about whether Natalie, the same woman who'd reacted with hostility and fear the first time he'd met her, was a coward or the bravest woman he'd ever met.

The tip of the pencil Mac was using to make notes snapped, and he cursed. He tossed it in the trash and stood, stretched out his sore muscles and left his office to stride into the detective pen that was the hub of SIG.

All bodies were accounted for except Jase, who was taking care of "personal business."

He snorted and shook his head. He supposed the guy still had youth and freedom, so why not take advantage of it? So long as it didn't affect his job performance, and it hadn't so far, it was his business.

Rubbing his neck, he told himself to focus. Focus on the case. Focus on catching the bastard who'd preyed on at least two women and who knew how many more since he'd absconded from parole.

Reaching the coffee station, Mac frowned at the small package of coffee beans proclaiming today's selection to be Tropical Thunder. The sound of stifled laughter made him turn. Carrie Ward, her red hair slicked back into a ponytail that accented her high cheekbones, cheerily raised her mug. "We thought of you when we made it."

Bryce DeMarco, who stood next to her, nudged her and chuckled.

"You two are a riot. Thanks." Muttering another curse, he reached for the pot. Before Jase had joined SIG, Mac and his fellow special agents had drunk Hills Bros. Simple. Predictable. Strong. Now if Mac wanted uncomplicated caffeine—one that didn't come with a hint of macadamia nuts, or hazelnut, or some other candy-ass nut—he had to walk to the break room and the coffee pot there was invariably down to sludge.

Partly because he needed the caffeine and partly because he didn't want to give Ward or DeMarco another laugh, he poured himself a cup of coffee, took several flavor-filled swallows, and stoically hid his grimace.

Whoever had opened that first Starbucks in Seattle should be shot.

"Hey, Jase," DeMarco called, "Nice threads."

Mac looked up to see Jase strolling into the office. He was wearing a snazzy gray suit with a cobalt-blue tie. Mac had seen Jase working at his desk a little after three in the morning. It was almost twelve hours later but Jase looked ready to conquer the world.

Leaning back against a desk, Mac nodded. "You're not quite as ugly when you're all cleaned up."

Jase grinned and did a piss-poor imitation of Vanna White. Catcalls and wolf whistles echoed around them. Mac raised his brows at the other three SIG members.

"You like?" Jase asked. "I can get you one for four hundred bucks. My nephew Nick just got a job at Macy's."

Four hundred bucks for a suit was a deal? Not in Mac's book. "Thanks, but no thanks."

"Suit yourself."

Mac groaned. "Cheesy."

"Going to have dinner at your mommy's house, Tyler?" DeMarco asked.

Unfazed by the taunt, Jase twirled—as much as a six-foot-three-inch guard with size thirteen shoes could twirl. "I'm testifying in court this afternoon. Then I'm meeting a date."

"Who's the lucky lady today?" DeMarco asked while waggling his brows. The handsome Hispanic man had almost as much luck with the ladies as Jase did, but he liked to give Jase a bad time. Simon Granger, the strong, silent one with secrets in his eyes, had a slight smile on his face, but it was the most amusement Mac had ever seen him express. He never grinned. Certainly didn't laugh. Yet he still managed to have a sense of humor. Now standing next to him, Ward made a sound of disgust and turned away.

"What?" DeMarco chuckled, but the sound suddenly seemed strained. The man's amusement false. "I'm working a tough case right now. I could use a break."

Carrie turned back and looked at DeMarco. They all did, taking his words seriously. Probably far more seriously than he'd intended.

They knew what a tough case he was working. The murder of one child and the disappearance of his sibling. The ones involving kids were always the hardest, particularly when said kids' mother had just become a prime suspect.

Carrie's features reflected sympathy for only the barest instant. Then she snorted and looked at Jase.

It happened like clockwork. She was going to use Jase to distract DeMarco. And Jase would play right along.

"Who she is doesn't really matter," Carrie stated. "The question should be if she knows old Tyler here is a one-night wonder?"

DeMarco laughed out loud, and even Mac couldn't help smiling. Jase grinned, but it wasn't his standard trust-me-to-make-it-good-for-you smile. It was a feral come-a-little-closer-and-see-what-happens smile he'd never directed at Carrie before, despite the way she liked to razz him. It raised Mac's radar. Could it be…?

"Jealous, Agent Ward?" Jase raked his gaze up and down Carrie's body.

Collectively, the men in the room—including Jase, Mac suspected—held their breath. To Mac's shock, Carrie turned away without drawing first blood—without even replying. Whoa.

Not knowing when to quit, Jase drawled, "What's the matter, Ward—?"

Mac's cell phone rang, drowning out Jase's words. He took it out of his pocket. "McKenzie."

"This is Natalie Jones."

Immediately Mac glanced at Jase. "What can I do for you, Ms. Jones?"

Jase's eyes widened, and he stepped next to Mac.

When she remained silent, he prompted, "Did you remember something about Lindsay? Or about the man who attacked you?"

"No. I mean, yes, but…your number. It's not local. You're in the bay area?"

"I'm based in San Francisco, but my job takes me all over the state."

He heard the deep breath she took, as if she was bracing herself. He straightened. "What's wrong?"

"I—I— Nothing."

This time there was no mistaking it. She was upset, although she was clearly struggling to stay composed.

"Natalie, talk to me. Why are you calling?"

"I talked to a friend of mine yesterday and I might have some information for you, but I need to talk to you about it in person. Can you drive to Plainville tomorrow?"

His first instinct was to ask why she couldn't tell him on the phone. He stifled it. He sensed right away she wouldn't tell him until they were face-to-face. And while it was true he didn't want to upset her, the fact was he wanted to see her again. Tomorrow seemed too far away as it was. "I'm only a few hours' drive away. I can drive up today and be there—"

"No," she interjected. "It's already late and I'm not sure the information I have is really relevant. I need to think about things. Look some…things over. But you're so far away. I—I can just speak to Officer Munoz—"

"If you have something you feel is relevant to my case, you'll talk to me." He said it firmly, indicating he'd be there whether she wanted him to or not.

"Then I'll come to you. I—I mean—" Her voice got a little squeaky, as if she'd just told him a dirty joke. It made all kinds of interesting images pop into his head. "I'll meet you at the local police station."

It was on the tip of his tongue to argue with her, but he didn't. The lady was recently blind and lived alone. Clearly, she was independent. Could take care of herself and get around. So why did he feel so uncomfortable with the idea of her "coming to him"? Why did he feel protective of her? "How's your neck?" he asked abruptly.

The sudden change in topic seemed to surprise her. "Uh…fine. I guess."

"Your voice sounds better. If your throat is still sore, I've heard tea with lemon works. Or you can try a salt water rinse."

"Okay," she said hesitantly. "Thanks."

Jase, DeMarco, Carrie…hell, even Simon was looking at him funny. He scowled and turned away. "How about I arrange for a car to pick you up?"

"No, thank you," she said, her voice downright chilly. "I've arranged for a ride."

Okay, so she had her shit together. He hadn't meant to imply otherwise. The lady had a chip on her shoulder, all right, and she wasn't about to let anyone lighten even part of the load. It made him wonder whether she let anyone close enough to help. To share her fears with. Somehow he doubted it. "Can you make it to the station by noon?" That would give him time to talk to a few witnesses before they met.

"Yes, but… It'll be you both? You and Agent Tyler?"

Her need for clarification—clearly a request more than anything else—made him frown. Was she hoping to see Jase again? For personal reasons? "Does it matter?"

"I just…I'd like to speak to you both, if possible."

Jealousy spread through him, slow and insidious. Grimly he tamped it down and tried not to glare at Jase. Deliberately, he said, "I'll see you at noon, Natalie."

CHAPTER TEN

ARTHUR CLEMMONS stuffed the last of his things in his duffel bag before turning to see his wife, Allison, walk into the bedroom. He admired her graceful movements and neat, pretty appearance. Even with her belly just beginning to swell with the precious life of their third child, he still saw in her the sweet college girl that had sat beside him in his Anatomy 101 class twenty years ago.

He'd almost finished medical school when he'd gotten his calling to serve God. As such, he'd already completed the rigorous courses designed to desensitize students to the sight of blood and human tissue. He'd never been overly queasy or one to faint during the dissection of a human cadaver. Still, every time he saw Allison's rounded belly, he couldn't help imagining her blood covering his hands as he lifted the baby out of her womb. It made him nauseous to even think about it—

"Evan's still dragging, but Eric's all set to go and waiting downstairs. Can you believe it?"

He took a shallow breath and smiled while shaking his head. "He's way too excited about this retreat. Makes me wonder if he's got a crush on one of the girls. There's a new one. Pretty but shy."

"Shy's good. It's what you liked about me, remember?" she teased. Then her expression grew stern. "Not like that Lauren Winthrop girl."

Lauren—

Clemmons stiffened but hopefully disguised that fact by picking up the duffel and hauling it onto his shoulder. Again, there was a gruesome flash of blood. A heartbeat of indecision about what to do. For himself. For God. "Who?"

"You know. Lauren. The girl the reverend was counseling before she took off and disappeared. She was in your youth group for a while. Pushy. Always said what was on her mind. Eric really admired that about her." She slipped her arms around Clemmons's waist from behind and laid her cheek against his back, her swollen belly resting against him, as well. "I was glad she moved on, but I wonder what happened to her? She seemed to be getting along so well at the church…."

"We knew she had a family somewhere. Maybe she went back to them. That would be wonderful."

"Only assuming her family was a good one. Which reminds me. I don't think I ever told you, but I saw something on the news. Something about a girl from Sacramento being murdered. They showed a picture of her. She had long blond hair instead of a black pixie cut, and she didn't wear all that makeup Lauren did, but for a second I thought it was her."

"Who's this?" Clemmons asked, feigning distraction. He glanced at his watch.

Sighing, she backed away and slapped his shoulder. "Lauren, silly. The girl we were talking about."

"Hmm?" He looked up. Shook his head. "I'm sorry, hon. I'm just keeping track of time. I want to make sure we get to the bus to greet all the participants. That's horrible about the girl who was murdered, but like you said, she was a blonde. I'm sure wherever she is, Lauren is fine." Only she wasn't. Clemmons knew that. But it was too late to change, and revealing what he'd seen would only result in further disaster.

"I pray you're right. I wouldn't want her as a daughter-in-law, but I wouldn't want any parent to suffer the murder of one of their children. If anything ever happened to one of the boys or to—" She put a protective hand against her belly and Clemmons quickly covered it with his own.

"Now, don't go getting all frazzled, little lady. The boys are going to be with me all week, enjoying nature and getting closer to God. They're blessed, just as we are."

"You're right. You're right. I know you're right." She hugged him tight, then leaned back and smiled. "The kids—and I don't mean just ours—are so lucky to have you. It's a shame your brother didn't have you as an example when he was growing up. Things would have fared so much better for him with you to guide him. Have you heard from him lately?"

Clemmons leaned down and gave her a peck on her adorable nose. Closing his eyes, he leaned his forehead against hers, praying for her strength and goodness to infuse him. To infuse both him and the younger brother he hadn't even known about until last year. He and Alex had finally been reunited, and his brother had proven how devoted he was to family and church. It didn't erase his sins, but to Clemmons it showed he was on the right path. "Not for a few days. But he's doing good. Definitely staying close to God."

"Wonderful."

He turned toward the bedroom door, freezing when she spoke again.

"I'll keep an ear out for him while you're gone."

Panic pulsed inside him, swift and all-encompassing. "No," he snapped, turning toward her and dropping the duffel on the floor. He grabbed her by the arms and shook her slightly. "I've told you before. You stay away from him when I'm not here."

"I know, but it's been almost a year," she said with wide eyes. "Don't you think—"

"You will obey me in this, Allison. My brother has found God, but a year of faith doesn't erase a lifetime of violence. I don't want you anywhere near him while I'm gone. If he comes by, don't answer the door. If he calls, don't pick up. If you don't promise me this, then I won't be going on this retreat. There are things that—"

"Hush now," she said, laying her palm on his chest. "Lord, your heart is beating so fast. You really are worried about me, aren't you? I didn't mean I'd seek him out, just that I'd keep an eye out. But I promise to do as you say. You're the man of the house. My man."

He kissed her, reassured by her promise. Allison

never broke promises. She was a kind, God-fearing woman.

"Thank you." He caressed her hair, then cupped her cheek. "You mean everything to me, Allison. You. The boys." He dropped his hand to curve it around her belly. "This girl."

"You've always cared for us. Provided for us. I know it. God knows it. And so does the Reverend. That's why he chose you to take over as the church's state leader." She clapped her hands. "I still can't believe it—finally, all your hard work and sacrifice is going to be recognized."

"Yes, well, sometimes I can't believe it, either. I appreciate his faith in me, but sometimes Reverend Morrison seems to forget he'll be moving on soon. I've asked him to let me preach to the congregation, but he's dragging his feet. It's as if he wants the seat his father-in-law will be vacating, but to keep his old one, as well."

"It's hard to let go of children," Allison teased. "And the congregation has been his for so long, it's very much like a child to him. Now he has Matthew. And as soon as he and Shannon take over as the church's national leaders, the Reverend will find himself too busy to micromanage things here."

She turned to put away a couple of shirts he'd decided not to bring with him and left on the bed.

"He's always been too busy," Clemmons muttered.

"What's that?"

"Nothing. You're right. You're always right."

She smiled at the way he echoed her earlier words.

"Dad!" A voice called up from downstairs. "Are we going?"

He rolled his eyes. "Sounds like Evan's ready now, as well. Better get this show on the road." Again, he turned. Again, Allison stopped him.

"Wait! You've forgotten two things."

"What's that?"

"First, this." She leaned up and gave him a long, tender kiss. Then, pulling away, she picked something up off the bed and handed to him. "And this."

It was his favorite ten-gallon hat. The one she'd given him for their twentieth anniversary. Cream with a gold cross embroidered on the front.

CHAPTER ELEVEN

MELISSA WAS LATE.

They'd agreed to meet at eleven thirty in the morning, and it was already quarter of. What was keeping her? And why wasn't she answering her cell phone?

With an annoyed sigh, Natalie fiddled with her clothes, tugging at her collar and smoothing out her skirt with sweaty palms. After talking to Mac on the phone yesterday, she'd once again returned to her photographs, doing everything she could to make the images visible to her. She'd made them black-and-white, darkened the edges in Photoshop and zoomed in on them under her magnified screen. It hadn't mattered. The only thing she'd seen were blobs of black and gray, with the hint of an occasional figure peeking through the mess. For the third night in a row, she'd gone to bed frustrated, Agent McKenzie's words echoing in her head.

I'm through coddling needy women.

Her Google searches about him hadn't come up with anything about his personal life, so she wasn't sure what woman he'd been referring to. Probably a girlfriend. Even a wife. The very thought of those possibilities made her feel worse about her attraction to him. She imagined any woman worthy enough for the tough, charismatic detective would be strong and sexy. Capable of being independent, even if she actually wasn't. Everything she no longer was.

Still, in an ironic twist, the same Google searches had fed her attraction, giving her insight into the man whose shadowed form had been enough to have her pulse pounding. He was clearly a talented and well-respected law enforcement officer. The Department of Justice's website described its elite SIG unit as "the best of the best" in law enforcement, with its agents having training and experience similar to that of many FBI agents. Agent McKenzie led the unit, and according to his bio, he'd been a decorated homicide detective for fifteen years prior to that.

He sacrificed so much of his life to help others. That spoke volumes about his character and made her twice as anxious to help him if she could.

Even after she'd given up trying to find clues in the farmers' market photos, getting to sleep had taken longer than usual. She'd spent an hour trying to remember details from that day, but they were pathetically few and hardly anything worth breaking into her house for. She'd finally been too exhausted to think of anything else, so she'd gone to sleep, but not before choosing her outfit for today—about five different times.

When she'd first started losing her vision, she'd paid a personal shopper, not just to buy her clothes, but to organize them by color. Even so, she had an electronic color detector and used it before leaving the house—

just in case. She kept her wardrobe simple, with fewer options, but with multiples of the same things. Even at home, she always changed after eating. Always. She couldn't bear the thought of food stains down her shirt. Outwardly, at least, she would remain the same, even if inwardly she never would be.

One person who disagreed with her was Bonnie, the adaptive specialist who worked with her once a week on increasing her living skills. She'd been the one to recommend the personal shopper and household reorganization, she'd arranged for a tutor to begin teaching Natalie Braille, and she constantly counseled Natalie that she was the same person she'd always been. "Sure, your life has changed, but believe it or not, you can still jump out of planes, Natalie. Plenty of blind people have done tandem parachuting. You can start with that. Eventually."

Eventually. There was the rub. Bonnie's confidence that Natalie could live a fulfilling life was conditional in many ways on keeping her caged in. For now. To Bonnie, the world was a traumatic place for someone still adapting to a disability. It was far better to isolate oneself for months—even years—until you felt confident in every aspect of your home life before venturing outside it.

She hadn't told Bonnie what her plans were for today, not wanting the other woman to try and talk her out of them. No, despite her prior fears, she'd actually been looking forward to venturing outside the corners of her home and yard. To walking, chin held high, past a bunch of cops. To coming face-to-face with Agent McKenzie, proving to him she was more than the bitchy, defensive woman he'd met days before. She was competent. Independent. Strong.

Standing on the curb waiting for Melissa, she no longer felt that way. And as unfair as it might turn out to be, her friend's failure to show today seemed to be yet another betrayal.

She lived in a quaint neighborhood but one that bisected a main street with a lot of car and foot traffic. People consistently detoured past her house in order to reach the small bakery down the block. She'd once enjoyed how peaceful it was in the mornings, but how alive it became later in the evening. Since she'd traveled so much, she'd barely known her neighbors. It didn't surprise her that none of them bothered to talk to her now. Still, every time she heard voices nearing, she tensed. Part of it was the same old self-consciousness, anticipation of how they would react at seeing her cane, but the other part of it was unease. It was hard to feel safe knowing someone, anyone, could come at you before you sensed them.

Which was silly, of course. It was broad daylight, and no one except one man wanted to hurt her. And it wasn't as if he'd attack her in full view of the world.

With a sigh, she checked her watch, confirmed it was five minutes to noon and, even though she had her cell phone in her pocket, made the slow walk inside. It was unseasonably warm weather, so she downed a glass of iced tea—as much to waste time as to hydrate her body, she knew—then forced herself to call Agent McKenzie. He answered his phone right away, his voice edged with impatience.

"McKenzie."

Fool that she was, her pulse immediately spiked as she recalled his touch. His scent. The compassion in his voice when he'd asked her about her throat and suggested she drink some tea with lemon. He'd seemed so…sweet.

Idiot. Even blind she could tell Liam McKenzie was about as sweet as he was harmless to her. And he was more dangerous than any other man she'd met. She'd never before felt the pure sexual pull that she did toward him. She'd never been more afraid of it.

His partner was so much less threatening to her peace of mind. She hadn't noticed a thing about *his* smell. Despite everything, she almost smiled at how the man on the phone might interpret that isolated thought.

She cleared her throat and said calmly, "Um, hi. This is Natalie Jones."

"Yes?" His tone didn't soften. If anything, it got rougher. Deeper.

"My ride's running a bit late. I'm not sure when I'll get there, but it should be within the next hour. I'm sorry but… Well, I don't want to keep you. We can reschedule?" She threw out the offer at the last second, waiting with half dread, half anticipation for his agreement, knowing it would be ridiculous to schedule another appointment since he'd driven all the way up from San Francisco.

Instead, he blew out a breath. "I'm here already. I'll wait around." His words softened at the last moment, as if he was deliberately trying to rein in his surliness. Be kinder with her again. Gentler.

Maybe he had sweetness in him, after all. The thought loosened the anxiety that had constricted her chest since Melissa had failed to show up. "I'm sorry to be a bother."

"It's no bother, Ms. Jones. I appreciate you coming in. Besides, a tardy witness is just another part of the job."

Well, that certainly put her in her place, she thought. Which was exactly where she needed to stay. "I'll see you soon."

As she hung up and walked back outside, she imagined how the conversation—how her *entire* acquaintance with Agent McKenzie—might have been different if she still had her vision. Her response to him had rattled her and had caused her protective wall to slam in place before she'd even realized it.

If attraction had made her act differently, perhaps Agent McKenzie's—Mac, as Jase had called him—occasional lapse into rudeness had been caused by defensiveness, as well. But defensiveness against what? Her own rudeness? An answering attraction? Both?

Just as he had seconds earlier, she blew out a breath, but she couldn't dispel the image that had formed in her mind. The image of her fighting with a man, then kissing him.

To her right, she heard a door slam, close enough

that it must be one of her neighbors. She waited for footsteps that never came. Instead, silence hailed down on her. She heard nothing but the occasional sound of cars driving by, and what she imagined was the subtle inhale and exhale of someone breathing.

Shallow and controlled. Deliberate, with a slight rush at the end. As if the person, like a lover trying not to orgasm too soon, held himself back even as he wanted to rush forward and—what?

Her skin tingled the way it did when she knew someone was watching her.

Why did she assume it was a man?

She frowned at the continued silence. Was someone playing her? Anger ignited. She wasn't helpless. Despite the blindness, she'd sworn never to be helpless. She refused.

"Who's there?" she asked sharply. Déjà vu. Wasn't that exactly what she'd asked when she'd heard a sound coming from her home office?

A soft rustle of fabric confirmed someone was indeed there. Squinting, she tried to focus, but like always, she saw only the melding of darkness and slightly lighter darkness. She stepped toward the sound, knowing the closer she got the greater chance there was to see details.

She stumbled slightly when a sudden sense of self-preservation made her pause.

People always commented how closing your eyes made everything pitch-black, but it didn't. Not really. Even as a child she'd noticed the gradations of light and color behind her lids. It hadn't stopped her from being afraid of the dark, but it had given her some solace when she'd been trapped in it.

Humans could be far more dangerous in the day than bogeymen and vampires at night.

Fear pressed into her, stealing her breath.

She no longer heard voices or the sound of cars coming from the main road.

Where the hell was everyone?

Her heart pumped blood and adrenaline through her veins so fast it reminded her of the day she'd driven that race car. Everything had been a blur then, too—an exciting, high-speed blur, but one that had made her feel alive, not scared.

Her anger and bravado left as if they'd never existed. "Hello?" she whispered, more pleading than questioning. Nothing. No one.

She was clearly imagining things because of the assault. With her hand protectively clutching her throat, she once more made her way back inside. She'd call a cab. Get another drink. Calm herself down before hitting the road.

It took a good thirty minutes before the cab honked from outside.

About time. Grabbing her cane again, she made her way to the curb.

She heard a car door opening and closing. She practically felt the driver's gaze on her and her cane, which had become as heavy as a thirty-pound ball manacled to her wrists. He spoke to her from several feet away, his voice slightly muffled by his footsteps and the cab's idling engine.

"Sorry it took so long, ma'am."

She paused. His voice seemed familiar....

A cat screeched from close by. Too close. She jerked and dropped her cane. "No," she gasped.

She remained frozen, arms extended in the reflexive gesture newborns made when startled. Embarrassment clung to her like sap oozing from a tree. Her heaving breaths echoed in her ears. Slowly, she bent her knees, not stopping until she squatted with her palms on the ground. She circled her palms in front of her the way she'd been taught. "Damn it, where are you?"

Her hands hit something solid and she patted it. Smooth, rounded end. Knotted strips of leather. Laces. She jerked back. A shoe.

"I've got it."

As she straightened, the cab driver cupped a gentle hand under her elbow and helped her up. "Thank you," she said when he placed her cane in her fingers.

"Easy now." He guided her into the cab. A hand, large and callused, covered hers before he shut her door, then got in himself. "Where to?"

"The police department, please." She took a deep breath, almost choking on the cab's musty smell. Leaning forward, she reached out, curious if the cab had the Plexiglas divider that had gotten obsolete in recent years. It didn't. But she heard the sound of the cab's radio crackling, the dispatcher occasionally giving instructions to his drivers.

The car jerked forward, and she leaned her head back against the seat and closed her eyes. In her mind, she drove, counting stop signs and naming streets.

"I didn't know you were blind the other night. I'm sorry, Natalie. I'm sorry the cab company left you waiting for so long. I told the driver that was rude after I saw him pull up."

The man's odd question made her brow furrow. What was he talking about? Did he mean he'd told the dispatcher it had been rude to keep her waiting? "I'm not sure—"

"I was sorry about Lindsay, too, but I have to protect God's kingdom. She's there now."

Once again, his words made no sense. Her mind struggled to comprehend them. When she finally did, the terror was staggering. Fragments of memories hailed down on her like bullets. Sixteen years old. Lindsay murdered. Her body dumped and found. Her broken cross pendant found inside Natalie's home.

Her mind spun. His voice had sounded familiar. Now she knew why. He was the same man who'd tried to kill her.

"What are you—?" she choked out.

Automatically, her hands reached out to stabilize herself. To her right, she felt the door. Tendrils of disbelief quickly gave way to fear.

She had to get away. Only, she was in a moving car, with nowhere to go.

Think, Natalie. Think. What are you going to do? That was her voice.

You. It's because of you I can't see. Someday you'll know. Someday you'll get what you deserve. That was her mother's.

She took several quiet, shallow breaths.

They hadn't traveled far. Given the short amount of time that had passed since she'd climbed in the cab, as well as the number of turns he'd made, she knew he was still navigating his way out of the downtown area and toward the freeway. It felt as if he was driving the posted thirty miles per hour, but he'd soon be moving much faster.

"I'm not mad about my eye anymore. You were scared. I just need to know what you know. What you've told the police. Why you're going to see them again. And whatever happens, I'll make it quick. God would want me to."

He wasn't *mad?* The bastard! The crazy, murderous bastard, using religion to justify the way he hurt others!

Nausea had her closing her eyes and battling not to throw up. She took several deep breaths, then slowly folded out the end of her cane until it was partially extended. Long enough, she hoped, to reach the driver's seat.

A fraction of light edged into her vision, and she squinted, trying to see him.

She couldn't. Not even how tall he might be while sitting behind the wheel. She could hear him humming, though. *Humming.*

It was "Singing in the Rain."

"You like Gene Kelly?" she asked even as she thought that was odd for a murderer…wasn't it?

The car jerked as his foot on the gas did. "Shut up," he snapped.

No way. "Why? Why did you have to kill Lindsay? She had a family. Someone who loved her." Somehow, although Agent McKenzie hadn't said so, Natalie knew someone had loved her.

Again, she thought of her own mother. How she'd longed to be close to her. How her mother had rejected her at every turn even before she'd no longer been given the option of loving anyone again.

Shifting subtly, she touched the cool metal of the door handle against the back of her fingers, judging its location. She leaned against the door, pretending she was scared and sick, resting her face against the cool-ness of the window glass. She positioned her body so it leaned slightly forward, thinking it would help her land beyond the reach of the vehicle's spinning tires.

"Abraham had a son and God ordered him to kill that son. Despite his struggles, Abraham knew he had to comply. God's Word. God's kingdom. We can't ask why."

Abraham? She tried to remember the story about a man ordered to kill the son he adored. What had been the son's name?

Isaac. Yes, that was right. And if she was remember-ing correctly, Isaac hadn't died. "God didn't let Abra-ham kill Isaac," Natalie pointed out.

Unbelievably, the man seemed pleased with her answer. "That's right. He stopped him. Rewarded him for his obedience. With Lindsay? God would have stopped her death if he'd wanted to. He didn't. He could give me a sign for you, but He hasn't done that either. Not yet, anyway, but who knows? We need to talk first. I need to know what you saw. There's plenty of time."

Even at his seemingly calm words, his breaths were erratic, as if he was struggling to maintain control.

Her body fell slightly back as he stepped on the gas.

Shit. Now. She had to get out of the car now.

If she could see, she'd have scoped out as soft a landing spot as possible, preferably grass or even dirt. Of course she couldn't, just as she couldn't be sure she wouldn't be throwing herself straight into oncoming traffic. But the traffic was what she needed. Witnesses. Help. In a crowd, he wouldn't stop and come back for her. It would also increase her chances of someone calling for help once they saw she was injured.

She had no doubt she'd be injured. That she might even die. But it would be by her own means, not someone else's.

"You want a sign?" she asked. With a cry of rage, she swung her cane, putting the force of her desperation behind it. He cried out and the car swerved.

She'd hit him!

"Here's your sign!" she yelled. Before she could give it another thought, Natalie pulled the car handle, swung the door open hard and flung herself out and forward.

It was probably a blessing she couldn't see the asphalt coming toward her. The blast of air and noise slamming into her was frightening enough as she curled her body into as tight a ball as possible. Vaguely she heard a distant curse, then screams, but whether they were her own or someone else's she couldn't be sure.

The impact took her breath away. All thought went with it. Pain exploded then spiked, then vanished—its absence, not the darkness, was how she recognized she was about to pass out.

Incredibly, her last thought was of sandalwood and citrus.

And the way she'd felt when Agent McKenzie had touched her.

CHAPTER TWELVE

RUBBING HIS HANDS over his face, Mac was torn between feelings of disappointment, anger and escalating worry. It was just past the hour Natalie had predicted it would take to get to the local police department. He'd already called her cell and home numbers with no answer.

He had no doubt that if she *had* answered, she would have been snippy with him. Again. It seemed to be her go-to mode where he was concerned. When she'd called to tell him her ride had fallen through, his natural instinct had been to offer to pick her up. But she'd responded so poorly to his previous offer of assistance, seeming to take it as a personal affront, that he'd held back. She obviously wanted to prove, either to him or herself, that she was still independent. And she was. She'd been getting along just fine without him.

At least that's what he kept trying to tell himself. It was just taking her longer to get here than she'd thought. If she'd changed her mind she would have called. If she'd been hurt, someone would have—

His cell phone rang, and he flipped it open. "McKenzie."

It was Jase. "I'm on my way to Natalie Jones's house right now."

He shot to his feet. "What?" he growled, instantly sensing from Jase's voice that something was wrong.

"She called my cell. Said she was contacted by Lindsay's murderer."

Disbelief seized him first, then something close to panic. "That's impossible. Why would he contact her? How? She told us she doesn't know—" Mac shook his head to clear it and stop his pointless rambling. "Where was she calling from? What else did she say?"

"Her house and that's it. She sounded pretty shook up. You said she called an hour ago, right?"

"Yes. To say she was going to be late." In turn, Jase had said he had something to do and would be back shortly thereafter. If Natalie had encountered trouble, why had she called Jase instead of Mac?

As if he could read Mac's mind, Jase said, "Look, I don't know what's going on between you two, but she sounded bad, Mac. Shaken. Maybe in shock. And when I mentioned calling you…she tried to talk me out of it. Said I could ask her any questions that needed asking for a report."

Disbelief. Rage. Appreciation. He wasn't sure what he felt most, but he felt all of them. Silent understanding passed between them over the line, both professional and personal. "Thanks, Jase. How far are you?"

"I wasn't too far when she called. I'm pulling up."

"I'll be there in less than twenty."

He hung up and immediately ran for his car. For this trip, Jase had driven his own.

On the drive, he forced himself to catalog what he

knew. All the evidence. He'd assumed Lindsay's murderer had been looking for something specific but that his attack on Natalie had been a result of her coming home and interrupting him. What if he'd wanted to hurt her all along? What if he wasn't going to give up until he succeeded in killing her?

When Mac arrived at Natalie's house, Jase immediately opened the door. He motioned to the hallway to his right. "She's in the sunroom toward the back of the house."

Mac stepped in and shut the door. "What the hell happened?"

"A man posed as her cab driver. Melissa Callahan was supposed to accompany Natalie to the police station, but never showed. When I arrived, she wanted me to drive her to her friend's apartment. It took me a while to convince her she needed to stay put. I've got an alert out for her friend now, indicating officers are to check her apartment, workplace and relatives and friends for any sign of her. But from what he said to her…" Jase's expression, if possible, turned even grimmer. "She jumped out of the car. Said she knew it was her only chance."

Mac sucked in a breath. The possibility of Melissa ending up being another murder victim was disturbing, but right now his focus had to be on Natalie and the fact *she* very well could have died if she hadn't acted. Again. That was assuming, however, she'd been right about the danger she'd been in and hadn't just freaked out. It wasn't unheard of, and it was his job to think of every possibility.

"Have you talked to witnesses? Can anyone confirm whether she was actually in a cab or not?"

"I've got some patrol officers over at Artisan Park now. There's a witness who saw a cab driving away. Natalie landed on a grassy incline that rolled her down into a softball diamond, where bystanders helped her."

"Did you identify the cab company?"

"Plain Cab Co. She called for a ride at about twelve-fifteen and dispatch says the cab should have been there around twelve-thirty, but they lost contact with the driver, a man who's worked for the cab company for about ten years. We have his info and are on the look-out for him, as well."

An hour had already passed since the driver had gone missing. Mac could only hope that wherever he was, he was still alive. "How is she?"

"Rattled, but trying to hide it. Holding it together. Scraped and bruised. She might have a sprained ankle, but otherwise she's fine. It's a miracle. At her insistence, no one called 911."

"Damn it, she should have gone to the hospital. She could have a concussion. Internal bleeding."

"That's exactly what I said. She refused. Threatened to kick me out if I kept insisting."

Mac dragged his hands through his hair. They couldn't force her to go the hospital so long as she was mentally competent; if they could, damn straight Jase would have already taken her, despite her threats to kick him out. In truth, if Jase really thought Natalie was seriously hurt, he'd have found a way to get her medical attention. The fact he hadn't done so reassured Mac somewhat, but didn't erase his need to see her for himself. Cursing, he started toward the room Jase had pointed at, then paused. "Get me copies of the witness statements. Have someone email them to me on my phone. Then check again on the status of her friend."

"Got it. I have other calls to make, too. Let me know when you're ready to roll."

"Have you checked into a safe house?"

Jase shook his head. "My next move. I haven't talked to her about it to get her consent, but—"

"If we've got solid proof the driver was connected to Lindsay, she's going to a safe house with or without her consent."

Jase nodded. "Understood."

Mac walked down the hall, then paused in the doorway of the sunroom. His chest didn't loosen until he saw her sitting near a round dining table.

With her long yellow skirt, cherry-red top and bare feet, she looked ready to have tea with a good friend— at least, she would have if one of her sleeves wasn't torn, her arms and legs scraped up, and her lip cut and swollen. His first thought was she'd made some effort to accentuate her natural beauty—because she'd been coming to see him?—but any sense of curiosity or foolish pleasure was swiftly overshadowed by an almost violent wave of anger.

She still had bruises on her face and finger marks on

her neck from the earlier attack. That made her newer injuries seem particularly grievous.

In addition to the new abrasions and puffy lip, her right ankle definitely looked swollen and was an angry shade of red; she fussed with a bag of frozen peas against it. She had a doozy of a bruise on her right cheek, and he could still see the old bruises from her fall on the treadmill. Banged up, but what had Jase said?

A miracle. It was true. Mac had been raised Catholic. Despite his skepticism about certain aspects of religion, he still believed in miracles. Something or someone had to have been watching over her for her to have suffered so few injuries. His next thought, however, wasn't at all Christian-like.

He wanted to kill her attacker.

That someone would attack any female, let alone a blind one, was an abomination. Some asshole had now done it twice. But what he was experiencing wasn't simply anger at mankind's general willingness to hurt each other. It was a possessive feeling he barely recognized, one that intensified every time he spotted another cut or bruise on her face or body. The only way he could describe it was a "this time, it's personal" feeling.

It didn't make sense. It didn't jibe with his desire to be on his own, answering to no one, meeting his own needs during his personal time, instead of someone else's.

None of that seemed to matter.

To give him time to get his emotions under control, he switched his attention from her to the room she sat in. It was large and airy, with lots of windows that looked out onto a beautiful garden complete with intricate pathways trimmed with boxwood hedges. It would take a lot to keep it up, and he suspected she must have a gardener.

Unlike the sterility of the house inside, which boasted none of the trinkets or colors most women were fond of, her garden was a lush paradise of textures and every shade of the rainbow. Whimsical benches and figurines peeked around rose bushes and cherry trees. It was, he suspected, far more reflective of Natalie's true personality. The fact she still paid someone to tend it spoke volumes.

Moving slowly, as if the action pained her, Natalie placed the bag of peas on the table. She lifted her arms to support a makeshift ponytail and sighed. Mac stared at the delicate skin at the side of her throat. The subtle muscles in her arms made him think of the sinuous ripple of a slow-moving river. When she released her hair, it fell like a curtain of silk to her shoulders, and his fingers itched to explore the soft-looking but mussed strands.

"Are you going to stand there much longer, Agent McKenzie?"

His eyes narrowed, more at her calm tone rather than her actual words. But for her slightly visible injuries, no one would guess this woman had jumped out of a moving car to escape a murderer. Just like before, his natural instinct was to poke and prod at her until he rattled that damn composure of hers. This time, however, he didn't give in to the temptation. She'd been poked at enough for the time being, and he could tell from her coherent, steady speech that she probably didn't have a concussion. Matching and probably exceeding her neutral tone, he murmured, "Eyes in the back of your head, huh? You forgot to tell us that. How'd you know I wasn't Jase? Or another officer?" Or a killer?

She shrugged. "Most people aren't as quiet as they believe. And you don't breathe like him." Her last few words sounded a little cross, but then he realized her swollen lip was making it difficult for her to pronounce her words.

Because he suddenly had to wrangle down his re- newed anger—anger at her, this time, for refusing med- ical treatment—he remained silent for several long moments. She didn't break. Didn't start babbling ner- vously the way most people did after a shocking event. Didn't make another sound, in fact. She seemed content to just sit there. So content that she might as well have pulled out a file and started buffing her nails.

His eyes immediately dropped to her fingers. Her fingernails were clipped short but painted a perfect shell-pink despite the havoc caused to the rest of her body. Understated yet polished, like everything else about her. Once again, even as he was relieved to see for himself that she was okay, he resented the hell out of her composure. It proved how much practice she'd had hiding her true emotions. From the world. From men in general. It pissed him off.

He walked into the room until he stood directly in

front of her. "What's with you not wanting to go to the hospital?"

She turned her face away from him, the action instinctively evasive. "Please. I've gotten more bruised up taking a fall mountain biking. I'm fine."

Her casual dismissal of her injuries was laughable until he remembered she was the same woman who'd traveled the globe and jumped out of an airplane a time or two. "Then you need to take better care of yourself. Let's go. Jase is still here making some calls. He can—"

"No."

"Natalie, I'm not joking. You need to be looked at. If you want me to tell the hospital you're mentally incompetent to make that decision—"

She lurched out of her chair so violently she almost knocked it over. "Don't you dare! You try that, and my days of cooperating with the police are over, do you hear me? Over."

Whoa. She'd gone from mulishly calm to blazingly irrational in two seconds. Her breathing was fast and jerky, and she looked ready to run him down on her way out the room. Somewhere in her past, there was a reason for that. He raised his hands in a placating gesture even though she probably wouldn't be able to see it. "Okay. Take it easy. I'm sorry I said that. I'm just worried about you."

She sat down as quickly as she'd stood, turning her head toward the light streaming through the windows. "I'm not crazy or incompetent, so don't ever suggest otherwise."

Stepping toward her, he said, "Believe me, I've got it. But if you won't go to the hospital…I'm going to check your ankle now." He crouched down and reached for her.

"You don't need—"

She hissed when he touched her foot. Instinctively she jerked back.

"Easy," he murmured. "I just want to make sure you're okay." Gently, he rotated her ankle, watching her face carefully. Beneath his hands, her cool skin warmed, echoing the faint pink blush that now covered her neck and cheeks. Although she took a swift breath and crinkled her brow slightly, she didn't appear to be in a huge amount of pain.

"See? It's not even sprained. Tomorrow I'll be running again. As not gracefully as ever."

He noticed her attempt at humor, might have appreciated it at another time, but right now he couldn't let go of the image of her diving out of a moving cab.

"Did you walk to the house or did someone carry you?"

"I walked. With guidance. I told you, I'm fine."

It grated him to concede she was right, but she seemed to be. "I'm going to look into your eyes now. Make sure you don't have a concussion."

"Jase already—"

She sucked in a breath when he gently cupped her face in his hands, moving her head so he could look directly into her eyes. Her breathing escalated at the same time he fought to keep his own steady. He stared into those witchy amber-and-green eyes of hers, marveling at the way they seemed simultaneously cool and hot. Just like her. To distract them both, he asked, "Did you lose consciousness at any time?"

"Just for a minute. But I—I knew who I was, where I was, immediately."

He grunted. "You're not in pain?"

"No," she whispered.

Her expression seemed guileless. Without deceit. But maybe that was a result of her blindness. Hell, he didn't know what the disability did to one's ability to cloak their feelings. Even staring at her now, if he didn't already know she was blind, he wasn't sure he wouldn't be as clueless as he'd been on the first day he'd met her. Shaking his head, he stood and tried to get back on course.

"Raise your arms and twist your torso."

"What? Why?"

"Because I want to make sure you're not hurt in other places, but I don't think you want my hands all over you at the moment."

Her eyes rounded, getting so huge it almost made him smile. She'd definitely caught his equivocation. Swiftly she raised her arms and did as he asked. He could tell by the way she moved and a quick visual exam that, other than the ankle and scrapes, she wasn't seriously hurt. Barring internal bleeding, of course...

"Satisfied?" she asked, lowering his arms.

He bit back his automatic retort. "Please stand."

"At least you said please this time," she mumbled.

He had to bite back a smile, knowing even as he did so she wouldn't be pleased by the amusement she was causing him. "Easy now. I'm putting my hand on your waist," he said. As he'd anticipated, she tried to pull away.

"What are you— You just said you wouldn't touch me!"

"No," he said softly, not taking his hand off her, but keeping his grip light. Nonthreatening. "I said I didn't think you'd want my hands all over you right now, and I understand that. But I need to rule out signs of internal bleeding."

"Where'd you go to medical school?"

"Just basic medic training for police officers," he responded lightly, refusing to let her bait him. "What I know can't cure you, but I can at least assure myself you're not endangering your life by refusing to go to the hospital. Unless you're willing to reconsider?"

She quickly shook her head.

"A few seconds, then. I'm just going to press against your sides. Is that okay?"

She mumbled something.

He leaned closer. "What's that?"

"I said, just get on with it," she clipped out, but he saw the way her lips quivered. She was trying so hard to act tough, but he wasn't buying it. Swiftly he palpated her sides and abdomen for tender spots before concluding she wasn't in imminent danger.

Drawing back, he caught her almost imperceptible sigh of relief. He flexed his fingers, then placed his hands on his hips. "You're lucky all you suffered is a sore ankle and some cuts and bruises."

She pressed her lips together and blinked, as if she was fighting back tears. Sat back down. "Believe me. I know that."

She was thinking about her friend, he realized. Wondering how badly she was hurt. Whether she was even alive. He hoped like hell she was. For everyone's sake. Because he needed to know and because he wanted to distract her from her fear, he asked, "You were coming to see me. Let's start with that first. Why?"

NATALIE TOLD HIM EVERYTHING, including about the photos that had run in the *Post*, the open photo file and error message on her computer, Melissa's plan to go with her to the police station but not showing up, and even her fumbling on the ground for her cane just before her so-called cabbie had helped her. She'd been tempted to exclude the latter, but couldn't let pride interfere with his job. He'd stayed silent during her explanation and remained so now. She clenched her teeth tightly so they wouldn't rattle, only relaxing her jaw when he began speaking.

"You think your attacker took these farmers' market photos, but you don't know that for sure, do you?"

"No, but it seems to be the only explanation."

"You don't use a password on your computer?"

"No need, since I'm the only one that's ever here."

"Surely not always. Are you telling me there's no

one ever in this house who could have accessed those photos on your computer?"

"Well, if you're talking hypothetically, I suppose my adaptive coach Bonnie and—"

"Adaptive coach?"

"She's helping me adjust to my vision loss. Works on everything from practical living skills to posi— I mean, she's basically helping me cope."

"Living skills to… What were you going to say?"

"Positive imaging," she almost choked out. "So I don't hate myself so much I end up slitting my wrists."

He met her lame attempt at humor with utter silence. After several heartbeats, he asked, "Who else?"

She cleared her throat. "Melissa, but she was the one who asked about the photos in the first place, so she didn't take them."

"So Melissa Callahan was your photography assistant? She's the friend you haven't been able to reach?"

He'd chosen his words carefully, she thought. Even though she'd told him Melissa hadn't shown and that less than an hour later a killer had come after her, Mac—when had she begun thinking of him as Mac?— didn't seem to rule out the fact Melissa might be fine. She clung to that notion with desperation, even though he probably was just trying to keep her calm.

Still, she couldn't resist asking, "Melissa…?" Her voice trembled in spite of her best efforts to appear unaffected. She was cold and getting colder.

"We've got men looking for her. We'll let you know as soon as we hear something."

Please let that be soon. Good news soon.

"So let's assume your attacker took these photos. What's in them that he would want?"

"I don't know! I've left a flash drive with copies of the photos by the front door. You can take them. Examine them yourself. I looked but—" She shook her head, hating the helplessness she was once again feeling.

"It's okay," he said quietly. "You were there. You might remember something. Something that didn't mean anything at the time but—"

"No, you don't understand. I can't remember anything from that day. I never even clearly saw the pictures I took. I—I hit my head and blacked out."

"Wait a minute. Were you pushed? Attacked? You should have told me. How do we know it wasn't the same—"

"No one attacked me. I just—I freaked out because… because I was doing good. I had enough vision to walk and take pictures. Just enough. But then that changed. I felt pain and everything went dark. Completely dark."

Once more, he was silent. Probably just registering what she was saying, but in that silence she heard doubt. Not about what happened on the day of the farmers' market, but about what might have happened earlier today.

"He said he killed her to protect God's kingdom," she said. "That he killed Lindsay."

"He admitted it?"

"Yes. He said he needed to know what I did. What I'd told you. He said he was sorry again, but that God hadn't stopped him. He seemed open to not killing me, but only if God gave him a sign. Otherwise..."

"Shit." Mac's curse was followed by a rasping sound that suggested he'd rubbed his hands against his face.

"It was the same man who attacked me two days ago."

"You recognized his voice?"

"Yes. But only after I got into the cab. He saw it pull up. Told me he even chastised the driver for making me wait—" she said with a broken, disbelieving laugh.

He stepped closer toward her, and his smell—that heady, masculine, comforting combination of sandalwood and fresh oranges—made her inhale deeply.

"Look, I hate to ask you this, but I need to be sure. Sometimes people hear things when they're under great stress. It's not uncommon. I've seen it numerous times with witnesses and victims of violent crimes. Plus, my wife was a psychologist before we married. With everything you've been through—"

"You're married?" Yes, she'd considered the possibility, but when push came to shove, she really hadn't thought of him as being married. As crazy as it sounded, she'd thought of him as being...hers. Her horror was too pronounced to miss, and she wanted to shrivel up and die.

"Divorced," he murmured.

She just nodded, feeling foolish—not just because of her revealing slip about his marital status but because he clearly thought she had mental problems. "I didn't misunderstand him, Mac. I swear. He killed Lindsay and he was going to kill me, too."

He hesitated, and she suddenly realized she'd used his first name. But he didn't comment on her slip. Instead, he focused the conversation on his priority—his job.

"Okay. You said he helped you with your cane. Were you able to see anything about him? His shadow, maybe. Was your impression of his height the same? Did you see whether he had a larger frame or not?"

There was no hint of criticism in his voice, and once again she realized kindness wasn't uncommon for him. He might fumble once in a while, but he was a protector, not just because it was his job but because it was who he was. A part of him, like his eye color or height. Even now, she felt safer, safer than she had with just Jase for company.

That made no sense. She'd called Jase because she hadn't wanted to deal with her crazy reactions to Mac, not with what she'd just been through. But now she wanted to luxuriate in those crazy reactions. Her body warmed and her eyelids grew heavy. She was tempted to sleep. To ask him to lie down with her. Hold her.

No. What was wrong with her? Why was she obsessing about this man?

"Natalie?" he urged, reminding her of his questions.

She struggled to focus on their conversation. On the fact that someone wanted to kill her.

"He got close to me only when he helped me into the cab. But I—" She bit her lip. "I wasn't paying that much attention because I was distracted." Rattled by dropping her cane and feeling self-conscious. "I'd still say he's a few inches shorter than you."

He hadn't been as broad, however. Nor had he had Mac's naturally confident carriage, either.

"Voice?"

"Not too deep or high. There was something…" She stiffened. "He hummed. 'Singing in the Rain.' You know, from the Gene Kelly movie? He got pissed when I asked him about it."

"Pissed how?"

"He told me to shut up."

"And I'm sure you did, of course."

She narrowed her eyes, hoping it made her look mean, not just squinty. "Was that a joke?" Because it had sounded like one. Had she imagined the faintly teasing tone?

"Anything else?"

She paused, shook her head, then remembered. "Wait. His hands. I remember his hands. They were large and callused. Like he worked with them a lot. Maybe a carpenter. Or a construction worker?"

"Okay, good. That's good." She heard scratching noises and realized he was taking notes. The fact he used pad and pencil rather than his cell phone or a PDA seemed telling. He was savvy enough to research her on the internet, but old-fashioned enough to still enjoy the feel of writing by hand. That just made him more attractive to her. Duncan had been all about his Black-

Berry, even when they were on a date. Even when they were in bed.

"How long have you been divorced?" she asked. Her eyes immediately widened in surprise. What the hell?

The scratching paused, then resumed.

"Just under a year."

She didn't respond. How could she? She was appalled by her runaway mouth. Now he *really* would think she was needy. Needy and desperate.

Maybe she was. Why else would she be thinking about the width of Agent McKenzie's shoulders in comparison to a criminal or asking him how long he'd been divorced?

She was still beating herself up when he murmured, "I'm single and available, too. In case that's why you were asking."

Her face flamed with heat. Was he playing with her, or did he just want her to know because he was attracted to her, too? Did it matter? She didn't want to desire him. To crave him with every fiber of her being.

But like it or not, she did.

CHAPTER THIRTEEN

MAC STUDIED Natalie's face as she took in his outrageous statement. Shock was still running through his own system. He didn't know why he'd said it. To startle her? To judge her response? No matter. He had to get things back on track.

"What I mean is, I'd be available *if* I was looking for a relationship. I'm not. That's the last thing I want."

She stared at him—in his direction, that is—before clearing her throat. "How come?"

"I'm not good relationship material. Most cops aren't. I'm particularly bad at it, apparently. Ask anyone who knows my ex-wife."

"She thought you worked too much?"

"More like I loved work more than her."

"Was that true?"

He knew he should probably equivocate, but staring at her, all bruised up, her eyes filled with genuine curiosity, he didn't. "Yes. It was." It hadn't always been that way. But the more clinging and demanding she'd become, the faster his affection for her had died. Partly because of stubbornness and partly because of how he'd been raised, he hadn't wanted a divorce. Nancy had been the one to make that decision and file the papers.

Still, he couldn't deny that when the divorce was final, he'd been grateful. Relieved.

Her eyes flickered, either at his honesty or the un-apologetic nature of it. Either way, he saw the way her expression closed up this time, as if she'd gotten his message loud and clear. It was for the best. Whether she was right about having met Lindsay's killer or not, neither one of them could be distracted by sexual at-traction right now. Or at least, they couldn't be *more* distracted than they already were.

"So what now, Mac?" she asked.

The way she said his name once more, short and sweet with a hint of breathiness, threw him and had him scrambling for a response. "I need to go over the situation with my team and watch commander. We'll set up a protective detail, of course—"

"Even though you're not positive it was really Lind-say's killer?"

"Even then. I trust your instincts. Believe you heard him confess. Plus there's the cross pendant. Together, it's compelling evidence. So we'll play it safe for now."

"I just—I just don't want to leave my house."

"The man knows where you live. He's been here twice. Inside at least once. I'm surprised you even came back here instead of going straight to the police station the way you were supposed to. It would be better if—"

"I'm familiar with my house," she said curtly, ob-viously not liking the way he'd chastised her. "I know how to get around. That's how I got away from him the first time. And this time, too. Because I could guess where we were. That we were still in my neighborhood. Put me someplace unfamiliar and I'll be helpless. Even *more* helpless."

He hesitated, wanting her as safe as possible but acknowledging she made a good point.

"Don't get me wrong, Mac," she said. "I want protection. But unless you think it's absolutely necessary, I don't want to be moved from my house. My routine."

He thought about it, then said slowly, "I don't think it's absolutely necessary. Not yet."

She nodded. Forced a small smile. "Okay. See, that's good. We'll play it safe, but we won't dismiss the possibility I overreacted. Who will stay with me? Not—not you or Jase."

Ah, Jase. He didn't like her bringing up his name, but he'd figured out why she kept doing it. He threatened her on a level—a primal female-to-male level—that Jase didn't. Given their circumstances and that she was clearly fighting her attraction to him, he could hardly relish the knowledge. "You have a preference?" he asked mildly, curious what she'd say.

"If someone's going to stay with me, I'd prefer a female officer if possible."

There was no "if" about it. "That's valid. We'll see what we can do. Right now, I need to talk to Jase, but…" He paused, wanting to reach out and smooth her hair and straighten her rumpled clothes. "You did the smart thing, jumping out of that car, Natalie. The brave thing."

The stubborn woman shook her head. "I'm not brave. Not anymore."

"I don't think you're giving yourself enough credit."
He could tell his statement pleased her. Her blindness
had shaken her confidence, but inherently she was a
warrior. He wanted to give that back to her. Wished he
could give her so much more. If he was capable of it.

But he wasn't. Not anymore. Now he just wanted
to concentrate on his job. Do what good he could and
still maintain some freedom. Some breathing room…

He looked around, suddenly feeling the need to
loosen his collar. Because if he kept looking at her,
wanting to put his hands on her… "Are you okay here?
I need to find Jase." He didn't want to leave her, but
he wanted to see those reports. And he needed to stop
thinking about her as a woman and start thinking of
her as just another clue in the case.

"Sure, but…" She paused and looked away again,
blushing until her cheeks were a rosy pink. He noticed
she only tended to blush when she slipped up, showing her attraction to him, or when she needed to ask
for help.

Sensing what she'd been going to ask, he said, "I'll
be back in a flash." When she said nothing, he prodded,
"Aw, come on. Camera, flash. *That* was a joke. Cheesy,
yes, but all the more reason to make you smile."

He got nothing.

"Natalie?" He stepped closer. She was clasping her
hands together so tightly they'd turned white. Outwardly, she was holding it together. Inwardly, she was
losing it. "Nat—"

"Can you stay for just a minute?" The words rushed

from her lips, as if slowing down might mean never getting them out. "Say something to distract me? Because I just started thinking of Melissa and how she thanked me for always taking care of her...." Her voice broke. "And I—I don't want to think about someone coming after me again because he thinks—"

He crouched in front of her, his knees pressing against her legs through their clothes, and took her hands, which were ice-cold despite the sun shining through the windows. He rubbed his thumbs in light circles against the tops of them. "Evidence to the contrary, we're going to protect you, Natalie," he assured her.

"So you said. But can you distract me? Please?" Her hands turned, and her fingers tightened on his. He wondered if she even realized what she was doing.

He struggled for something to say to her. Battled with the knowledge he needed to get the protective detail rolling. That her safety was his priority. Then again, she was with him. How much safer could she be? Because he knew he'd protect her, just as he'd protect any witness. Even though she brought out feelings in him no other witness ever had.

"You asked me how Jase breathes," she choked out.

"Yeah," he said cautiously. He wasn't sure, with his protective instincts bouncing around inside him, that he really wanted to hear her thoughts in connection with Jase at all.

"Despite the fact he's more laid-back than you, he doesn't always take time to breathe. He gets caught up in whatever's captured his attention at the moment. He holds his breath, then gulps it in. He needs to pace himself a bit more, before he burns out."

He smiled, imagining how Jase would react to her description. "So, he's what? Flighty? Shallow?"

"No. He just hasn't fully found himself. What is he? Thirty-two? Thirty-one?"

"Twenty-nine."

"So he made special agent—detective, right?—early. That makes sense. When he finds something he values, he takes care of it. He's a good guy, if a little fast on the trigger."

"Not the way a man generally wants to be described," he murmured, sensing immediately how his innuendo thickened the air and caused a spark of heat where their fingers still touched. Again, that telltale blush spread across her cheeks.

Releasing her, he stood. He thought of the way Jase had called him out the day they'd met her. Definitely a good guy, but Natalie was right. Despite his slow drawl, he could be rash. Then again, given his own recent actions, Mac couldn't exactly cast stones.

He stared at her, disturbed by her insight.

If she saw Jase that clearly, what did she see in him?

He walked around to the other side of the table and dropped into the chair across from her, noting how she seemed to track his movements through the sound he made. "How much of me can you see, exactly?"

She breathed a sigh as she realized he was indeed going to stay and give her the distraction she'd asked for. "Why?"

"You said sometimes you can see details. Can you see them now?"

She shrugged. "I can see your shape. Like I'm seeing you through a lens, one covered with a gray veil or a thick gel. I can see clearer if you're against a light background, because that creates a more definable contrast line."

"Is that how you can still take your photographs?"

"I don't—"

"I saw your camera on the console table. With its cap off this time."

She looked embarrassed that he knew. "Very observant, Agent McKenzie."

Ah. So they were back to him being Agent McKenzie instead of Mac. "Is that a yes?"

"No. Yes. I haven't taken pictures for a while. I did the other day. It felt good even though I'm sure to anyone else, those photos would look like a jumbled mess."

"But you're doing it for you, so that doesn't matter."

She tilted her head quizzically. "You're right. I'm just hard on myself." Her face grew serious. "I used to travel the world photographing important people and life-changing events. Now I'm lucky if I can get a shot of an inanimate object. Pathetic, isn't it?"

"You are many things, Natalie, but pathetic isn't even anywhere close to the list." The compliment surprised both of them. "So how do I breathe?"

She pressed her lips together. Under his gaze, her cheeks flushed.

He narrowed his eyes. What exactly was she thinking? About him? Them? Together and sweaty and naked? "You don't want to tell me?"

She shook her head and smiled. "You breathe slow and steady. Enough but no more. Like you know you take up a lot of space and don't want to take up more than your fair share. Like you always have something to prove. To make up for. Like other people need it more than you and you'd rather leave it for them."

Mac jolted. He felt as if he'd been sucker punched. Standing, he moved to her side again, immediately aware of how he towered over her. How she had to look up at him. How small and fragile and feminine she was compared to him. "Who the hell are you? *What* are you?"

Her smile vanished. "I—I don't know what you mean."

"Yes, you do. I'm naturally intuitive, but you—you see things no one else does."

"What did I see in you?"

Mac remained quiet. Then, because it was true, he said quietly, "Too much. I—I need a drink. How about you?" Before she could respond, he moved to the doorway and yelled, "Jase—!"

"I got a call. Be there in a sec," Jase yelled back.

Mac stifled a curse. "I'll go get—"

"Mac?"

He stiffened when he felt a light touch on his arm. Carefully he turned. How had she walked up and touched him without him even realizing she'd gotten up from the table? What the hell was wrong with him?

She stared up at him, the inner ring of her eyes a clear, pristine green, like the waters in the Bahamas where he'd fished for a month by himself before college. He'd always intended to visit again.

"I'm sorry if I said something to upset you, Mac."

With her words, his gaze moved to her lips. They were full, the top lip crested with a button at its center that practically begged to be kissed if it weren't for the cuts and swelling next to it, reminding him how close she'd come to serious injury. Possibly death. Reminding him why lifting a finger to her face to see if her skin was as soft as it looked wasn't an option for him. God, he wanted to kiss her anyway.

Jase stepped into the hallway and walked toward them. Shaken, Mac stepped back as if she'd suddenly caught on fire.

Having read his mind about needing a drink, Jase handed Mac a cold can of pop. "Here." He held out a second can. "I got you one, too, Ms. Jones. I thought the sugar might do you good."

He met Jase's gaze. Jase shook his head, silently telling him he hadn't heard anything about Natalie's friend.

"Thank you." She held out her hand and Jase took it, gently wrapping her fingers around it. He guided her back to the table.

Mac had the almost irresistible urge to cut Jase's hand off at the wrist. *Holy fuck,* he thought. *I have truly lost my mind.*

She sat down, then carefully opened the soda can. Mac took a long swig of cola. All three of them jerked when Jase's cell phone rang, but she was the only one who spilled soda on herself and the table in front of her.

"Oh, no!" she exclaimed, color flooding her cheeks. "I'm sorry. Did I make a mess?"

"It's okay, Natalie," Mac soothed, immediately moving toward her.

"Sorry. I've got to get this call." Jase took the call, his eyes on Mac. "Yes. Yes, sir, I hear you. I'll have him call you in five." He closed his cell. "DeMarco just got a break on the case he's working on. The child abduction. Watch commander says he needs the whole team at headquarters. He wants you to call. Why don't we bring Ms. Jones down to the local station so we can—"

Automatically, Natalie shook her head. "No. I don't want to leave."

"Natalie…" Mac began, understanding her need to hide her head in the sand, but knowing they shouldn't leave her alone.

"I said no. You both go, but I'm staying here. I've had enough of…of…well, anyone else, right now. Thank you."

Amazing. Despite her earlier willingness to accept police protection, she actually expected them to leave. He was certain the spilled soda, not to mention the electric current that had spread through them while they'd held hands, had something to do with that.

Sure enough, Natalie lifted the hem of her long skirt, flashing an enticing amount of thigh, and frantically tried to find the spilled soda on the tabletop.

He gave Jase a "hold on" gesture, and the other man nodded. "Natalie. Listen to me."

She froze, looking confused, and that made him feel like shit. He rubbed his hand soothingly on her arm, but that just seemed to increase her agitation.

She started to shake.

He focused in on her button lip again and wondered what it would feel like to hold this woman. Whether she'd be shy and sweet if he kissed her, so that he'd need to coax her mouth open with his tongue before she fully relaxed and melted against him. Or whether she'd burn hot and fast, using her tongue to spar with his own, being as quick and agile with her body as she was with her mind.

He turned and stepped away. Paced and ran his hands through his hair even as he felt Jase's gaze. *What is going on here? I can't feel this. I can't do this.* He was looking into the murder of a teenage girl. This woman was caught up in a killer's web somehow...innocent... but it was never wise to—

"Mac?"

He must have been out of her line of vision, because she'd stood, and she sounded frightened. Even so, his name on her lips caused his gut to tighten. His cock to swell. His body to break out into a sweat.

He fought back his desire and turned to Jase. "Tell Stevens I'm going to stay longer. You can head back and fill me in when I get there."

"He's not going to like it," Jase said sotto voice. At Mac's earthy reply, Jase left without another word.

Before he could change his mind, Mac ruthlessly forced himself to lay his cards on the table. She had enough cause to be jittery without having to deal with the blazing attraction he felt for her. She was probably picking it up in spades, unsure what his next move would be and whether it would be personal or not, when personal was completely inappropriate at this point. He stepped up to her. "I'm attracted to you, Natalie."

It was obviously the last thing she'd been expecting him to say, and the breath whooshed out of her. Her eyes were rounded, her lips slightly parted to reveal white teeth and the barest glimpse of her moist, pink tongue.

"I'm just telling you because it seems dishonest not to. But I'm a cop and you're a witness—" one targeted by a killer, he thought "—so there's nothing you have to worry about with respect to my attraction. In fact, I won't mention it again. We need to concentrate on finding Melissa, catching this guy and figuring out how we're going to keep you safe. We need to—"

She held out her hand as if to gauge the distance between them and stepped closer. He stepped forward until her palm rested lightly on his chest. When she didn't lower it, he felt his pulse pick up speed. Knew she could feel it thumping against her own skin.

"I need to forget about what's happened to me," she breathed. "Today. Eight weeks ago. The past year. I need to feel normal for just a few minutes. I hear you. I don't know why you'd be attracted to me—"

He frowned and lightly gripped the wrist of the hand still touching him. "Now, hold on—"

She talked over him. "I know nothing can happen between us. But I'm attracted to you, too, Mac. That's why, I—I want you to distract me again. Please? With no expectation of more. Can you just do that?"

Frustration ate at him, causing him to pull her slightly forward until her body barely brushed against him, making him ache and her gasp. "What are you asking for, Natalie?"

She licked her lips and forced a smile. "Nothing major. No big deal. Just a kiss. Will you kiss me, Mac? Please?"

For a stunned moment, he said nothing. He stared into her luminous eyes, wishing it was her passion for him that made them look dazed. Given her plea, maybe it was.

One thing he was certain of—he couldn't go another second without knowing what she tasted like. Despite his screaming instincts, which were telling him to back away—*now*—he slowly lowered his head until his forehead rested against hers. She gasped again but didn't move. He breathed in deep.

Inhaled her wonderful scent.

Cinnamon.

It seeped into his pores.

He gently rocked his head back and forth. With his free hand, he caressed her upper arm.

Slowly, he lowered his mouth to hers.

Oh, God.

She'd been expecting color. An explosion of fireworks in those autumn-hued tones that just being in his presence brought to mind. Instead, the moment Mac's lips touched hers, Natalie's entire world went dark. Darker. It wasn't the bleak kind of darkness she feared with all her heart, the one she knew she'd have to face someday, but the rich, dense darkness of chocolate. The kind to sink into. The kind to savor.

Where there was no past.

No future.

Just the moment.

And the incredible sensations that come with it.

His taste exploded on her lips, spreading through her body with such delicious warmth that she immediately opened her mouth for more. His tongue slipped in, wet and agile, rubbing against her own. Then, with a light flick against her lips, he was gone.

She whimpered as he lifted his head. "No," she gasped, clutching his shirt and trying to pull him close. "More."

"Natalie." He placed his hands on her shoulders. "We've got company."

A voice came from behind him. "I'm sorry. I called out when I came back in, but you—uh—didn't hear me. I have to talk to Mac. Now."

Natalie's eyes popped open. Jase's voice broke her out of her passion-induced trance, but she was still disoriented. Turning her head, she saw the faint outline of a very tall man. Her entire body stiffened.

Jase.

Agent Tyler.

Mac kissing her. Because she'd asked him to. *Begged* him to.

Her hand flew to her mouth.

Oh, God. Oh, God.

"Easy," Mac murmured. "It's going to be okay."

She shook her head and tried to get past him, but his nearness and her own embarrassment caused her to lose her sense of direction. She flung out an arm, trying to find the table they'd been standing next to, but all she encountered was warm, male flesh. She jerked back as if he'd burned her.

"I need you to leave."

"Natalie—"

Her phone started ringing now, and she grasped her head, its shrill ringing tone making her wince.

"Shit. Jase, go answer the phone."

"No—"

Jase muttered a low curse himself, then once more left the room. In some distant part of her mind, she heard him close the sunroom door. Probably to muffle the ringing phone while he ran to answer it, but it didn't matter why.

She lost it.

She was disoriented. Her body and emotions spinning out of control. She forgot they were detectives and that a moment ago she'd been trying to pull Mac into another kiss.

Panic licked at her from all directions. Logic fled. All she knew was that she was vulnerable. Helpless.

Just like before. In a park, thrust into total darkness. In this very house, with fingers wrapped around her throat and squeezing the air out of her. In the closet attic, screaming for a mother who hated her.

Lindsay. Murder. Melissa.

She'd been so desperate for Mac's touch, she'd forgotten it all. Hadn't even heard Jase return when he had.

Her arms flew out as she tried to navigate her way toward the door. Her legs slammed into something hard, and she almost fell.

"Careful!"

She felt a hand at her elbow and wrenched away. Her breathing kicked into overdrive. Fast and shallow.

"Natalie. Stop!"

Something wrapped around her waist from behind and pulled her backward. She whimpered and struggled, flinching when she felt a hand cup her face. "Out," she moaned, the crazed fear in her voice making her panic spike. "Out."

Please let me out, Mommy. I'm scared of the dark. Please.

Her childish pleas, memories from the past that still haunted her, echoed in her brain, transporting her back twenty-plus years.

But in the present, warm breath fanned her ear. Grounded her.

"Nat. Listen to me. You're okay, baby."

She felt something touch her forehead.

"It's Mac. Agent McKenzie. You're safe."

Slowly, he released her. "You can leave if you want. You're safe. Do you understand?"

Mac. Agent Mac McKenzie.

Safe here. In her house. Not left alone in a closet by her mother. Not alone in her home with a killer.

She felt some of her panic subside. "Sit," she managed to say.

"Here you go. I'm scooting a chair behind you right now. That's it. I've got you."

She felt the chair at the back of her legs and sat down. Pressing her face into her hands, she concentrated on breathing. In and out. In and out.

Her fingers relaxed. Her heartbeat slowed. Soon, she was breathing normally, and the room was completely quiet.

Quiet enough for realization to hit her.

She'd lost it. Freaked out because they'd closed a door in her own house.

Mortification filled her.

"I—I'm sorry," she clipped out, wondering how many times she'd humiliate herself in front of this man before she learned her lesson.

WATCHING NATALIE try to gather her composure after her panic attack was more painful than he would have ever thought possible. He wasn't known as a softie. He'd had all kinds of people cry in front of him. Badass criminals. Worn-down hookers. Tormented victims. Even his ex-wife. Few moved him. It wasn't that he was unfeeling, exactly, just realistic. Life was about pain far more than it was about pleasure. He figured everyone came to that realization at some point, and he had to remain emotionally removed in order to do his job.

Natalie's frantic attempts not to cry in front of him moved him more than he could ever have imagined. "Natalie, sweetie—"

Someone cleared his throat. Jerking his gaze up, Mac saw Jase in the doorway. "I called for a security detail and she's here. It's Officer Liz Lafayette."

A pretty blonde cop in a blue uniform peeked out from behind Jase and waved. "Agent McKenzie. Ms. Jones." Obviously realizing she'd just waved at a blind woman, she winced, then smoothed her expression into neutrality. Even so, there was no missing the curiosity in her gaze.

"I need to talk to you, Mac. *Now.*"

Swearing under his breath, he said to Jase, "Look, give us a minute—"

Natalie cleared her throat. "Go. You need to go. I'll be fine."

Turning to look at her, he shook his head. Her face was once again a blank slate. His refusal was swift. Instinctive. "No, we need to talk about—"

"No. We don't," she said firmly. "I'm fine now."

"You weren't fine a few seconds ago," he snapped, lowering his voice only slightly despite the fact Jase and the officer would hear him anyway. "That wasn't normal, Natalie."

"Haven't you learned by now?" she said softly. "Nothing's normal about me. I just panicked for a bit. That's all. I'll be fine by myself. I always am."

"Nat—"

"Don't you get it?" she said, raising her voice. "I want you to leave. As we discussed, I'm a witness, not an invalid. Go smother someone else for a while."

Mac stared at her and accepted that pushing her much further would likely cause her to break. But no way was he letting her completely off the hook. He'd warned her. Given her an out. Tried to do the professional thing. In response, she'd asked him to kiss her. Had melted in his arms when he had, setting in motion a heady addiction that made every other need he'd felt pale in comparison. She would damn well deal with it now, because he would be kissing her again. Plenty.

He straightened and took a step back, making sure his voice held an appropriate amount of admiration. "You're good, you know. You might stumble, but you've mastered the cool bitch facade better than most."

Behind him, the officer gasped. Jase let out a slight groan.

Natalie merely smiled tightly. "Thank you, I try. Now, while I appreciate what you've done so far…" She lifted her head, her eyes scanning the room. "What you're *all* going to do to keep me safe from here on out, you need to go."

Knowing she was trying to put him in place, back into the safe little box he'd been in before today, Mac bent down and spoke softly in her ear, making sure that, this time, the others in the room wouldn't hear him. "The thing is, I've seen what lies underneath your mask, Natalie. I've tasted it. So I'll leave you in Officer Lafayette's capable hands for now. But don't get too comfortable hiding in the dark again. Because I'll be back. We're going to find the man who threatened you, and we're going to catch Lindsay's killer, regardless of whether they're the same person or not. And when we do, you won't be a witness anymore. You won't be part of the job. You'll just be a woman who's attracted to me as much as I am to her."

"A *blind* woman," she reminded him, her voice snotty and not all that quiet. "Try to think about that before you return. It'll save us a lot of trouble if you do."

He stepped back and straightened. "No trouble, believe me," he said almost cheerily. "They say that when a person loses one of her senses, it enhances the others. That leaves us at least four we've got to work with. And they're pretty damn good ones, if you ask me."

She gasped, her mouth dropping open.

Satisfied, Mac turned to find Officer Lafayette and Jase watching him with matching expressions of fascination. "Take care of her, Officer. I'll be back soon."

It was a promise. One he fully intended to keep.

CHAPTER FOURTEEN

"THAT'S MY PRECIOUS LITTLE BOY. My little prince." Shannon Morrison laughed in delight when her son, Matthew, smiled at her again. "He's smiling. Honest to goodness smiles. He's right on track according to what the books say."

"That's wonderful, dear."

At her husband's monotone response, Shannon glanced up at him. He was sitting at his huge glossy desk, his head bent over a pile of papers, his glasses perched on his strong Roman nose as he wrote this week's sermon.

Although his dark hair was now steely-gray, Reverend Carter Morrison was as handsome as the day they'd met. He still drew the eye of every female who came within fifty feet of him, young and old. Together, they made a blindingly attractive pair, with comparable intellect, charm and eloquence adding to the whole package. They'd risen through the ranks of the Crystal Haven Church just as she'd known they would, and although they'd been stymied for a time, as much as she hated to admit it, that had been more her fault than his.

Her inability to conceive had been her shame, and it was the reason she'd put up with his weak nature for so long. Still, even when her ability to be surprised or hurt had faded, her respect for him had continued to diminish. Over the years, she'd been forced to become hard. Cruel. It was what he'd driven her to, otherwise everything they'd worked so hard for would have disappeared.

Now, things were heading in the direction they always should have.

They had their son, which meant Shannon's father would no longer deny them their due—a leadership position with the church on the national level.

They had their son, which meant she no longer had to disguise her shame with steel.

They had their son, which meant they could learn to love one another again.

As she watched her husband, she felt a trace of respect returning. Alongside it flashed something just as unexpected—desire.

He'd done what he'd promised. He'd given her the thing she wanted most in the world—a child of her own—and he'd done what he needed to in order to ensure their family's destiny was fulfilled. He might have faltered for a time, but in the end he'd proven himself loyal to her. When forced to choose between his baser instincts or his place beside her, he'd chosen *her*. He no longer had reason to seek out others.

She could give him everything he needed.

Standing, she picked up Matthew, kissed his cheek and handed him to Adele, his nanny. "Have a good nap, my sweet little prince," she said softly. "Once you've put him down, you can take the rest of the day off, Adele. Thank you."

Adele nodded and carried Matthew out of the room, leaving Shannon alone with her husband. She waited until she heard Adele leave, and then she closed the study door. She stepped behind Carter's chair and began to massage his shoulders. He stiffened when she touched him, but she didn't retreat. As she continued the massage, he relaxed slightly, letting her knead the knots out his shoulders.

"You're tense, Carter. I think the past few months have been hard on you. Why don't you let me help you relax?"

She smoothed her hands, first one, then the other, down his chest. Then she did it again. Then again. With each caress, she stretched her arms farther, until soon her fingertips grazed the front of his pants and the flesh that was hardening at her attention.

He said nothing, didn't move, but his breaths quickened and grew louder.

She walked her fingers to the front of his shirt, then quickly jerked on the separate panels, causing his buttons to fly off. She tugged his shirt out of his pants and once again teased him with the back-and-forth slide of her hands, this time on his bare skin.

She felt her own breathing escalate. Felt the welcome warmth and moisture between her legs increase. Slowly, so slowly, he pivoted around in his chair until he faced her, and she stood between his splayed legs, his hands on her hips.

"What's going on, Shannon?" he asked.

"Can't you tell? I want you. I want to feel your hard shaft, your delicious shaft, the marvelous shaft that gave me my beautiful son, inside me. I want you to take me. Hard. I want you to fuck me, Carter, the way you've fucked all your little whores."

His eyes flared with desire. She'd never talked dirty to him before. Never intimated that she wanted sex between them to be anything other than traditional missionary position. But things were different now.

She was a mother. She was one with the earth. Fertile. Passionate. Primal.

And she wanted to be fucked by her husband.

He kicked his feet in between hers and knocked her legs apart. His hands tightened on her hips, and he pulled her down until she was straddling him. Then he wound his fingers in her hair and pulled, yanking her head back, hard.

She gasped, the sharp pain frightening her even as it stoked her desire to new heights.

"You want me to fuck you? Are you sure about that, Shannon?"

She opened her mouth to answer, but just then her cell phone rang.

He didn't release her hair. Cautiously, she retrieved her cell phone from her pocket and lifted it up so she could see the screen.

It was Alex Hanes.

Carter looked at her, his mouth twisted in a sardonic grin. "Aren't you going to get that?"

Shannon smiled. She pressed the button to "ignore" the call, then tossed her phone behind her. Carter loosened his grip on her hair, just enough that she could move. With one hand, she caressed Carter's chest, then reached down to cup him between his legs.

"He can wait. Right now, this is the only thing I want."

CHAPTER FIFTEEN

"WHAT'S GOTTEN INTO YOU?" Jase asked quietly as they walked from Natalie's house to their cars parked at the curb. "Being attracted to a witness is one thing. Acting on it with a *blind* witness who was just kidnapped is a whole other story."

Nothing Jase had said had ever been truer, but no way was Mac going to be lectured. Especially not with that kiss still playing through his head, alternately filling him with joy and dread. "You telling me you've never had something going with a witness, Jase? Because I won't believe you."

"She's *blind,* Mac. And even if she didn't have to worry about some nut trying to kill her, she's obviously having a hell of a time dealing with that."

"I'll worry about the nut. Her blindness has nothing to do with this." It was funny how that was true. Hell, he'd thought he'd been attracted to Natalie before. When they'd kissed, he'd felt exactly how Alex Hanes must have felt when, after fifteen years in prison, he'd walked back into the world as a free man. Disoriented. A little apprehensive. But beyond grateful for a second chance to experience life again. "Mind your own business, Jase."

The other man's brows rose. "This is my business. You asked me to assist you on this case, remember?"

He finally stopped to face Jase fully. "And I'm asking you, very nicely, that if your questioning isn't related to the killer we're tracking down, to back off. If you continue to push, I'm going to stop being nice and push right back.'"

"What the hell does that mean?"

"It means, when a guy can't go a week without banging at least three different women, he's obviously got impulse control problems and shouldn't cast stones." He turned to his car. "Now, let's—"

"Hell, no—" Jase grabbed his arm.

Mac reacted instinctively, whirling and grabbing him in return. With a quick twist and flip, he tossed Jase to the ground, shoved his arm behind his back, then straddled him while he pressed his face halfway into the cement walkway and half into the immaculate green lawn on either side of it.

"Jesus, Mac—"

"Listen to me, you little shit," Mac hissed in his ear. "I have been doing my job for a hell of a long time without your guidance, and I will continue to do it when you decide you want to run for office or take a desk job because it'll make you more money. Do not tell me how to do my job and don't try and get physical with me either."

"You're going to hurt her." Jase cursed as Mac pressed his face harder into the ground.

"Like hell I am. I'm going to keep her alive. There's something between us, yes. And I let it get out of hand.

But I'm not an idiot." Disgusted, Mac released his hold and stood. "Evidence to the contrary aside," he added grudgingly.

They stared at each other for several tense seconds. "Shit." Mac swiped at his hair before extending his hand. After a brief pause, Jase took it and rose to his feet.

"You say that now, but you should see the way you look at her."

Mac glanced away, afraid Jase would see more than he wanted him to. "I admire her. Despite her issues, she's facing some pretty tough shit. She's not whining and she's not complaining. She's hell-bent on proving that her blindness hasn't changed who she is."

"Maybe it hasn't changed who she is," Jase said quietly, "but it's changed how she needs to approach life. Whether she likes it or not. You gonna help her accept that?"

His denial was instinctive but still slower than it would have been yesterday. "She doesn't need my help. A woman brave enough to jump out of a moving cab isn't going to let an eye disease bring her down. She'll figure that out eventually."

"I hope so." Jase tugged at his clothes and swiped dirt away. He glanced at Mac from the corner of his eye. "Just so you know, I could've taken you to the ground with me if I wanted to."

"I don't doubt that." Silently, he reached out his hand. Silently, Jase shook it.

"Good thing Officer Lafayette got here so fast. Because if she hadn't, I'm not sure you'd have been able to tear yourself away from her. You were stuck to her like white on rice."

Mac grunted and frowned, not because he could deny what Jase was saying but because... Turning, he scanned the surrounding neighborhood.

"What?" Jase asked.

"She called a cab when her friend didn't show. Our perp told Natalie he saw the cab driver pull up. That he chastised the man for keeping her waiting. He was close by then, close enough that he could overpower the driver and get control of the cab without Natalie or anyone knowing about it."

"The police already swept the neighborhood for potential witnesses. You read the reports. But—"

"But that doesn't mean they confirmed each house was occupied or that Hanes wasn't hiding inside one of them." His gaze skipped over one house after another. Unlike the cookie-cutter track homes that were most common these days, each house in Natalie's neighborhood had a unique upscale design with well-maintained landscaping. Only one lawn bordered on unkempt, indicating it hadn't been mowed in a few weeks. His eyes narrowed on the cream ranch-style house with blue shutters. He crossed the street to walk toward it, Jase right beside him. Off to the side, obscured by some bushes, was a foreclosure sign that had either blown down or been deliberately hidden.

"I'll take the back."

Mac nodded.

He approached the front door from the side, hugging the wall nearest to the door handle. There was a smear of something on the front porch as well as on the lower door casing. It looked like fresh blood. Swiftly, he drew his weapon. "Blood evidence," he called to Jase.

"Got it. Back door's been jimmied."

Carefully, he touched the doorknob to "soft-check" it; it was unlocked. He rapped on the door. "Police. Open up."

There was no response.

Still standing to the side, he turned the knob and pushed the door open. He pivoted and leaned in, giving himself a clear line of sight while protecting himself as much as possible. More blood stained the carpet leading to the back of the house. "Police! Drop any weapons and come out with your hands up," he shouted.

Again, nothing. He heard Jase enter from the back and announce himself, as well.

A moment later, Jase called, "Shit. I've got the cabbie."

His adrenaline spiked even higher. "I'll finish the sweep," he called. One by one, he cleared every room in the house, making sure no one was hiding in any of the closets. The place was an abandoned mess, with clothes and boxes strewn everywhere. Hanes had obviously set himself up in the front living room. It was notably cleaner than the rest of the house, as if he hadn't been able to stand living in filth himself. A blanket and pillow were folded into a neat package, and there were fast-food bags and empty cups folded and stacked on one table. There was also a small flip video camera set up on a tripod nearby. Cursing, Mac joined Jase in the back family room next to the kitchen.

His eyes went instantly to the unconscious vic on the floor, a portly man with thinning white hair stained by blood. Jase crouched next to him, remnants of rope and tape lying close by. "He hit him pretty hard. His head injury is probably the source of the blood you found."

Mac nodded. "You call it in?"

"Yeah. An ambulance and patrol car are on their way."

"He was here all along. Probably has been since the burglary or even before it. Watching her. Watching us. He's even got a video camera set up."

"The local police did everything they were supposed to. No one could've known he'd be this bold."

Maybe, Mac thought, but reasonable or not, it was an oversight that could have cost Natalie her life. "We know he's plenty bold now. And we're not going to underestimate him again."

ALEX DITCHED THE CAB in the back of a supermarket parking lot. He walked several miles to the public bus depot where he'd left his own car—the car Clemmons had bought for him—then got on the freeway toward Sacramento. He'd driven almost thirty miles before he stopped checking the rearview mirror.

Not since prison had he felt so lost. Even so, in prison he'd had the chaplain. To teach him, in spite of what he'd done. To pursue him, despite Alex's initial rudeness.

To patiently guide him toward the light and show him the paradise that awaited him, if only he was willing to repent his sins and trust himself to an almighty God.

But now Alex didn't have the chaplain to guide him. He had something better, someone better, or so he'd thought. Without someone to interpret scripture or point out the signs for him, things had become confusing. Gray.

Alex didn't like grayness. He liked things black and white. It was in grayness that the devil lurked, tempting humanity and encouraging sin. Fabricating excuses. Mucking things up so you were never quite sure who was talking to you, God or the devil in disguise. Alex missed the comfort of certainty. Of knowing that what he was doing was right. Because it was what He wanted.

But now Alex wasn't sure. Not since the woman had escaped him. Escaped his plans for her. God's plan. Or had he misunderstood?

It had been easy for him to pick up Natalie Jones. Far easier than he'd ever anticipated. He'd seen her walk outside, shocked at the sight of her walking cane. He'd stared at it, confused. Why was she using a cane for the blind?

The answer, of course, was that she *was* blind.

He'd laughed out loud at the beauty of it. She'd seen something she shouldn't have. Something God didn't want others to see, so He'd struck her blind because of it. Then He'd sent Alex to her to guide the way.

He'd barely been able to contain his excitement as he'd watched her, waiting and waiting some more. Then she'd gone back inside. When the cab had shown up, he'd known exactly what he was going to do.

It was a bold move, he knew. Some would say it was beyond foolish for him to overpower the driver in broad daylight and take his place. He'd waited for someone to call out, or for the police to arrive, sirens blaring, guns drawn, but that hadn't happened. It had all made sense. He had cleared the way for him, which was yet another holy sign that what he was doing was necessary. Right.

While he'd watched Natalie from the cab, he'd been struck by how truly beautiful she was. Beautiful enough that his body had responded in a very unholy way. It had distracted him. Made him long for material things. Secular pleasure. It only took spotting her cane, and her dropping it, to remind him that he was more angel than she. She needed guidance, and he was the one who could give it to her, just as the chaplain had done for him. But only after getting Him the information He needed.

He'd served his sentence. Sacrificed in order to find salvation. It seemed reasonable that Natalie Jones would have to do the same.

But then she'd rejected him. Rejected his words. Struck out at him with her cane. Escaped. His anger had been all-encompassing, leaving only enough room for humiliation. Fear. He'd failed. And how could failure result in anything but eternal suffering in the flames of hell? Had he lost his chance at redemption? Suddenly the faces of all his past victims—men, women and children—had swarmed before him, making him dizzy.

There had been too many people for him to turn around and go after her. He hadn't wanted to take that chance. Be caught. He'd doubted God's power to protect him, and he knew that's why he was being punished now.

Whimpering, Alex jerked the car to the side of the road, not even hearing the blast of horns that came from other drivers. He squeezed his eyes shut and grasped at his temples. There were two voices inside his head now. Two voices that warred. One telling him to fulfill his original task, the other telling him to see the signs that urged him to change his course. Yet both voices were His.

And then there was a third voice. His own voice. The voice from his past. Telling him that ending his confusion would be simple. Easy. The matter would end. Even without answers, he would be saved. Safe.

All he had to do was kill Natalie Jones.

CHAPTER SIXTEEN

NATALIE DIDN'T THINK ANYTHING could be worse than being trapped in a car with a homicidal maniac, but being trapped in her own home with Officer Liz Lafayette came close. Although the woman was exceedingly professional and polite, even friendly, everything she was and did served only to remind Natalie of her own shortcomings. She was young, but obviously smart, ambitious and strong. She'd have to be in order to have gotten through the police academy. She could go anywhere and do anything she wanted. And no one would dare feel sorry for her.

Natalie would also bet she was pretty. She had the type of bearing that only a confident woman had—not arrogant, but self-assured—plus she wore earrings that occasionally caught the light. The scent of Estée Lauder's *Beautiful* perfume was a pleasant cloud around her when she moved. Natalie had an old bottle of it somewhere in a drawer, but she'd stopped wearing it months ago. She'd meant to throw it out but hadn't gotten around to it.

She could be in her bedroom right now, sorting through that box and throwing away the last vestiges of her past—or more likely huddling under the covers and pretending morning hadn't come—but because she hadn't wanted to appear rude, or worse, that she was intimidated or hiding, she'd come out and asked the woman to join her for breakfast instead. Now they were done, and Natalie searched desperately for a topic of conversation to alleviate the awkwardness in the air. She couldn't come up with one. All her thoughts were on Mac and that kiss and how she'd made a fool of herself by freaking out on him. Something both Jase and this woman had seen.

"So…" Liz cleared her throat. "Agent McKenzie called a while ago. He's checking into a Plainville hotel later today."

Natalie's pulse suddenly went into overdrive. "A hotel?"

"He often works out of the Bureau of Law Enforcement Building in San Francisco. But given what happened yesterday, he's setting up shop at our police station. Both he and Agent Tyler."

It made sense. The female officer had explained what Mac and Jase had discovered after leaving her house yesterday. That her attacker had been holed up right across the street, waiting for the perfect opportunity to pounce. She'd handed it to him on a silver platter. With bells on. But even the knowledge that he'd been that close didn't disturb her as much as the idea of Mac checking into a Plainville hotel. Of him leaving the comfort of his own office and home for the sole purpose of being closer to her. Granted, it was only because of the case, but…

"He—he told me he was based in San Francisco, but from what I heard yesterday... I mean, I thought they had a more important case they had to work on...."

"I guess he convinced his watch commander he was needed here." Liz's shrug was soundless yet explicit. And although there was no hint of innuendo in her voice, Natalie imagined it was there nonetheless.

"Why is he working this case? Isn't this something your staff can handle on your own?"

"SIG handles special investigations, and this is certainly one of those. The girl who was killed, Lindsay Monroe, her father has special political connections."

"And if she didn't? Her case file would get shoved to the back burner?"

"Along with a whole bunch of others. It's a sad truth, but there aren't enough good cops to handle all the cases that get thrown our way."

"Are you a detective, too?"

"Nope. Not yet. One day, I hope to be."

"Do you know Mac and Jase? Personally?" She closed her eyes. *Yeah, that sounded subtle, Natalie.*

But Liz seemed to think nothing of her question. "My supervisor worked with Mac on a case a couple of months back. Has a lot of respect for him, and that's enough for me."

"Do you know—"

There was a knock on the front door, and she heard the sound of Liz's chair scraping back. "You expecting anyone?"

An edge of tension in Liz's voice was immediately apparent, one that hadn't been there just seconds before.

"No," Natalie said, instinctively stiffening and fighting the urge to flee. "I'm not."

"Let me just go check. Please stay here."

Her footsteps tracked her movements to the front door where Natalie could hear her talking with someone. Then the sound of Melissa's voice drifted toward her.

"—need to talk to her. Please!"

Natalie hesitated and bit her lip as Liz firmly denied Melissa entrance. Although she'd been relieved when Melissa had finally called her yesterday, making excuses about why she hadn't shown up, Natalie hadn't been able to stifle her hurt and disappointment. She'd been cold. Distant. Told Melissa she'd call her later.

Now, she listened as Melissa continued to argue with Liz. The officer's tone was becoming more and more aggressive even as Melissa's became more desperate. Natalie sighed, stood and called out, "It's okay, Liz. It's my friend, Melissa. Please let her inside."

Their arguing abruptly stopped.

"I need to call Mac first," Liz said.

Mac, Mac, Mac. He certainly wielded enormous authority with the local police. But she supposed that wasn't being fair. After all, the man was the lead agent on this case, trying to solve the murder of a young girl. Trying to prevent him from murdering again.

Shakily, Natalie took her seat once more. Mac was trying to protect her, she acknowledged, because it was his job. But he hadn't kissed her because of his job. Granted, she'd *asked* him to kiss her, but when she'd tried to emotionally back away from the connection she'd felt, he'd made it plain he wasn't happy about it. She recalled his words clearly, the same way she'd recalled them throughout the night.

We're going to find the man who threatened you, and we're going to catch Lindsay's killer, regardless of whether they're the same person or not. And when we do, you won't be a witness anymore. You won't be part of the job. You'll just be a woman who's attracted to me as much as I am to her."

Could it be true? That such a virile, strong man could be attracted to her, the same disabled, needy woman he'd been determined to stay away from? But perhaps it was because he was so strong that he was attracted to her. He was a modern day warrior, with hard sleek muscles that she'd felt herself when they'd embraced. She'd wanted to sink into him. Lose herself in his arms where she could feel both daring and safe, something she'd never quite been able to manage before, not at the same time.

She knew it was the allure of his strength that drew her to him, and likely what drew scads of other women to him, too. As a cop, he was a natural-born protector, one who enjoyed saving the day. Perhaps that's what she was to him. Just one in a long line of the weak and needy. Despite his declaration that he didn't want that, his need to protect was probably inbred so deep he couldn't get away from it. That had to be it.

She heard a noise and looked up. "Melissa?"

"No, it's just me. Liz. I'm sorry, Natalie, but Mac gave me orders to not let Melissa in."

"Did you tell him I wanted to see her?"

Natalie didn't need to see her to sense Liz's deep discomfort. "Well, yes, but…"

"But what?"

"He overrode that request."

She inhaled a breath, trying to contain the temper that flashed through her. "He overrode…" Natalie stood. Damn him. It was bad enough she saw so little of her friend, anyway. Yes, that was her choice sometimes, but that was the point. She saw who she wanted to when she wanted to, and she wasn't going to let Mac or even some freaky religious nut change that. She couldn't. If the blindness hadn't completely destroyed her, and it hadn't, not yet… "I'll just let Melissa in myself."

"She already left, Natalie."

Her anger was so strong she half expected her body to ignite. "So I'm not allowed to see anyone. I'm to be kept a prisoner in my own home. Unable to talk to anyone or see any of my friends."

She heard a faint, low male curse and hissed in surprise.

"Mac's still on the line. He wanted to talk to you in the event you were mad. Actually, he knew you would be mad so… Would you—er—would you like to talk to him?"

"Yes." She held out her hand for the cell phone, which Liz gently placed in her palm. She raised the phone to her ear but didn't say anything. She heard Liz walk away, heard her own rapid breaths.

"I'm sorry you feel as if you're a prisoner in your own home, Natalie. That's not what's happening."

She licked her lips and closed her eyes. Lord, his voice... The man had such an incredible voice. And mouth. And body. She shook her head slightly as if to clear her head. "Then why aren't I allowed to see my friends?"

"You can see your friends, but not Melissa. Not until I have a chance to talk with her and clear her story."

"Clear her story? What does that mean?"

"It means Melissa was the one who left you standing on a curb so that a murderer could pick you up, Natalie. It means I have to rule out the fact that she might have been involved with your abduction. Which means she might even have had something to do with Lindsay's murder."

"Are you insane? Melissa's not a criminal. She had nothing to do with this!"

"If that's the case, then she'll talk to me, we'll clear the whole thing up. By the way, I looked through the pictures you gave me."

"Did you see anything that can help you? With Lindsay's case or mine?"

"They were more than helpful, Natalie. I believe I've identified both Lindsay Monroe and Alex Hanes in the photos. They weren't standing together. Alex was hanging out by the playground while Lindsay strolled the grounds. IDing her was a bit more difficult because she changed her hair color, and I can only see a partial profile of her face, but I think it's her. If I'm right, your pictures place them together on a specific date just before she was murdered, and along with the evidence we already have, it'll make a strong case for Hanes's conviction."

She heard his unspoken words. It would make a strong case when they finally caught him, but she didn't doubt they would. Mac and Jase were good cops. Dedicated. They wouldn't let the murderer of a sixteen-year-old girl go unpunished.

"It's also proof that the man who attacked me is the same man who killed Lindsay," she said. "Well, wow... That's great then, right? You have everything you need from me...." Why that realization depressed her, she didn't even want to know.

"Not quite."

She jerked at his unexpected answer. "Wh-what do you mean?"

"The pictures are evidence, but they need to be authenticated in order to be admissible. Since you're the person who took the pictures, we're going to need you to testify at trial. I also need to consider what Hanes said to you when he got you in that cab."

"He said a lot of things. What are you referring to?"

"Even though he didn't copy all the photos off your computer, chances are he saw some of the same shots I did. He'd see he was in them. That Lindsay was, too. Yet he took the chance of coming back. Why? Why resort to kidnapping you? You said he wanted to talk to you.

To find out what you knew. What you'd told us. That tells me he's afraid you saw something, something that might not be in the photos. I want to go over that day with you. Go over the pictures with you, too."

"But I already told you, I don't have clear memories of that day! And I can't see the details in those pictures."

"I can. We'll look at them together and I can describe what I see. You're not alone in this, Natalie. I can help you." For a second, his words made her melt, just the way hearing his voice did.

She told herself she was a fool.

Because she *was* alone. She always had been. Alone to deal with the fear of what was coming for her. Alone to deal with the reality of it.

Her pictures had made her forget that for a while.

Her pictures had given her the illusion of belonging. To the world and the people she shot. Now she didn't even have that. As much as she'd enjoyed the feeling of being part of something when she took her pictures, part of different people and places across the world, she'd always been an outsider, now more than ever. Now she couldn't even pretend. She couldn't be part of something she couldn't see because, for all intents and purposes, they didn't exist for her.

She especially couldn't belong with a man whose voice and scent she gravitated to but whose visage she couldn't form. How could you truly be with anyone when you didn't even know the color of his eyes? The expressions on his face?

"Natalie?"

She sighed. "We can talk some more, even though I don't think it'll help. In the meantime, am I allowed to talk to Melissa on the phone? I mean, she can't hurt me over a phone line, right?"

His silence before he answered highlighted his struggle for patience. "Yes, you can talk to her, but don't tell her specifics of what happened and don't coach her on what to say. That's important, otherwise you could just delay her being cleared. I'm not trying to control your every movement. I'm just trying to do my job and protect you."

His words hung in the air, verifying what she'd thought earlier. He was simply doing his job. She had to remember that.

"Thank you for clarifying that for me. I'm not trying to be difficult. Despite my behavior yesterday, I know I'm just a job to you."

"Damn it, that's not what I mean and you—"

His voice, a dark growl, radiated immense frustration. She felt guilty for causing him grief, but she had her own frustration to deal with. Her own confusion.

"Please. Don't. Your job is all that matters right now." It was all that *could* matter. She'd never felt so conflicted in her life. She wanted to cooperate with him, but she didn't. She wanted his help, but she didn't. She wanted to be more than just part of his job, but she didn't.

She *couldn't*.

Hell, there were so many things she wanted. From her body. Her life. From Mac. What she *wanted* didn't matter. Dreams and desire weren't a part of her world anymore, at least not right now. She doubted ever.

She had to be realistic about what she could have and what she could handle. A tough male like Mac, one who clearly guarded his freedom and independence, wouldn't—even if he was open to a relationship, which he'd already told her he wasn't—want a relationship with someone like her. And even if he was attracted to her, which she was smart enough not to deny, she wasn't going to be a charity case, an easy lay or the pathetic disabled woman giving a man his kinky thrills during secret booty calls. Not ever. She'd rather die first. "I'll do everything I can to help you find this person. You'll do everything you can to keep me safe. That's enough on both our plates. We don't—we don't need anything else getting in the way."

His silence was charged. Instead of agreeing with her, he said, "Stay safe." Then he hung up.

She palmed the unfamiliar phone, unsure where the end call button was. She cleared her throat and laid the phone on the table, then stood. "Officer, I'm—I'm going to my room for a bit."

The first thing she did was go to the drawer where she knew she kept the bottle of *Beautiful* perfume and threw it in the trash.

MAC BARELY KEPT himself from flinging his phone across his office. The woman was driving him crazy, and the journey had only just begun. He'd known the second their lips had met that she held the power to drive him to his knees. And of course, even before Jase had started in on him, he'd known he couldn't give her that power.

Not now. Maybe never.

He had a job to do. And he had reality to face.

She was a prime witness in his murder investigation.

That was all he could rely on her for.

He couldn't rely on her to ease the ache in his groin that flared whenever they were around each other. And he couldn't rely on her to give him that sense of peace that had floated through him when he'd been kissing her.

Despite her steely core, the woman was as needy as they came. More to the point, she was going through an incredibly difficult time, physically and emotionally. No doubt, she needed to know that, despite her disability, she was still desirable. He'd felt her uncertainty in her touch and in the hesitant play of her tongue against his. He'd also felt her *need* as she'd trembled against him. Right before she'd moaned and lost herself to the sparks between them. She was going to latch on to whatever bond she could make right now, like a duckling bonding to his mother, and it would be cruel for Mac to take advantage of that.

He wasn't the type of man who could devote himself to anyone the way Natalie needed. Hell, he hadn't managed to meet Nancy's needs, and she'd been fully sighted, because his career had to come first. He wasn't good at nurturing people, but what he did *was* important. Necessary. He couldn't take time off to be at her beck and call even when she legitimately needed him.

Which was why Jase was right.

Despite the brash promises he'd made the day before, even after this case was over, he couldn't let the passion go any further between them, no matter how much his body rebelled at the thought.

Still, that hadn't stopped him from fantasizing about the two of them last night. Together. Against each other. Sweaty and hot. In a bed. On the floor. Against a wall. Outside in the rain. Hell, he'd managed to pack more creativity and more variety into those few hours of sleep than he'd ever managed to do in real life. And her blindness hadn't slowed them down one bit. He'd woken with a hard-on that had literally had him clenching his teeth in pain and fighting to keep from spilling on his sheets, something he hadn't done since he was thirteen. But it was the hollow ache in his heart when he'd realized it had all been a dream that had shaken him.

He'd met the woman twice. Interacted with her briefly on both occasions. And waking up to find her absent from his bed, *when she'd never even been there,* was enough to make him feel…what? Lonely? Longing?

It wasn't possible, and even if it was, it couldn't be allowed to continue. Hell, he'd never felt that way about Nancy. Ever. But he had loved her once. He didn't relish the idea of spending any significant time loving Natalie, actually sleeping with her beside him, and then having to deal when she suddenly wanted to end it because he wasn't enough for her.

So, no, he'd chalk up his reactions to Natalie as chemistry and a white knight complex. He'd get things back on track professionally, just like he'd tried to do on the phone.

Yet he didn't want her thinking that all she meant to him was a job, either.

He'd heard the hurt in her voice when she'd said that, and he'd hated it.

"You ready to head out?"

He turned to Jase, who had his roller suitcase next to him. He had to blink several times before coming out of the fog his thoughts had shrouded him in. Memory of their present plans returned.

He'd offered to go to Plainville on his own. Jase had a new case, one that would take his considerable attention. But Jase had insisted on accompanying Mac. "I can review the files on the new case while I'm there. Make some calls. That way, if you need me as backup, I won't be too far away. I can handle Natalie, too. If anything else comes up with her."

Mac had understood what the other man was saying. And offering. He'd been smart enough to agree.

Both he and Jase would continue to work the case together and follow leads. Natalie would continue to be guarded by the local police, and if they needed to interview her for further information, the one to get it from her would be Jase.

It wasn't what he truly wanted. He wanted to stay close to her, close enough to do his job, but even closer than that.

Which was why he was going to stay as far away from her as he could.

"Yeah. I'm ready. Did Plainville PD finish with the house?"

"They processed it and are testing for Hanes's fingerprints now. It's gonna take some time. We don't even have the DNA results from Lindsay's pendant yet."

Mac knew that, but he had no doubt Hanes's fingerprints and DNA were going to be found. Joe Casey, the cabbie who'd been carjacked, had positively identified Alex Hanes as the man who'd attacked him.

They were going to be holing up in Plainville until this case was solved, or at least until they knew Natalie was safe.

It looked like one wasn't going to happen without the other.

CHAPTER SEVENTEEN

"Natalie, I've left a thousand messages on your phone," Melissa said when Natalie finally answered her cell.

"And I told you I'd be in touch," she said coolly. "That I was a little busy dealing with another attempt on my life."

"You're also mad at me, and I don't blame you. I'm so sorry. I swear, I never thought something like this would happen."

Natalie gripped the phone tighter. *No,* she thought, *you just thought I'd be stuck standing in the middle of the street looking like a fool.* She didn't say anything, however. She couldn't have, even if she'd wanted to, because Melissa was still talking.

"It was just...I thought I'd be a little late, but then I got hung up in traffic because of that accident on the highway and my cell phone battery was dead. When that policewoman answered the door, I—"

Natalie's head was throbbing, and she pressed her fingers to her temples. "It's fine, Melissa, really."

"But you were kidnapped. Taken by some weirdo because of me."

The same weirdo who tried to strangle me to death.

She'd told Melissa the connection, but that was it. As Mac had ordered, she hadn't told her what he'd said or even that she'd ended up jumping out of the cab. "It wasn't because of you, Melissa. It was because of my own bad luck. Now, you be sure and tell Agent McKenzie that when he talks to you. Remember, it's just a precaution he's taking. He has to talk to everyone. You didn't do anything wrong."

When Melissa didn't say anything, Natalie frowned. "Melissa?"

"I'm here. It's just, how can you be so damn noble all the time? Don't you ever get angry? I fucked up, Natalie. You have a right to be mad."

"Well, I'm not mad," she said, her voice strained. "I'm just tired." She forced her tone to be slightly more cheery. "Thanks for coming by today. We'll talk later, okay?"

She hung up before Melissa could say anything else. A pinch of guilt made her chew her lip, and she struggled with whether she should call her friend back. Despite her words, she had sounded mad at the end, hadn't she? But she'd been through so much. Wasn't she entitled to be a little cranky, given what had happened to her?

Besides, she had some things to do. Like once again go over her copies of the photographs she'd given Mac. She hadn't seen anything the first twenty times she'd looked at them, but maybe…

A faint knock made her look up.

"Natalie, is it okay if I come in?" Liz asked.

Natalie was sitting in the sunroom, where she and Mac had shared that disastrous kiss, and the idea of Liz inhabiting the space made her feel weird, so of course she said, "Yes, please do."

"So, that was your friend, Melissa? The one who stood you up yesterday?"

Natalie didn't miss the hint of censure in the woman's voice. She raised her chin. "That was Melissa, yes."

"You spent a lot of time reassuring her that you're okay."

"Why wouldn't I? I *am* okay."

"You'll *be* okay. There's a difference. You're allowed to be mad at her."

"I'm not mad at her! Everyone messes up. Melissa was running late because of her boyfriend. They have a complicated relationship."

"It was still a lame thing to do. Standing you up. Doesn't mean you can't be friends with her anymore, but friends can tell each other how they really feel."

"What would it matter if I told her it was lame? It can't change anything. Besides, it was my own fault. I should know better than to rely on anyone."

Her words surprised her. She hadn't meant to say them.

"That's not any way to live."

She knew that. Deep down, she did. But such thinking was for normal people. People who had unlimited options. People who could afford to rely on others. People who didn't know better. The fact that this woman— this sighted, competent woman—was lecturing her suddenly became too much. In a tight voice, Natalie asked, "Do *you* rely on anyone, Officer?"

"Of course I do. When I'm out on the streets, I have to rely on my fellow officers to watch my back."

"But that's part of the job. It's quid pro quo. They have to rely on you, too, right?"

"Right. But what's that got to do with it?"

"It means everyone does what they need to survive. They ultimately do what's right for them."

"Cops put themselves on the line for people every day."

"For three very important reasons."

"What's that?"

"Money. The thrill. And third, because no one ever thinks it's going to happen to them. If you did, if you knew you were going to get shot and killed on the job, wouldn't you choose something else?"

She heard her answer in Officer Lafayette's hesitation, but she took no satisfaction in it. In fact, it made her feel so tired she suddenly wanted to simply go to sleep and never wake up.

"That's not fair," Officer Lafayette protested, though weakly. "That's self-protection."

"That's right. And that's exactly what I'm doing. I know who I can rely on. Myself. Anyone who thinks otherwise is a fool."

BEFORE CHECKING in to his hotel, Mac stopped by the Plainville Police Department to give the press an update on Lindsay Monroe's murder investigation. Although he deliberately didn't mention Natalie or her photographs, he specifically named Alex Hanes as their primary suspect. Updating the public wasn't his only objective, however. He wanted Alex Hanes's photo plastered on every news channel in the nation. He wanted the man to know Mac and a hell of a lot of other police officers were looking for him. He wanted him to get jittery, to imagine himself locked up in prison again, so that he'd get careless. Make a mistake that would get him caught. At the very least, he'd think twice about kidnapping a woman in the middle of the day if he felt there was a greater chance someone would recognize him.

Once he was at the hotel, Mac pulled out the photos Natalie had given him. Frustration drilled painfully at his chest along with something else—an uneasy feeling that he was missing something. That there was more in the photos than he was seeing.

Yes, the photos proved that Lindsay and Hanes had attended the same farmers' market. Perhaps that's where he'd first seen her. Still, other than putting them in the same location, the photos weren't incriminating in and of themselves. Not that he could see, anyway. Yet Hanes had wanted them badly enough to burglarize Natalie's home. He'd wanted to know what Natalie had seen that day, enough to kidnap her in broad daylight.

That told him something important had happened, something that either wasn't depicted in the photos or, if it was, something Mac was missing.

But what was it?

Since he didn't know, he ticked down his mental list of what he *did* know:

They knew Lindsay had attended the Plainville Farmers' Market on the date Natalie took the pictures.

Lindsay had been killed sometime after that.

Since she didn't appear to be wearing orange, and her body had been found with a swatch of orange fabric, that increased the chances she'd been killed on a different day but didn't guarantee it. The orange swatch of fabric could have been from a scarf, or handbag or jacket she'd put on after the photos were taken.

They still didn't know if she'd been killed in Plainville or somewhere else, if she'd gone to the farmers' market with Hanes or someone else, or if Natalie had seen something she shouldn't have and simply didn't remember.

Basically, what they didn't know sucked.

He and Jase would continue to study the photos for clues, and Jase was planning to go over the photos with Natalie. But for now, the Plainville Police Department had been given their orders, with clear instructions to call Mac if something turned up. First they were going to interview regular vendors at the market. Show them pictures of Lindsay, Alex and Natalie. Ask if they recognized anyone in Natalie's photos, maybe even a local who could then be interviewed, as well. As tedious as link analysis was, it was a methodical procedure that resulted in useful evidence far more often than not.

Everything that could be done was being done and by a very competent crew. He knew that from having worked with the Plainville Police Department in the past. He'd thought about hitting the pavement himself, certainly had no qualms about doing whatever grunt work was necessary to get the job done. But there were already so many loose ends that Mac needed to deal with. He had phone calls to make. Witnesses to interview.

He'd be plenty busy, but part of him was rethinking his decision to stay away from Natalie. Mac's main concern was finding Alex Hanes. His strongest connection to the man was the woman he'd tried to kill even *after* he'd had her photos. Staying away from her simply because of their shared attraction no longer seemed smart, but a chickenshit move that could interfere with him doing his job. Maybe instead of staying away from her, he should stay as close to her as possible. Even if that very closeness distracted him on a personal level.

The shrill ring of his phone made him jerk. When he glanced at the screen, he grunted. Alex Hanes's parole officer was finally getting back to him.

"McKenzie."

"Agent McKenzie, this is Cora Concannon, Phoenix Parole Department."

"Thanks for calling me back. Anything new on Hanes?"

"I'm sorry, but no."

"Did you get my message about the cross pendant found in a woman's home in Plainville, California?"

"Yes, I did. I'm sorry, but I've been out of town before now. You said the pendant belonged to your murder victim?"

His murder victim. It was how many people often referred to the dead whose killers Mac tried to hunt down. The wording never failed to impact him. It was a reminder that he did have a personal stake in every case he worked. That he stood and spoke for those who couldn't do it for themselves.

"That's right. Lindsay Monroe's father said she always wore a cross pendant he gave her. One with a very unusual engraving on it—Litsy. It was a term of endearment the family used. The pendant was found, chain broken, in the home of a woman who'd just been assaulted. I have reason to believe, now more than ever, that that man was Hanes. I think he kept the pendant as some kind of memento."

"I think you're right."

Her quick and easy agreement took him by surprise. "What makes you say that?"

"I only spoke with Alex a few times before he absconded from parole, but when I did, he was quite vocal about having found God. He peppered his vocabulary with scripture and said he owed his release from prison and his bright future to a higher power."

"And yet his DNA was all over a sixteen-year-old murder victim. And I'll bet all over the house across the street from that of the blind woman he tried to strangle to death just one month later."

"A blind woman? Is she okay?"

"She's fine for now." And Mac was going to make

sure she stayed that way. "So Alex was religious. Did he mention a particular religion? A church he was attending? A pastor he spoke to?" Was it possible he'd confessed his crimes to someone under the protection of religious confidentiality? The very thought left a sour taste in Mac's mouth. He was all for spirituality, still believed in God even if He wasn't quite the same one he'd learned about in Sunday school.

When it came to organized religion, however, he couldn't help being a skeptic. In his line of work, he knew how often those who claimed to worship God could do the unthinkable and then rely on their inherently sinful natures as an excuse. Forget about questioning how a creator could allow such horrible things to occur in the first place, but the idea that criminals could have their sins washed away through confession and repentance? It seemed a little too easy for Mac to swallow.

"No, nothing so specific. He was staying at a halfway house for recently released inmates, however."

"I remember. Amber House. I talked with the owner soon after I first contacted you. I've got a call out, but haven't heard back from him yet, either."

"It's a particularly hard time to catch people, given all the last-minute vacation plans before the school year starts again."

Mac caught the note of defensiveness in the woman's voice. "That wasn't a jab at you."

Two seconds passed before Concannon continued. "Anyway, it was his brother who arranged for him to

stay at Amber House. Maybe he'd know whether he attended a particular church."

Mac shook his head. "What brother?"

"Excuse me?"

"I said, what brother. None of the documents I have,
including Hanes's parole sheet, lists a sibling."

"Really?" Mac heard bumping sounds coming from
the other line. "Wait, I'm pulling out his file... Let me
check.... Well, you're right. For some reason, I remember him telling me about a brother, but obviously I could
be wrong about that."

"Or the records are just incomplete."

"That's always a possibility, too." Again her tone
was laced with defensiveness. Not good. Because his
jurisdiction was so broad, Mac's effectiveness hinged
on his ability to keep good working relationships with
all the different law enforcement agencies throughout
the state. Still, he couldn't overlook shoddy work or pull
his punches just because someone might take offense.

"Do you remember a name? Did Alex say where his
brother lived? What he did for a living? Anything?"

"No. Like I said, I think he mentioned a brother, but
I can't be sure now."

"Please let me know if you remember anything else,"
he said, striving to be as polite as possible, though it
was more difficult than usual. "I hope you enjoyed your
vacation."

"Goodbye, Agent McKenzie."

When he hung up, he immediately pulled out tran-
scripts of his interview with Lindsay's father. He flipped

through pages until he found the section he'd been looking for. According to Monroe, his family was devoutly
religious. Some tension had occurred when Lindsay
started expressing doubts and had refused to attend their
church. That tension had probably contributed to her
running away. And it didn't mean she hadn't changed
her mind afterwards, or that another religion hadn't
held more appeal to her.

Religious faith, especially when he wasn't sure what
faiths they were talking about, certainly didn't scream
a connection, but he had to consider that Hanes took
Lindsay's cross pendant, not to keep a memento from a
victim but because they shared similar religious beliefs.
If that was true, than maybe religion had had something to do with how they met or why he'd killed her
in the first place.

Picking up the phone again, he dialed the DOJ crime
lab. Henry Littlefield answered. "Hey, Henry. It's Mac
McKenzie."

"Yo, Big Mac. What can I do for you?"

"You can tell me you've got the results from the DNA
or fingerprint analysis we've requested in the Lindsay
Monroe case."

"Work, work, work. It's all about work with you,
man," Littlefield muttered good-naturedly. Mac took
it in good stride. If ever there was someone who em-
bodied a workaholic, Littlefield was it. It didn't help
with the crime lab's backlog, however, because new
requests were made every day, and invariably most of
the requests were designated as rushes. First priority

was always given to cases currently at trial, however. While the lab did its best, the techs weren't miracle workers. That's why Mac wasn't surprised when Littlefield came back on the line and said, "Sorry. Not yet. Hopefully soon."

"Right. Thanks. Can you connect me to Tanzina in Tech?"

"Take it easy, Mac."

"You, too, Littlefield."

A quick click was followed by, "Ernest Tanzina."

Mac smiled at the heavily accented voice. Tanzina was Romanian, a good-natured man, devoted father and all-around likable guy. In all the years they'd worked together, Mac couldn't remember a time when the guy wasn't smiling. "Hey, Tanzina, it's Mac."

"Hey, Mac. How's it going?"

"Pretty good. But I'm working the Lindsay Monroe case and I was hoping you could do me a favor."

"Sure thing."

"You've been searching the vic's hard drive. Using key string search terms for internet predator evidence, right?"

"Standard stuff. Meet. Secret. Love. Trust. Nothing's hit so far."

"I want you to run a search including religious terms. God. Church. Mass. That kind of thing."

"You found something useful, then?"

"Won't know until you run that search," Mac drawled.

Tanzina laughed. "I'll call you back in twenty."

He actually called back in ten. "Payday."

Mac sat up. "Tell me what you've got."

"Last September, looks like she started chatting with someone with the screen name BLVR. I can access the dates and times of those chats, and I can tell you they include religious terms. But I can't access the actual chats themselves. To do that, we're gonna need a warrant for the company that owns the server she used. If they come up with anything useful and you want to find out BLVR's IP address, we're gonna need a warrant to get that, too."

"Shit. How long is that going to take?"

"You can write up a warrant and get a judge to sign off tomorrow. As far as getting the info from the companies, we're looking at days. Weeks even."

"Damn it, that's too long."

"So what do you want me to do?"

"Get started on it. In the meantime, I'll check things out here."

"Here being where?"

"Plainville."

"Ah. Small town."

"Right. Small town. Limited number of churches. Even though her body was found an hour north, in Redding, she attended a farmers' market here. Maybe she attended church here, too."

"Good luck, man."

"Thanks. Stay in touch."

Mac hung up, then rubbed at his forehead before making yet another call. The owner of Amber House was still "unavailable." "Tell him I need to talk to him as soon as possible. Special Agent Mac McKenzie with California DOJ." He repeated his phone number and hung up.

Shit, a few phone calls had resulted in yet another long list of tasks. He needed to look into whether Alex Hanes had a brother or not, one who might know whether he'd attended church. He needed to pinpoint churches in both Redding and Plainville and see whether anyone at those churches had ever seen Lindsay or Alex Hanes. And he still needed to interview Melissa Callahan.

Which to do first? In the end, it was an easy decision.

Natalie knew Melissa. Melissa had left her waiting so that a murderer was able to get to her. That murderer had killed Lindsay. Lindsay had befriended someone online, someone who she referred to as *M.*

Melissa's name started with *M.*

Granted, Lindsay had referred to *her* M in male pronouns, but that could have been a cover-up, meant to throw anyone who found her journal off track.

Chances were interviewing Melissa wouldn't amount to a hill of beans. In fact, he hoped that was the case. So while he waited for the owner of Amber House to call him back, he'd interview Melissa first. And if doing so meant she'd be cleared faster so that Natalie could stop worrying about her, that was just happenstance. But still a happenstance he'd be thankful for.

CHAPTER EIGHTEEN

DESPITE HER INITIAL DISCOMFORT with Liz's presence in her home, Natalie spent the day getting to know the other woman and found herself having a pretty good time. They played cards, talked about old movies, and worked in her kitchen together making tuna sandwiches. It had been so long since she'd experienced such steady female companionship that Natalie almost forgot Liz was a cop assigned to protect her, rather than a new friend she'd invited over for lunch. But then Liz got a call from work and had to excuse herself to another part of the house. For the next few hours, Natalie tackled a few household tasks she'd been putting off.

When late afternoon approached and Mac still hadn't shown up, Natalie tried to muster some pride for having run him off—her attempts had obviously worked. Pride wasn't anywhere close to what she was feeling. All she seemed to be able to do was envision herself alone as the years passed, never again feeling that mindless heat that had suffused her the moment her lips had met Mac's. It left a hollow feeling in her stomach, one she became desperate to fill.

To distract herself, she took another stab at the farmers' market photos. Again, she couldn't even identify what was in most of the photos, let alone whether there was something weird or incriminating about them. She'd hoped the more she looked at them, the greater the chance they'd jar her memory, like retracing one's steps often did, but—

Wait a minute. Retracing her steps. She hadn't even thought about that possibility until now. Yet the area where the city held its farmers' market was less than ten miles from her house. Granted, it wasn't like the farmers' market was running today, but if she walked the park's paths, maybe her brain would subconsciously fill in missing details. It was worth a try, wasn't it?

Only she needed a way to get there, and she wasn't about to call a cab.

Liz.

She walked to the dining area where Liz had last been. "Liz?"

"I'm right here, Natalie."

"I was wondering if you could drive me somewhere. I'd like to get out of the house for a while."

"Um, well… I don't know, Natalie. I'll have to check with Mac."

Even though the poor woman didn't deserve her annoyance, Natalie felt herself frowning. "Why? I'm not allowed to go anywhere unless you have his permission? He told me he wasn't keeping me prisoner, but maybe I misunderstood."

"You know I'm just trying to do my job, Natalie. So let me call Mac."

She blew out a breath at Liz's calm-as-ever, slightly chiding tone. "Fine. Call him."

She waited and listened as Liz did just that. "Hello, Agent McKenzie. It's Officer Lafayette. Natalie just asked if I could take her outside for a bit to get some air and I just wanted to make sure... Well, she didn't say, exactly— Yes, sir. Natalie, where is it you want to go?"

She gritted her teeth. Reminded herself that Mac was trying to keep her safe. *Trying to do his job.* "Tell him I want to go to a park and bring my camera with me, if that's okay with him."

"Uh, she says she wants to go to a park and bring her camera with her. If that's okay with you."

Tapping her foot, Natalie strained to hear Mac's words on the other line but could only make out a faint rumble. Even that sounded sexy. Damn him.

"Thank you. He said yes. I'm ready to leave when you are."

They took Liz's patrol car since Natalie had already disposed of her own vehicle. Less than ten minutes later, Liz announced they'd arrived.

EVEN THOUGH IT WASN'T DARK yet, Alex shone the lights of his car on the northeast side of the church and watched the play of light against the pale pink wall. When he'd first seen the massive pink building with its cheery white trim, he'd thought there'd been some kind of mistake. It looked nothing like a place of worship was supposed to look. And when he'd finally gotten the nerve to go inside, he'd discovered it wasn't like any other church he'd visited or heard about.

It was far better.

He gripped the steering wheel, alternately slapping and fiddling with it, as he stared out the windshield.

He was becoming desperate.

He needed guidance.

The urge to sin, to kill Natalie Jones despite the signs indicating he shouldn't, was overtaking him. But wasn't that a sign in and of itself? Hadn't the holy spirit guided him here? Wasn't the holy spirit guiding him now?

His gaze strayed to the car's glove compartment. Slowly, he leaned over and popped it open. With shaking hands, he pulled out the familiar gun. He traced the trigger as if mesmerized. It was loaded. Just in case.

Like the syringe he kept in the glove compartment was also loaded.

Just in case.

Both items represented his old way of life, and each time he turned away from them, he'd felt himself growing stronger. More confident that he'd changed. That he was on the right path.

Only now...

Now he wondered if the gun and maybe the syringe, too, were meant to *keep him* on that path.

He raised the gun and examined it in the slight glow created by the headlights. It felt heavy. Solid. A natural extension of his hand.

Killing Natalie Jones would solve so many problems. Help Alex. Help Him.

And if he killed for God, perhaps he could do other things, as well. Things he'd done in his previous life. Things that hadn't served a purpose because *he'd* served no purpose. Now that he was a servant of God, perhaps he was entitled to enjoy it all.

Drinking. Smoking. Fucking.

Killing.

All without fear of repercussion.

But wait, nothing was without repercussion.

God was the ultimate judge, and Alex had given all that up for a reason.

For Him. For a family who wasn't here.

His knees moved agitatedly up and down while he moaned and dropped his head in his hands. No, no, no. Those thoughts weren't good. Weren't right. The devil was in the car with him, working his way into his mind.

He had to be strong and resist.

He'd chosen the right path. Still had faith. But beyond that, he no longer knew what to do. Which voice in his head to trust. That's why he'd come to the church. To pray. To talk to Him. But He'd abandoned him. He hadn't granted his pleas for answers.

Dropping his hands, he chewed on his thumb and glanced at the open glove compartment. The baggie with the syringe and other supplies was hidden behind papers, but he knew they were there. Maybe—maybe if he could quiet the voices for just a little while, things would go back to the way they were. He'd stop questioning. Be certain again. Drugs had quieted the monsters in the past. Had rocked him in a hazy, surreal embrace, making him feel safe. Invincible.

The drug could make him feel that way again.

But no, that would be wrong.

Wouldn't it?

Would it?

He pounded the steering wheel with his fists now, his breaths sounding like sobs. He'd done everything He'd told him to do. He'd come here for help. And He wasn't here.

Him. God. Clemmons. Reverend Morrison. They were all the same in his mind. He owed his loyalty to them all.

What to do? What to do?

Silence the voices. That was it.

Still gripping the gun with one hand, he reached into the open glove compartment with the other.

CHAPTER NINETEEN

"OKAY, WE'RE HERE," Liz said.

Natalie opened her car door and stepped out, breathing in the fresh air and hearing the rustling of the breeze through the trees and bushes that covered the park grounds. She heard the other woman round the car and stop beside her. "Would you like to take my arm? If we link elbows, you can hold your camera and take pictures as you feel like it."

Natalie hadn't *really* been planning on taking pictures. She'd simply said that as an excuse. She hadn't wanted to tell Mac her true motives in case her field trip didn't pan out; no sense getting anyone's hopes up. But now that Liz had made the offer, she supposed it made sense. It'd be nice not to have to rely on her cane for a while. To walk and still have use of both hands.

"That would be…nice. Thank you."

"Here you go." Liz guided Natalie's arm through hers. "Anyplace in particular?"

The other woman was so matter-of-fact, any awkwardness Natalie was feeling quickly dissipated. "The gazebo at the north side." That's where she'd parked her car and started taking pictures. As they walked side by side, Liz effortlessly kept pace with her, guiding her past obstacles but only after giving her fair warning first. Natalie was surprised how fluidly they moved together. "Do you have a blind relative I don't know about?" she joked.

"Actually, yes. My mother is blind."

She stumbled at that, then quickly righted herself. "I'm sorry. I mean, I'm sorry I said that. How—?"

"She was born blind."

"And—is she okay?"

"Sure. She's great. Six kids and the love of my dad's life. She's competing in a judo competition next month. Took it up about a year ago and likes to brag that she can flip anyone anytime. I haven't challenged her on that. I learned a long time ago my mom never makes idle threats."

"Judo?" Natalie had heard that judo was a sport adaptable to the blind, but she'd figured that meant competitive athletes, with training in other martial arts, not the average woman with no previous training at all. The average woman was more like her own mother. Weaker. Wasn't she?

"Yes. If you're ever interested in talking to her about it, let me know."

"I—I will. Thank you."

"Here we are."

She knew they'd reached their destination even before Liz spoke. She could smell the roses that surrounded the gazebo, their sweet scent so powerful she could've sworn they were standing in the midst of them rather than on the concrete sidewalk. She pictured the rainbow the flowers had made when she'd last seen them—a frothy explosion of white and pink, peach and red, plum and orange mingled with dark, glossy green. A chaotic mass of colors that nonetheless always appeared deliberate and was always breathtaking.

She'd taken several shots of the roses, the adjacent gazebo, and… What was it? Oh yes, a magician! She'd remembered that in the hospital. A close-up of a magician doing card tricks in between making balloon animals for the kids. And then she'd taken the path to the east.

"Let's walk east. Toward the grove of redwood trees. Do you see it?"

"I sure do. Did you want to take a picture first?"

"Oh, right. Yes." She raised her camera, looked through the lens and sucked in her breath. Just as had been the case with Melissa, she saw blurry gray shadows, but somehow she managed to see the shape of individual roses, too. She knew it was partly memory and partly her mind playing tricks on her, but she didn't care. She took the picture, and when she lowered her camera, she was smiling.

"Let's go."

They walked and chatted, with Natalie occasionally stopping to take a photo while she tried to remember what she'd seen, heard, smelled, felt or tasted just two months ago. Soon, however, without her being aware of it, she stopped trying to remember and simply found herself enjoying the walk.

"Right there. There should be a bench under a big oak tree. Do you see it?"

"Yes."

"Let me sit there for a minute. It gives a great view of the playground on one side and the fountain on another. I remember when—"

A ringing interrupted her. "Sorry," Liz said. "That's my phone. Let me get you settled on the bench and then I'll take this call."

"Right."

As soon as Natalie was sitting, Liz answered her phone. "Officer Liz Lafayette. Yes, Captain, I'm with her right now. The Turner case? I already talked to the mother, sir. Yes, I told her…"

As Liz spoke, Natalie closed her eyes and lifted her face to the sun. It was a mild day, with a light breeze, but even the tepid heat on her face, combined with the airy smells around her, filled her with a rare contentment. She hadn't remembered anything helpful, but at least her mind hadn't replayed those moments of terror when she'd lost her vision. It was so peaceful now, but almost too quiet. She wondered how she'd feel if she was sitting in the midst of a crowd. Safe on her bench but close enough to hear dogs barking, kids playing, old Pete shouting at a couple as they walked by—

Natalie's eyes popped open. Old Pete!

He'd been shouting that day. And he'd been shouting at a man and a woman before the police had run him off. A woman with spiky dark hair and a man with neatly trimmed gray hair. She remembered thinking they were a couple by the way they interacted, but the contrast in their hair color and height had made them seem more like father and daughter than lovers. And there was something about the way the woman had been standing. Something that had distracted her...

She was sure of it. That part of her memory clear.

But what had Pete been shouting? Something weird that had diverted her attention from the unusual-looking couple. Something about being blind? A hypocrite? Granted, Pete had spouted out a lot of nonsense at times, but he was capable of rational thought, too. What if he'd actually known the man and woman? What if the dark-haired female was Lindsay, the same dark-haired girl Mac had identified in her photos?

Someone sat down next to her on the bench, and she turned, squinting at the shadow. "Liz? I was just remembering something. Nothing big, but something that might still help Mac."

"Mac?"

The voice wasn't Liz's, and it definitely wasn't a woman's. Her terror was immediate. "Wh-who are you?"

"Who are *you?*" the man answered, her panic causing her to ignore the teasing quality to his tone. She sensed movement just before she felt his hand on her face.

She moved instinctively, screaming and grabbing at his hand as he touched her hair. She latched on to his fingers and bent them backward. At the same time, she heard Liz shout, "Hey, what are you doing? Get away from her!"

The man screamed and tried to pull away, but she just hung on tighter. At the same time, she stood and tried to kick him. She was too close, however, to do any damage. "Stay away from me," she yelled. "Stay away!"

"Natalie, I'm right here. Let go of him. Now!"

At Liz's voice, Natalie instantly released the man's hand and backed away.

"Crazy bitch! What the fuck is going on?"

"What the hell did you do to her?" Liz demanded.

"Nothing! I just sat down next to her. The wind was in her face, and I nudged it out of her eyes."

"She's blind! She doesn't care if her hair is in her eyes."

"Blind? Shit, I didn't know. She looks normal," he mumbled.

"Get out of here. Now."

She heard the man walk away, muttering under his breath. Again, she caught the word *crazy.*

Crazy. Not normal. For a minute, she'd forgotten that's how people viewed her.

She didn't move. She stood rigidly, exactly where she'd been standing while Liz questioned the poor man who'd made the mistake of sitting next to her.

"I'm sorry, Natalie. I was only about twenty feet away. I started walking while I was talking, and when I turned around, he was sitting next to you. I came as soon as I saw him, but it was too late. I'm sorry."

"It— It's fine, Liz. Really. Can we go now?"

"But don't you want to keep walking? Take more pictures?"

"Actually, no. I'm really tired. I'd just like to go home."

MELISSA CALLAHAN WAS PRETTY. With light brown hair, albeit with a streak dyed blue at the front, she even resembled Natalie to a degree. They were about the same height and complexion, but that's where any similarities ended. Melissa was sweet, slightly naive and fairly gullible—Mac doubted Natalie had ever been any of those things, even when she was a child.

After confirming Melissa had been with her boyfriend at the time Natalie had climbed into that cab with a killer, he'd quickly realized she was exactly what Natalie had claimed she was—a good friend, a flaky one, but not one who'd left her friend out to dry so a murderer could take her. It was apparent from talking to her that she cared for Natalie and that she felt horrible about what had happened. In fact, it was probably her guilt that had her revealing so much unsolicited information about Natalie's personal life during their conversation.

It wasn't something that Mac had been inclined to stop. Even as he'd known Natalie would be horrified by her friend's candidness, Mac had encouraged it, playing on her fears that a killer was after Natalie and might somehow get to her unless Mac knew everything there was to know. What had surprised him in spite of his resolve was that he'd actually felt guilty about it, when normally he wouldn't have given it another thought.

He was just doing his job. Knowing everything possible about Natalie was necessary, especially given her unique vulnerability and foolish pride, in order to protect her. Still, there was also a personal part of him that took satisfaction in getting to know the *woman* better, not the witness, even if it was through the eyes of her friend.

Melissa told him about who Natalie had been before she'd lost her vision. Her genuine love for traveling and adventure that had bordered on desperate at times. About Duncan, "the selfish prick" who'd run out on her. About how different she was now, in part because of her adaptive coach and her therapist, who'd both told her that isolating herself was Natalie's best recourse for adjustment. Of course, Melissa had also told him how little she thought of that line of thinking, and Mac couldn't help but agree with her.

Some healing time, sure. Of course that was necessary. But Natalie had had half her life to adjust to the idea that she might go blind someday. Then she'd had months to deal with the actual fact. Given who she was, given everything she'd done in her life, hiding out had to be more harmful to her than helpful. She was one of those women who thrived on sensation and challenges. If she hadn't been an artist, Mac could easily have seen her going into something like law enforcement and blowing all of his team to hell with her sheer guts and intelligence. Mac was amazed she couldn't see that herself.

"So is either the adaptive coach or the therapist blind?" Mac asked.

"No."

In and of itself, that didn't mean anything, but it still left him wondering. "Since losing her sight, has she even talked to someone who's blind? That you know of?"

"Not that I know of. And—" Melissa hesitated.

"What is it?"

"I get the impression that she doesn't really want to. I wanted her to take some Braille classes, at a local school for the blind, but she rejected the idea so quickly. I don't think it was simply not wanting to leave her house. As far as I know, she's never met a blind person other than her mother."

Her mother. Mac chewed on that for a second. "That's right. She said her disease was genetic. So her mother was blind?"

"*Is* blind."

She said it so softly that Mac barely heard her. But he did. "She's alive?"

For the first time, even with everything that she'd already told him, Melissa looked guilty. And reluctant to say more. "Never mind."

He shot her a chiding look. "Too late to stop now, Melissa. So her mother's blind. So what? Do they have an estranged relationship?" And did it have anything to do with how Natalie reacted when he'd threatened to tell doctors she was too incompetent to make her own decisions about treatment?

"That's Natalie's business. I've said enough because

I want to help you protect her. But her mother has nothing to do with any of this."

Melissa's vehemence only made Mac want to push more. "How can you be so sure?"

She didn't respond, but she didn't have to.

So, yes, they were estranged. Estranged enough that Natalie wouldn't seek support from the one person who would know exactly what she was going through.

As Mac left, Melissa asked, "So I can go by and see Natalie tomorrow?"

"That's up to her. But you won't get any objections from me. Not right now, anyway."

"I know I screwed up. She deserves to have someone she can count on, whether she knows it or not, and she finally decided to give me the chance. I blew it. It's just my boyfriend and I are having problems and—" Briefly, she closed her eyes and shook her head. "Never mind. No excuses. I just hope she gives me another chance. She's never been the type to trust easily, you know. When she lets someone close to Natalie, it's rare and it's a privilege."

Frowning as he left, he wondered if Melissa had been trying to tell him something. Did Melissa know about the kiss they'd shared? Had he taken something rare and special, the privilege of being close to Natalie, and squandered it?

While it might not be relevant to the case, he was going to have to satisfy his curiosity about Natalie's mother. First, however…he called Jase on his cell. "Your sister's friend. The one that's blind. Where does she live?"

CHAPTER TWENTY

WHEN SHE AND LIZ returned to her house, Natalie immediately excused herself. She didn't usually nap during
the day, but at that moment it was all she wanted to do.
To her surprise, as soon as she sank onto the bed, fine
tremors started in her hands and worked their way down
until her whole body was shaking. A chill invaded her
bones, causing the shakes to get even worse. Frantically,
she looked at her bedroom door, which she'd closed but
hadn't locked. Liz was outside, reviewing some case
files at the kitchen table. Natalie tried to sit up, so she
could lock the door, but her limbs wouldn't move.

It was as if the events of the past few days or months
or years had finally caught up with her, conquering her
strength, determination and resolve. As if her attempt
to relax and let down her defenses, even for a few minutes, had opened the floodgates to memories both new
and old, and to memories of people and events meant to
defeat her. Worse, it was memories of her mother that
were assaulting her most.

Katrina Butcher had always been an emotionally
distant parent, but after Natalie's father died, just after
she turned eight, her mother became abusive. At first, it
was just verbal put-downs or intense anger at the slight-

est infraction. Then it became a slap here or there. And then the worst, beatings followed by locking Natalie, who'd always been extremely afraid of the dark, in an attic closet. Every single time, she'd try to be quiet, biting her lip until she tasted blood because she knew her mother would increase her punishment if she called out for her. But eventually she'd imagine something coming for her out of the dark, something even scarier than her mother, and she'd start screaming, not stopping until her voice simply gave out.

Natalie told herself her mother just couldn't handle the grief of losing her husband. That she'd needed someone to direct her anger toward. That it wasn't personal.

By the time she was twelve, she finally learned it *was* personal.

That year, her mother suddenly lost most of her vision. What Natalie hadn't known was that the vision loss had been slowly worsening over the years and that her mother had always blamed Natalie for the onset of the retinal disease. Despite the doctors telling her otherwise, she'd convinced herself that the stress of pregnancy and childbirth had caused some kind of dormant injury that had then become active several years later, interfering with not just her daily living but ruining her dreams of being a world-renowned painter.

The ironic thing was, Natalie hadn't even known her mother was an artist. As soon as her eye ailment had started, she'd packed all her art supplies away, in the same attic where that horrid closet was.

Natalie's ignorance was shattered after one particularly bad beating. After shoving her into the closet, her mother had been the one to scream back at her, pounding on the door from the other side while telling Natalie everything she'd lost because of her. Her mother hated her. Wished she'd never been born. Wished she was dead.

Within months, her mother was completely blind. Even then, Natalie hadn't abandoned her. She'd hoped to show her mother, by being there for her every day, by loving her despite all she'd done and said, that she was worthy of being loved in return. It had never happened.

Her mother had spiraled into depression and psychosis marked by more and more frequent suicide attempts. Finally, when Natalie was fifteen, her mother had been committed by the state for mental incompetency. She was declared legally insane a month later and had been institutionalized ever since.

Every year until that horrible day at the farmers' market, Natalie had continued to visit her, but it was always the same. Her mother stared blankly into space throughout the entire visit, never once recognizing the daughter who had so desperately wanted to mean something to her.

The only people who knew about Natalie's mother, and not even half of the ugly details, were Melissa and Duncan. Even though Duncan had never said so, Natalie was sure part of the reason he had broken things off with her was his fear she would surrender to the same insanity that her mother had.

Clearly, he hadn't known her at all. Insanity might

claim her at some point, but not because she surrendered to it. Before that could happen, she'd do what her mother had attempted but had never been able to successfully accomplish. She'd kill herself.

But that wasn't necessary. Not yet.

Curling into a ball, Natalie swallowed hard and told herself that she couldn't fall apart. Not with Liz still in the house, anyway. Not when falling apart might lead to more falling apart until eventually there was nothing left of her.

When Reverend Carter Morrison pulled into the church parking lot, he bypassed the front spaces and drove to the back of the building toward the lot that provided easy access to the staff offices. It was half past seven and the grounds deserted, although the cleaners would be arriving at eight. He'd just miss them. It wouldn't take but a minute to get the baby blanket Shannon had left earlier in the day, the one so soft it reminded him of cotton candy. It had been a gift from her father, and he wanted to make sure they had it with them when they visited him tomorrow. It was to be their final meeting before the Grand Reverend officially announced Carter as his successor to the empire he'd built. The empire that he and Shannon would tend and grow into something even grander until it was time to pass it on to their son.

Their son.

He still couldn't believe he had a son. After all the years of fertility treatments and false hopes and crushing disappointments, it was something he and Shannon never thought would happen. But God had finally answered their prayers, giving them not just the child they wanted, but the key to building his life's work.

The knowledge had made her insatiable. After months of turning him away from her bed, *she'd* turned to him. Had even let him dominate her.

At first, when she'd stood behind him and begun to caress him, he'd been disgusted. But then he couldn't help it; his dick had responded to her teasing caresses. And then she'd asked him to fuck her, and he'd liked hearing that word come out of his proper little wife's mouth. He'd done things to her she'd never let him do before. And he'd felt something he hadn't felt in a long time.

Her respect and approval.

Not that he wanted either any longer, but the fact that she felt both for him was liberating. Intoxicating. It would make living with her a little while longer more bearable. But although he still needed her, although he'd given her the fucking she'd asked for and would do so again, he'd always feel disgust for her now.

He'd been too submissive with her, he'd finally realized. She was a strong woman and needed his strength in return. He'd damn well give it to her. He'd punish her for all the years that she'd tormented him, if only in his own mind.

To his surprise, there was another car already parked next to the church, a beat-up old Mazda with its headlights dim but illuminated. Flickering as if the car's battery was about to die. He recognized the vehicle immediately. It belonged to Alex Hanes, a member of the church, one who'd joined as part of their prison release program. He hesitated, then saw a shadow move in the car.

Idiot.

He was in the driver's seat, obviously waiting. Why?

If it had been up to him, ex-convicts wouldn't be allowed to join the congregation. It wasn't up to him, though. Not yet.

Grand Reverend Lester Phillips, Shannon's father, had established the prison outreach program early on. He believed that converting others to faith was spurred greatly by charity, not just spreading money on worthy causes, but actually taking in the downtrodden, the criminals, outcasts and troubled youth, and showing the world the miracles that could be performed. Carter had been skeptical at first, but in the end, as in most things, his father-in-law had been right. Ironically, it was through such service that he'd been able to meet Lindsay Monroe, although of course he hadn't known her real name at the time.

She'd been Lauren to him. Pretty Lauren.

Of all the girls he'd been with since marrying, she was the one he'd actually fantasized about leaving Shannon for. Of course, that would never have happened. He wasn't a rocket scientist, but even if the girl hadn't been so young, he'd always known how far Shannon and her family connections could take him. Plus, if he hadn't left her through those turbulent years of infertility and depression, he was unlikely to ever do so. She might not be the love of his life, in bed or out, but she was loyal to him and the church, and his career had exceeded all expectations. Even better, the job had come with all the perks that he'd previously fantasized about.

Money. Fame. The adoration of his congregation. They all looked to him as if he was a God himself, and *that,* more than anything, was intoxicating. In his own way, he'd become as addicted to it as Alex Hanes had been to heroin. He didn't ever want to do without, to go through the pain of withdrawals, and he wasn't going to.

Still, he missed Lindsay sometimes, even though he tried not to think of her. When he thought of her, he rarely remembered the way she'd smiled at him or how she'd opened her sweet body to the invasion of his. Instead, he remembered that horrible day. The day Shannon had swept into her father's cabin in Redding like the angel of death....

When Lindsay had first told him she was pregnant, his initial response had been joy. Finally, he'd have a child, a child that Shannon couldn't give him, just as he'd always wanted. Almost immediately, however, he'd realized the implications of his indiscretion. How everything he and Shannon had achieved would crumple like a house of cards when her father, the public, *everyone* learned he'd impregnated a sixteen-year-old girl. He'd broken down and told Shannon. Gone crying to her like the weakling she often accused him of being. But while her initial reaction had been disdainful, that disdain had quickly shifted to approval. Praise.

It was perfect, she'd told him. Their chance to be parents and give her father the heir he required before he'd announce Carter as his successor. All it would take was Carter using his considerable charm to convince Lindsay that he loved her, that he wanted the best of everything for her, and that allowing him to adopt the child and raise it in the church would give her the opportunity to go to college and see the world. Of course they would continue to see each other, love each other, behind closed doors, and she could visit the child anytime.

At least, that's what he told her.

To Shannon's great joy, Lindsay had agreed. Things had flowed smoothly from there. They'd promised Clemmons a leadership position in the church, something he'd been wanting for years, if he would arrange for someone to keep Lindsay company in a remote fishing cabin in Redding. She wouldn't be a prisoner, but she'd discreetly wait out the term of her pregnancy, and then Clemmons would deliver the baby to Carter when it was born. Pious man that he was, Clemmons had struggled with indecision. He clearly didn't respect Carter or Shannon, but he'd ultimately concluded that keeping the church free from scandal was in everyone's best interest.

He'd probably relished the idea of getting Carter and Shannon out of the picture, so he could run things right.

But Clemmons wasn't as perfect and moral as he thought. He'd asked his brother, an ex-felon just learning the teachings of the church, to watch over Lindsay, and Alex, exceedingly grateful and loyal to the "family" that had welcomed him with open arms, agreed.

Months had gone by without incident. In truth, Carter had almost forgotten about Lindsay. She'd been such a good girl, doing exactly what they'd planned. But then she'd started to have doubts. She'd wanted to see him. She'd loved him so much that she couldn't imagine *not* being with him or, worst of all, giving their baby over to another woman's care. Alex had called, giving them warning, and Clemmons and Carter had driven to Plainville so Carter could calm Lindsay down.

He'd almost succeeded. But then that bum at the farmers' market had pointed at them. Called him a hypocrite. Commanded Lindsay not to give him what he wanted. Staring into the man's eyes, Carter had suffered a moment of indecision, as if God was indeed speaking through the weathered-looking old fool. He'd been shaken on the ride back to the cabin, and once there, Lindsay had pleaded with him to let her keep their baby. He'd been wrung out, close to giving in, and that's probably what Shannon had sensed. Or rather, anticipated. She'd shown up, and it had all been over.

What had been smooth sailing for months had suddenly transformed into a disastrous tempest, one ending with Lindsay's blood staining the floor and all their hands.

It was nausea that pulled Carter out of his memories. He struggled for a moment, fighting the urge to vomit. He could imagine what Shannon would say about it. How she'd curse and belittle him for his weak nature.

Eventually, however, he pulled himself together. He always pulled himself together, no thanks to her. And someday, he wouldn't need her. But not yet.

Once Grand Reverend Lester Phillips retired, Carter's congregations and reach would multiply a hundredfold. So many sinners in need of saving. So many young girls among them. For as long as it suited him, he could fuck Shannon, dominate her in bed and have his little girls, too.

He winced as his dick shivered. He had to control himself. Stay off the radar for just a while longer. He couldn't ruin everything he'd worked for by giving in to his temptations again. Not yet. Not when he was so close to getting what he wanted.

Young, lithe bodies and dewy innocence were arousing, but power was the ultimate aphrodisiac.

Despite the violent crimes he'd committed in his youth, Alex Hanes hadn't figured that out yet. Either that, or prison had suppressed his memory. He truly got off on the idea of being a religious warrior, one who rejected the laws of man in order to protect the gateways to heaven.

Carter knew the truth.

He was a warrior with an agenda, a very selfish one. He didn't act for the church based solely out of religious fervor but desperation. It was what had made Alex, like so many like him, so biddable—his need for redemption. For assurance that all the sins he'd committed in the past wouldn't result in a fiery eternity in hell.

And of course, Carter didn't mind giving him that.

He, after all, was a sinner, as well. Weak and flawed. Yet in the end he'd been forgiven, too. It was all quite beautiful when you really stopped to think about it.

Still, hesitation seized him as he stared at Alex's car. He'd never met the man alone before. There'd never been a reason to, and besides, Carter wasn't the fool Shannon thought he was. The man was biddable, but he wasn't quite stable, either. Clemmons had been crystal clear about that, warning Carter that they couldn't push Alex too far. He was extremely protective of the younger brother he'd only recently learned existed. In turn, Alex adored Clemmons. But because of his position in the church, because of who and what he *was*, Alex adored Carter more.

Days ago, he'd come to Carter and shown him the pictures that had been printed in the *Post*, the picture that showed Lindsay attending a small town farmers' market, the same farmers' market that Carter had attended with her. He'd been on edge ever since. The photos hadn't shown Carter. They also hadn't shown Lindsay was pregnant.

Both omissions were a blessing, of course. All he'd wanted was some reassurance that none of the woman's remaining photos—she'd taken hundreds according to the newspaper article—had captured him or Lindsay's pregnancy, either. Once he got that reassurance, he'd truly be able to enjoy his victory when the Grand Reverend passed the torch and anointed him with that title.

But Alex had messed up. Failed to copy all of the

woman's photos. So perhaps he was here to tell him he'd completed the job.

Wonderful.

He pulled into a spot just behind and to the right of Alex's car. As he stepped out of his own vehicle, the air immediately fluttered and cut through his clothes, the sharp chill catching him unawares. He called out, "Alex?"

He didn't answer. Impatiently, he walked closer. "I told you if you ever needed to talk to call me and I'd meet you. How you can expect anyone to be—"

He'd just rounded the driver's side of the car when he saw Alex through the open window.

He was alive but just barely. His breathing was slow and labored, his lips blue and his open mouth framing his discolored tongue. His eyes were that familiar cocoa brown, but his pupils were barely visible, as small as the head of a pin. He was sweating and twitching, and when Carter gingerly peered inside through the open window, he saw that Alex's fingernails were also blue. In his right arm protruded the syringe he'd used to inject heroin into his veins.

The same heroin he was currently overdosing on.

He stared for several minutes as Alex's body continued to twitch. Surprise morphed into hesitation. Should he call 911? Drive him to the hospital himself?

Don't be a fool, Carter. He told you himself the police are involved. Be a man for once in your life.

The familiar voice, haranguing and disdainful, pricked his anger.

He wasn't a fool! Alex was the damn fool. Pulling a stunt like this at Carter's church when what he should have been doing was keeping attention away from it. But there was no help for it now. The cleaners were going to arrive any minute, and he doubted he could successfully bribe all of them to move Alex's body and keep it a secret. Things had become far too unwieldy as it was.

Maybe that's why this had happened. Alex knew things. Things that could destroy the church right along with Carter and his family.

He was careful not to touch anything, and he couldn't tell if Alex knew he was there or not. His own breathing was harsh and his heart was thumping uncontrollably, but he forced himself to act, walking past his car and toward the building. He grew calmer the farther away from Alex he got.

His fingers were shaking, but only slightly, when he unlocked the back door and hurried to his office. Immediately, he spotted Matthew's blanket. Taking the blanket with him, he left the same way he'd come in. When he got into his car, started the engine and drove away, he did so without once looking back at Alex's car or the dying man inside.

CHAPTER TWENTY-ONE

DESPITE THE PASSING hours, Natalie still lay on her bed, drained in body and spirit by her trips to the park and down memory lane. She supposed it was evening now, and wouldn't you know it? Mac hadn't called or stopped by. Despite the promises he'd made after their kiss, he'd obviously had second thoughts about getting more involved with the sexually frustrated blind lady. Who could blame him? He now had the photos that were the real key behind the attack on her. Why would he spend time with her when he didn't need to?

And when had she gotten so pathetic? First her mother and now this. While she'd managed to stop torturing herself with memories of her childhood, Mac appeared to be her new favorite subject of choice.

Even when she deliberately tried to excise him and instead think about her favorite trips or her plans for the future, Mac muscled his way into her thoughts without mercy. Big and overwhelming and impossible to ignore. Without knowing anything about him except what she'd learned online, she knew everything. To her, he'd come to represent life in all its true glory. Everything she could never have.

How was it possible for someone to make such a huge

impact after so little time? She'd asked herself that question over and over again since meeting him. But in the end it was perfectly understandable. Mac was just one of those people, a rarity, who emanated vitality and sexuality without even trying. He wasn't so much a sleek panther, strong yet elegant and sophisticated. That animal seemed more reminiscent of Jase. Mac reminded her of a lion. The king of the jungle. She had no idea what he truly looked like, but what she did know had her imagining him in animal form.

He moved sinuously. Seductively. Muscles bunching beneath his short tawny coat. From the black tip of his tufted tail to his thick heavy mane, he beckoned her to stroke him. To tickle his soft, white underbelly. Roared loud and long to let her know what he wanted. That he wanted her.

Licking her lips, her head moved restlessly on the pillows and her hands fluttered beside her, unsure what to do. A memory soon had her fingers clenching. She'd once spent a week in the savanna taking pictures of lions, and she'd seen for herself how aggressively male lions took their females, straddling their prone bodies on all fours from behind.

She'd never allowed herself to be taken that way. Had always thought it was too submissive. But suddenly the lions she was imagining shifted and morphed. She was on her knees in the grass, her torso lowered and her elbows resting on the ground. A man who looked a little like Natalie's favorite cop show detective a few seasons back, only blessed with Mac's broader shoulders and squarer jaw, knelt behind her. His fingers gripped her hips, caressing them as he worked his enormous shaft into her from behind.

Her breaths quickened, and her legs shifted restlessly. Her thoughts had distracted her enough that her trembling had stopped. Warmth suffused her body, embracing her so thoroughly that her muscles loosened. She turned onto her back, her limbs stretching lazily. Her eyelids were heavy with exhaustion and wanted to close completely. Before she knew what was happening, they did. Reality fell away. She lay there, listening to her breaths and feeling her heart pounding fast in her chest. Gradually, she felt the same beating pulse getting stronger and stronger between her legs.

He pumped aggressively and steadily, relentless, holding her even tighter when the pleasure became too intense, and she tried to pull away. In response, she shoved her hips backward, meeting his thrusts with slapping sounds that kept time with her moans. God, she felt good. Alive. Feminine.

And best of all…

Oh. She grimaced as the throbbing between her legs intensified, and her entire body quivered again, this time with the overpowering pleasure.

Best of all, he was talking to her with that lush, dark voice of his. His hair fell into his face. He bent down to kiss her back, and she felt the smooth, silky strands caressing her skin.

"You're mine. To take when I want, as many times as I want, Natalie. Feel how hard I am for you."

Ahhh. A breathy moan escaped her before she could stop it, but she didn't even try to stop the next one. He was picking up speed, and because she was dreaming, because she was both observer and participant, she could not only feel his shaft penetrating her, she could *see* it, slick with her juices as he squeezed himself out of her, then swiftly shoved himself back inside, past the clenching tight muscles that both hindered and hugged him.

"You're beautiful. Strong. A lioness. I want you. I'll always want you. You'll never be alone, Natalie. Never again."

His hands left her hips. He licked his fingers before he cupped her breasts and found his rhythm there, too. He pinched her nipples when he took her. Released them when he retreated. The hard milking motions pulled at something inside her, tightening all that pleasure he was giving her into a pressurized ball that built and built and built until it had nowhere to go but...

She exploded. Pleasure ripped through her like a fireball designed not to incinerate but to light her up for an eternity. Her soul ignited, rejoicing in the power and heat that had revived it from its quiet slumber. Sensation kept going and going, and heightening and heightening, pulling screams from her that she didn't even realize she was making until...

"Natalie!"

At Liz's voice, Natalie's eyes popped open, and starbursts of light echoed the throbbing pulse still going between her legs. Breaths heaving in and out of her, she realized with horror that her hand was between her legs, caressing herself through her pants.

She'd brought herself off, coming so hard that she'd screamed, loud enough for the police officer working outside her door to hear. She whipped her hand away and jerked to a sitting position. "Liz—" she croaked out, even though she had no idea what she'd say. How she could ever face her again.

"Shit, Natalie. I'm sorry. I thought—I'm sorry," she muttered before backing out of the room and shutting the door.

Natalie could do nothing but listen to her own panting breaths, bury her face in her hands and do exactly what she'd been trying so hard not to do—fall apart.

She allowed it for approximately ten minutes. Then she locked her door and took a shower. Then she changed into her nightgown, climbed into bed and pretended she'd actually be able to fall asleep.

Some time later, when a soft knock came through her door, she closed her eyes but didn't respond.

"Natalie, I'm so sorry about what happened. I didn't mean to invade your privacy. It's just, you called out and I... Well, I wasn't sure...."

Liz's misery finally got through to her. Raising a hand to her heated forehead, she said, "It's not your fault. I...I was dreaming." And chances were Liz knew exactly who she'd been dreaming about.

"Yeah. I just want you to know... It's okay. And I won't say anything. To anyone. I swear it."

Natalie bit her lip and choked out, "Thank you." She

believed Liz meant what she was saying, but it didn't matter. She'd never felt so humiliated.

"One more thing. I called Mac and told him about what happened in the park. I'm sorry, but I had to. He wants to talk to you."

She turned over and pulled a pillow and then the covers over her head.

"Natalie. Did you hear me?"

She still refused to answer.

Finally, Liz gave up and left.

Natalie lay in bed feeling the same type of dread someone facing a firing squad would feel. It had been another lesson for her.

Letting her guard down, inviting pleasure into her life, always came with a price. No matter what promise thoughts of Mac brought to her, she had to remember that.

CHAPTER TWENTY-TWO

EARLY THE NEXT MORNING, as Mac spoke to Clive Henry, the owner of Amber House, he barely stopped himself from punching a wall. "So when I was asking you when you last saw Alex Hanes and whether he'd mentioned traveling anywhere in particular, you didn't think that, maybe, just maybe, you should have told me he had a brother? One who arranged for him to check into your establishment in the first place?"

"Uh, no. I didn't."

"And why was that?"

"Because he didn't tell me he was going to visit his brother. And his brother had already paid for his rent, three months up front, so as far as I was concerned, his brother already knew where he was supposed to be, and it wasn't with him."

The man's logic had Mac shaking his head in disbelief, but he simply said, "Do you have a record of this man's payments to you?"

"Yes, yes, I do."

When he said nothing else, Mac said very slowly, "Please get those records and tell me the man's name and any other information you have on him."

"Uh. Okay."

As Mac waited, his thoughts immediately focused on Natalie. He'd been beyond pissed when Officer Lafayette had told him what had happened in the park, even more pissed when he'd realized it was the same park where the Plainville farmers' market was held. "Damn it, what the hell is wrong with you?" he'd snapped before he could stop himself. "You're supposed to be protecting her and that means never letting her out of your sight, especially in a public place. I don't care how close by you are!"

"I know. I'm sorry, sir. I take full responsibility."

"Damn straight," he said, even though he knew it wasn't true. He had to take his fair share of the blame, as did Natalie. She deliberately hadn't told him which park she was going to, and he hadn't asked her. It hadn't dawned on him that she'd be so foolish to go back to the scene of a crime—well, not really, not as far as they knew, but pretty damn close—but she'd obviously known he wouldn't like it. Why else hadn't she told him?

"I want to talk to her. Now," he'd said.

Only Natalie hadn't wanted to talk. She'd gone to bed and wouldn't respond to Liz's calls. She might be asleep, Liz had said, even though, yes, she'd just talked to her. Or more likely, she was probably upset because of what had happened in the park. But something in Liz's voice had made Mac wonder if there was something she wasn't telling him.

He'd been tempted to go straight over there. To check on her himself. But he'd been right in the middle of an appointment, an important one, and one he was hoping could help Natalie in the end. One that might help him understand her better. She seemed hell-bent on flaunting her independence and abilities no matter the danger it might put her in. She was trying so hard to prove she didn't need anyone that her independent nature was giving him hives. Given his stance on needy women, how was that for irony?

He understood her recklessness revealed a different kind of neediness. One that still caused him strife. One that still interfered with his focus, so he couldn't give his full attention to the job. But oddly enough, Natalie's need wasn't pushing him away the way that Nancy's had. Instead, it kept drawing him in. He wanted to meet her needs for some odd reason.

But then he reminded himself that he'd wanted to meet Nancy's needs in the beginning, too.

"Hello. Are you there?"

Mac scowled at hearing Henry come back on the line. "Go ahead," Mac said.

"His name is Arthur Clemmons. He paid with a personal check."

"What's the address?"

"245 Morning Glory Lane, Sacramento."

"Do you have a fax?"

"A copy machine that doubles as one."

"Great. Fax a copy of the check to the Plainville Police Department." He gave the man the fax number, then took out his laptop and proceeded to search for information on Arthur Clemmons through police channels.

No prior record. In fact, the guy was squeaky clean, with no information about siblings noted, let alone one like Alex Hanes. It didn't take him long to bring up the man's employment history. "Bingo."

He was a youth leader at the Crystal Haven Church in Sacramento.

So he'd been right. Religion had to be the key to how Alex had met Lindsay. It might be how she met her friend, "M," as well.

He glanced at his watch. Eight-thirty. Early yet, but it was possible Clemmons was there, so he called the number he'd jotted down.

"Crystal Haven Church."

"I need to speak to Arthur Clemmons."

"I'm sorry, sir, but Mr. Clemmons isn't available. He's on a week-long retreat with his youth group."

Shit, Mac thought, before responding. "His youth group. Do you know if a girl named Lindsay Monroe was ever part of it?"

"Lindsay Monroe? Nope, I don't think so."

Didn't matter, Mac thought, since Lindsay might not have used her real name. He couldn't be sure until he visited the church himself and showed the staff, Clemmons in particular, her picture.

"My name is Special Agent Mac McKenzie and I'm with the California Department of Justice. I—"

"Is this about Alex Hanes?"

Mac's brows rose in shock while his adrenaline spiked. *This is it,* he thought. The break they'd been looking for. "Yes. Is Hanes there now?"

"Well, yes. I mean, sort of."

"I don't understand. Is he there or isn't he?"

"They took him away last night. After the cleaners arrived and found him. But the police came by this morning. They're here asking questions."

"Wait a second. What do you mean by 'they found him'?"

"He was dead." The woman lowered her voice. "They say he overdosed on drugs. I guess he hadn't really changed in prison, after all."

"I guess not," he echoed. "Listen, if the cops are still there, please get one on the line for me. Now." The cops must have been close because it was less than a minute before one came on the line.

"Detective Quinton Brass," a deep voice intoned.

"Detective, this is Special Agent Mac McKenzie with California DOJ's SIG unit."

"Agent McKenzie. We were just about to give you a call. Our patrol officers took the call of a DOA last night, and we just finished processing the scene about an hour ago. Our vic came up as a person of interest in one of your murder investigations."

"That's right. I just received information that his brother, Arthur Clemmons, is an employee of the church. The receptionist said he's out of town."

"We've confirmed that, and confirmed he's been at a remote campsite in the Yosemite Valley for a few days now."

"And Hanes?"

"Overdosed on heroin. No immediate signs of foul

play. We asked for security tapes, but the church doesn't have a system."

"That's damn inconvenient," Mac muttered.

Brass chuckled. "Yeah. But we spoke to the cleaning crew that found him, and then to some of the employees here. They said Hanes was part of the church's inmate rehabilitation program. That he appeared affable and devoted. No sign of alcohol or drug use. Someone who'd really turned his life around. He'd been gone for a while, but had recently returned to the church."

"How recently?"

"About two months."

Two months. Right around the time that Lindsay had been murdered. "And how long was he gone?"

"Let me check my notes. Let's see. Looks like it was about seven months."

"Shit," Mac breathed. "He was with her."

"You talking about your vic?"

"Yeah. A runaway. Disappeared around the same time that Hanes did. Only she didn't make it back."

"You thinking he killed her? That this might have been a suicide?"

"I don't know what to think. But he was my prime suspect, and I'm betting his DNA is going to prove he was up in Plainville before he died."

And that's exactly what turned out to be the case. After getting the full story from Detective Brass, he called Littlefield and Tanzina. Tanzina was still in the process of tracking down IP addresses, but Littlefield had struck gold.

"Hey, Big Mac. I was just about to give you a call."

"Yeah, that seems to be the refrain of the day."

"We finished the DNA tests. Your ex-felon rubbed the hell out of that cross, enough to leave skin cells. And his DNA was on the cup you found inside that abandoned house, as well. I confirmed with the criminalist at Plainville PD that his fingerprints were all over the place, too, as well as in an abandoned cab they found early this morning."

"Lock, stock and barrel," Mac said.

"What?"

"They just found him DOA of a heroin overdose in Sacramento. Sac PD is there now."

"And this is a problem why?"

"No problem," Mac said. "Thanks for the info, Tanzina."

"Sure thing, man."

Nope, no problem, Mac thought. In fact, on the surface, Hanes's death meant that Natalie wasn't in danger anymore. But there were still too many unanswered questions for Mac to feel comfortable with the way things were resolving.

What had Hanes thought he'd find in Natalie's photos? Why had he killed Lindsay? And had Clemmons known where his brother had been before he'd returned to the church? Had he even bothered to ask? He couldn't see a man of God not questioning where his ex-felon brother had disappeared to for seven months before letting him back into the fold.

No, it didn't matter that Alex Hanes was dead. This

case wasn't closed yet. Not by a long shot. Still, Hanes's death likely meant Natalie was safer, at least in theory. He wanted to tell her that, visit her as he'd been wanting to do all of yesterday. And he would. Despite the agreement he and Jase had reached, he'd known the instant he'd called Carmen Delgado, Jase's sister's friend, that his resolve with respect to Natalie had weakened. After he'd met Carmen and verified how unusual it was for Natalie to be so independent given her recent vision loss, his weakness for Natalie had amplified.

He couldn't be with her. Not in the biblical sense. He couldn't be the man she relied on for the rest of her life. Fine. But he could be her friend. Help her through a rough time in her life. And he would. Right after he drove down to Sacramento and checked out Alex Hanes and his church for himself.

NATALIE WAS ALREADY awake when the sun rose. As she did every morning, she turned on her side so that she faced her window. Warmth filtered through glass and cotton, but it didn't soothe her the way it usually did. For the first time in weeks, the idea of getting out of bed seemed too much for her to handle. Then she heard the muted jingle of the wind chimes hanging just outside her window. Thought of the little shop in the Philippines where she'd bought it. Remembered what she'd survived in her childhood, how much her life had changed, and how far she'd come.

She wasn't like her mother. She was stronger.

Yes, she'd gone to bed humiliated last night, and yes,

she'd freely opened herself to the bitterness and self-pity that had coated her like a tub of hot tar. But honestly, it wasn't as if she could just hide in her room all day.

Pity time is over, Natalie. Now, ask yourself the questions.

Taking a deep breath, she did. Out loud, she asked the same two questions she'd asked herself every morning for the past year.

"Am I a quitter? And would that be such a bad thing?"

Head hanging down, she gripped the edge of her mattress, her answer not coming immediately to mind. Once again, she turned toward the window and tried to picture the view of the garden she'd once loved to tend. Somehow, her mind recalled with excruciating detail its nooks and crannies, including the detailed iron bench tucked into a corner and surrounded by passion vines and camellia trees.

Was she a quitter?

Maybe, she finally concluded. But not today.

She sat up, swung her legs to the side, got up and dressed in the ugliest sweats she had. After tying her hair into a ponytail, she walked to the kitchen.

"Good morning, Natalie."

She jerked at the sound of Liz's voice behind her, her cheeks automatically flushing. "G-Good morning. Have you eaten?"

"I sure have."

The woman's voice was, as always, calm and

friendly. To Natalie's eternal gratitude, she didn't betray by word or inflection what had happened last night.

"I'm just doing some paperwork at the dining room table. Call out if you need me."

"Thank you. I will. And Liz…" She paused, but then decided that ignoring it wouldn't change the fact that it had happened. "Thank you. For everything. I don't think I've told you that yet, but I appreciate you staying here with me."

"You're welcome, Natalie. And for the record, I think you're an amazing woman. I hope when this is all over, we can get to know each other better personally."

Natalie felt the tightness in her chest loosen. Liz was down-to-earth, smart and good company. The idea that she would want to keep in touch when there was no longer a professional reason made her feel almost…normal. "I'd like that." When she heard Liz walk away, she retrieved a banana and some yogurt from the fridge and ate her breakfast while standing at the counter.

She negotiated the twenty steps that would take her to her living room and the treadmill. One, two, three, four, five—she passed the doorway to her bedroom. Six, seven, eight—she passed the painting on the wall, the one she'd bought in Russia from the woman who'd watched her children play with empty eyes. Natalie hadn't been able to coax a smile from her, not until she'd returned the next day and given her a picture of her children. Nine, ten, eleven, twelve, thirteen, fourteen, fifteen—Natalie's hand rested on the dark green chenille sofa that was piled with colorful pillows, in-

cluding the one she'd bought in Thailand with the intricate basket weave pattern in gold and red silk. Sixteen,
seventeen, eighteen, nineteen—she touched the curved
arm, steel covered with nubby plastic, that afforded a
handhold when she used the treadmill.

Slowly, she bent down, made sure her shoelaces
were tied tightly, then stepped up onto the machine.
She hadn't been on it since she'd fallen and Mac had
come crashing through her door. She hated the fact that
she was a little reluctant to get back on it now. She'd
had a bad moment last night and it had bled into the
morning. But she was determined not to let fear stop her
from doing what she loved. From living, whatever that
life looked like. She took a deep breath, programmed
in her usual workout, completed the five-minute warm-
up, then started running.

As she ran, she thought about the oddly matched
couple at the farmers' market. She thought about Pete
and what he'd shouted out to them. And she tried to
remember what it was about the woman's posture that
had caught her attention....

CHAPTER TWENTY-THREE

SHANNON'S EXPRESSION WAS almost comical. Her eyes were as wide as saucers and her normally clear complexion was mottled and red with fury. "You left him there? For the whole fucking world to find? Are you crazy? You brought the cops down on us!"

"What was I supposed to do?" Carter said, hating the whine in his own voice. "The cleaners were due any minute. Plus, it was all over the news—he was the prime suspect in Lauren's—Lindsay Monroe's—murder. *He* was the connection. I figured if we severed that connection, we'd be safe. You and me. Matthew. I wanted to protect us."

"Protect us? You've gutted us. You didn't even search his car to see if there was anything inside that could incriminate us. You stupid idiot. You fool."

His head began to throb, and rage settled into his bones. "Don't call me an idiot. I thought things had changed between us." He put a hand on her arm. Stroked her skin. Tried to bring back the connection they'd made when she'd seduced him. Tried to calm both of them down and resist the sudden temptation he had to choke the air out of her body.

She flung his hand away. "I thought so, too. I was

wrong. I just pray that Matthew doesn't grow up to be as much of an idiot as his father!"

He lost it then. He struck out at her. Slapped her hard enough that she fell back. He saw the blood on her lip, but it was the look of utter shock on her face that filled him with pleasure. She thought she was the strong one. No more. "Don't you talk to me that way. I'm through with you demeaning me. I'm the man of this house. The leader of the church. The head of this family. You will obey me and show me the proper respect."

She laughed. "I'll obey you? And how do you think you're going to accomplish that?"

He felt a flash of hesitation before he crouched over her and shoved his hand between her legs.

More shock in her eyes. But there was also fear. And desire.

He liked it. He liked the expression of uncertainty on her face.

He liked the way she watched him unbuckle and unzip his pants.

He liked the way she fought him when he shoved up her skirt and ripped her underwear off her body.

He liked the way she cried out when he dug into her, pushing past her dry, resisting muscles, and how she grew wetter and wetter as he powered into her.

And he liked how she climaxed as he poured his seed into her barren body.

Afterwards, when she was struggling to catch her breath, her sobs blending in with the sounds of Matthew crying from his cradle, Carter stood and buttoned his pants. He looked down at her, filled with the triumphant knowledge that things had finally changed. He was running the show now. Not her. "I will take care of this. I'll make sure it gets done. That's all you need to know. Do you understand?"

When she didn't answer, he kicked her just hard enough to show her he meant business.

She gasped. "Yes. Yes, I understand."

"Good. Now, get up and tend to Matthew."

CHAPTER TWENTY-FOUR

MAC TOLD JASE about Hanes's death, then proceeded to do some research on the Crystal Haven Church. What he discovered didn't reassure him. Rather, it merely fed his concerns that Alex Hanes's death wasn't the end of things. On a hunch, he pulled up the names of the church's leaders and, along with Arthur Clemmons, ran the names for property records in both Redding and Plainville. Nothing.

After throwing his stuff into his bag, he walked to the hotel lobby. There, he was surprised to see Jase, who had said he was heading back to San Francisco immediately after they'd talked. Instead, he was leaning against the reception desk, a thick pile of papers in one hand and a wide, flirtatious smile on his face.

Didn't the guy ever give his dick a rest?

"Hey, Tyler," he called. "Did you decide to stay another night and lose your room key?"

Jase glanced up and jerked his chin in greeting, then leaned closer to the woman behind the reception desk. "See what I have to put up with? I'm telling you, I could really use some TLC. What do you say?"

The bubbly, well-endowed blonde actually giggled. Her gaze jumped back and forth between Mac and

Jase, an assessing gleam in her eye. "I don't know, your partner looks like he could use a little loving himself. Maybe the three of us—?" Her gaze landed on Mac's crotch and stayed there.

Wow. He'd been hit on plenty, but never so blatantly. He was a little embarrassed to admit, even to himself, how flustered it made him feel. Heat flooded his face but no place else. He kept his expression stony. "Sorry. Not my thing."

Obviously enjoying the show, Jase's grin widened. He turned back to the woman and tsked. "You're a naughty girl, Eve. I'm afraid we don't come as a package. You probably can't tell by looking at him, I know, but Mac here's a little…old-fashioned."

Eve pouted, then shrugged, quickly moving on. "Call me when you've got some time and we'll get better acquainted."

"Awesome." Jase straightened and joined Mac. "Looks like you've still got it, old man."

"Another word and you won't be able to make the date you just made."

"Hey, if you're interested, after all—" Jase laughed when Mac glared at him. "Probably for the better. I mean, I wouldn't want you to feel bad when you can't keep up."

"Listen, Hanes is dead, but it doesn't mean this case is closed. There are plenty of loose ends we need to tie up."

The amusement swiftly left Jase's face, and he

frowned. "Relax, Mac. We've been working nonstop. You know what they say about all work and no play."

"Yeah. That it makes for a great case closure record." God, he really did sound old. Lighten up, he told himself. At least a little. "With the exception of Ward, my closure record is better than anyone's. And the only reason she's leading is she recently closed a case with multiple vics. I plan on catching up, so help me out." His attempt to lighten the mood aside, Mac didn't miss Jase's eyes flicker when he mentioned Carrie Ward. For a moment, Mac almost felt sorry for him. It was obvious Jase's feelings for Ward went deeper than his normal carousing, but it was none of his business. He glanced at the papers Jase held. "Anything of interest in there?"

"Some. I just did some research on Crystal Haven. Turns out it's part of a huge network, just one small satellite of a national organization that's been growing like kudzu. I made an appointment to meet with the church leader, Reverend Carter Morrison, at two. Four and a half hours from now," he pointed out, obviously still irked by Mac's implication that he was slacking off on the job. It was a point well taken.

"I did my own research, too. Morrison could be Lindsay Monroe's *M,* but the website lists a dozen church employees with first or last names starting with *M.*" Mac rubbed the back of his neck. "But Morrison's obviously the best place to start. Sorry. I was out of line. It's just this case is going in so many different directions my head is starting to spin."

"Whether it was Hanes or not, you'll figure it out, Mac. You always do."

"Thanks, Jase."

He gave him a two-finger salute. "Anytime. So, did your research on the church prove fruitful?"

"I probably came up with the same stuff you did."

"I know you're headed down there next, but since I've already got an appointment with the reverend, why don't you let me handle that side of things?"

Mac's first instinct was to say no. He was used to doing things on his own. Sure, he relied on other cops now and again—that was part of the job. But he was itching to see Crystal Haven for himself. The problem was, he was itching to see Natalie, too.

That was telling. When was the last time a woman had ever seriously competed with the job? He couldn't remember another time. On the one hand, that concerned him. Made him wonder if he was losing his edge. On the other hand, it made him wonder if perhaps he was finally getting his priorities straight.

Despite his snide comments about Jase's hound-dog ways, he knew Jase was a good cop. Maybe it wouldn't be a bad idea to let Jase take this part of the investigation. In a way, it might get things back on track between them. "It's bugging me that the church doesn't have a security system. Like I told Detective Brass, it's damn inconvenient for us. But at the same time…"

"It seems pretty damn convenient for someone else?"

Mac grinned. "Stop. You're scaring me."

Jase shrugged. "Dude, I'm not just a pretty face. I thought you knew that already."

"I guess I forgot. Won't happen again." The look they shared assured Mac that whatever damage had been done to their relationship had been repaired. "Anyway, I checked the system and the church has been hit several times over the years. Two burgs. A few vandalisms. Even an attempted rape on an employee, the church secretary. The church is loaded. So why no system?"

"It'll be one of the first things I ask Carter Morrison."

"Good. Let's shake them up a little. Let them know we're on the trail. Call me and let me know what you've got. And what you think of him."

"Him specifically? Any reason for that?"

Was there? Anything other than a bad feeling, that is? "I pulled up some YouTube videos of a few of his sermons."

"Good thinking. That never even occurred to me."

"It would have eventually," he said, and he meant it. Jase was smart. He obviously didn't say it enough, because the other man looked slightly surprised before he wiped his expression clean. "The guy's got what it takes. He's charismatic. An impressive orator."

"But?"

"He's got a wandering eye. Seemed to me he focused a little too much on certain members of his audience. The young, pretty type."

"Lindsay?"

"Maybe, but we don't even know if she attended the

church yet. Given the connection with Hanes, it's likely she'd been there at some point. It's worth checking out, that's for sure."

"I agree. In fact, you might be interested to know that the lovely Eve is more than just a pretty face, as well. Turns out she used to live in Sacramento, and while she never attended Crystal Haven or met Reverend Morrison personally, she has a cousin who used to sing for the church choir."

Mac's brows rose. "Small world."

"Isn't it, though? Although Morrison never tried anything outright, Eve's cousin seemed particularly outraged by his wandering eye and the rumors of more, given that his wife was several months pregnant at the time."

"When was this?"

"About six months ago. She's since had the baby. I'm going to get in touch with the cousin, too. Her name's Nina Parker. I'm wondering if Morrison has changed his ways now that he's a father or if he's even more hellbent on proving his masculinity."

"Good work. So I'll leave it to you. Call me after you talk to them."

"Will do. Hey, did you ever get in touch with Carmen?"

"I did. She's an amazing woman." Unlike Natalie, Carmen Delgado was completely blind and had been from birth. He'd spent the better part of three hours talking with her last night, about what her life was like, what her limitations were and whether she thought she could help Natalie adjust to her new life. She'd been interesting, smart, beyond kind. Beautiful, too. But just as had happened with the hotel receptionist, Mac hadn't felt a spark of attraction for Carmen. The only woman he seemed interested in at the moment was Natalie.

"No problem. Tell Ms. Jones I said hello, would you?"

His words were innocuous, but the tone he used made Mac mutter, "Bite me."

Jase laughed. "Careful. Eve might hear you and take that as an invitation."

Shaking his head, Mac turned before Jase could see his grin. Then he thought of something. "Hey, Jase."

"Yeah."

"You said the church is a satellite of a national organization. Find out the name of the conglomerate's leader and do a property check in both Plainville and Redding. We're still looking for the place Lindsay was killed. When the church secretary told me Arthur Clemmons was off at a church retreat, it got me thinking that churches have retreats plenty of places. Why not up here?"

"Makes sense. I'll let you know what I find out."

WHEN MAC SHOWED UP at Natalie's house, he couldn't help frowning at the coolness with which she greeted him. Yeah, she was pissed off, all right, but why? Because of their kiss? The way he wouldn't let her blow it off? Because he'd stuck her with Liz and hadn't let her see her friend? Or because *he'd* tried to blow off their kiss?

Hell, he was so all over the place, he couldn't blame her for being mad. Didn't matter.

Yes, he could understand her fear at the first two, and her anger at the latter two. But frankly, he wasn't feeling particularly charitable, either. She'd pushed that kiss, and whether she knew it or not, she still might be in danger despite Hanes's death.

Plus, they still hadn't talked about the stunt she'd pulled when she'd tricked Liz into driving her to the same park where a killer had likely first set his sights on her. Didn't she understand that he couldn't do his job and worry about her safety at the same time? Or maybe women were incapable of such rationality. His ex had loved to play games, starting fights just when he was getting ready to leave on an important call. Getting even more pissed when he couldn't stay to talk things out, despite his reassurances that he'd call as soon as he could.

After a couple of minutes of awkward silence, during which Officer Lafayette made herself scarce, Mac asked Natalie to sit down with him. She took the same chair she'd chosen the first day they met, and he sat on the sofa next to her. He studied her for several quiet moments.

She was still a little flushed, and she'd obviously just worked out. Much like the first time he'd seen her, her tee was still slightly damp from her sweat. Her workout clothes were bulky and drab, and he wondered if she'd donned them in anticipation of seeing him. As if she'd wanted to reestablish boundaries by making herself as unattractive as she probably imagined herself to be in her own mind.

She needn't have bothered.

According to Carmen Delgado, the fact that Natalie was living independently and doing the things she did was pretty unusual for someone who'd recently suffered the degree of vision loss she had. She'd also agreed, however, that given the extremes to which Natalie had lived her life before losing her vision, her current tendency toward agoraphobia was a sign she wasn't fully dealing with her situation. He saw that clearly. He saw her.

It didn't matter what Natalie wore or how grubby she was. She might be blind but he wasn't. He saw her and he wanted her. More than anything he'd ever wanted in his life. He hated that he couldn't have her. But he could at least enjoy being with her, even as he worked the case. And maybe, just maybe, he could help her see herself—her true self—again, too. "Do you remember me asking you about Alex Hanes, the man we believe killed Lindsay and attacked you? Well, we found him. He was a parolee out of Arizona."

He watched the play of emotions on her face. Surprise. Relief. Curiosity.

"Where was he?"

"In Sacramento."

Her brow crinkled. "Is that where you were last night? Why you didn't come by like you said you would?"

He could tell immediately she regretted the way she'd phrased the question. So she'd been looking forward to seeing him and had been disappointed when he hadn't shown? The knowledge filled him with far too much pleasure for comfort.

"Actually, I was interviewing someone last night. I called. Wanted to talk to you. But Liz said you were asleep."

She plucked at the edge of her shirt, and the small movement, both inherently stubborn and jittery, made him almost smile. "This morning, I tracked Hanes's brother to Sacramento, and when I called I discovered that Sacramento PD was there."

"And they'd taken him to jail?"

"No. He's not in jail. He died of a heroin overdose sometime last night."

"A drug overdose?" She seemed to reflect on that for a few seconds. "I don't know how I'm supposed to feel about that."

"Forget how you're supposed to feel. What *do* you feel?"

Automatically her hand rose to her throat, where the bruises Alex had left on her were fading but still visible. "He hurt me. I really think he would have killed me. But something about him, something I heard in his voice, told me…" She shrugged. "I don't know."

He leaned forward. "No, go on. Please."

She licked her lips before saying, "Something in his voice told me he thought he was doing the right thing. What God really wanted him to do."

"He was crazy then."

"Yes," she agreed faintly. "Crazy."

He winced. Okay, so he'd used that word again, even though he now knew better, but she didn't seem to take offense. "Many say that most criminals hurt others only because they're not right in the head. That society or biology has left them incapable of rational thought."

"But you don't believe that?"

"It depends. In rare situations, I think mental illness can make someone do things he wouldn't normally do. But most of the time, I think people just don't try hard enough to fight temptation. They give in too easily, because they're afraid of the alternative."

"Hmm," was her only response. "So I guess this means you and Liz can go now. Thank you for everything you've done for me."

Her calm dismissal angered him and not just because it wasn't what he wanted to hear at the moment. The thought of hearing those words at *any* point in the future bothered him. "Are you religious, Natalie?"

She was obviously surprised by his sudden question. Confusion formed on her face first, then resignation. She must be getting used to him questioning her. Assumed it was because of his job. And, of course, part of it was. But it was more than that. He was curious about this woman. Even with the information Melissa had given him, even with what he'd found out about Natalie's mother, it wasn't enough. He desperately wanted to know what made her tick. What she thought about when she shut herself in the dark and away from prying eyes and inquisitive, relationship-shy cops.

"I was very spiritual at one time. Now, not so much. You?"

"With a name like Liam McKenzie? I was raised Catholic. Sunday school. Mass. Confession. The whole nine yards."

"Yes, but that doesn't answer my question. Are you a practicing Catholic?"

"I believe in God. I try to attend church on Easter Sunday and Christmas Eve. But no, I'm not religious, if by religious you mean I believe everything the church preaches. My wife was fonder of strict interpretation. She wasn't when we met, but she became increasingly so throughout our marriage. I guess you could say I drove her to it."

"So you're saying religion led to your divorce?"

"We'd already been having trouble, which is why she sought the church out, I think."

"Do you blame the church for your divorce?"

He jerked, startled by her persistence. "Truthfully? Maybe I did a little, in the beginning. I didn't want a divorce. I thought the church would be committed to helping us. Instead, I think it was more interested in spreading dogma than truly helping us work out our problems. But I've always viewed organized religion somewhat suspiciously. It always seems to be about exclusion, or terrifying someone into acting a particular way."

"Kind of like penal laws, don't you think?"

He smiled despite himself. "Touché. But in the end, the law is more about trying to be the floodgates, trying to make living in the here and now as safe as possible, than actual judgment."

"Hmm. I guess I can't argue with you since I'm not a lawyer. But seems like that's what religion is about, too."

Something about her was different, he thought. She'd challenged him from the very beginning, but today, she seemed confused about how to handle him, alternately pushing him and slipping into an almost flirtatious repartee. Was she even aware of the shift? Or was she simply becoming more comfortable with him despite herself? The idea pleased him.

"Why the sudden theological discussion? What did you find out about Lindsay's pendant?"

She'd seen the connection right away. Smart, but then he'd already known that.

"I talked to Hanes's parole officer. He was born again when he was released from prison. Lindsay's family was also religious, although she'd started to stray from the beliefs she'd been raised with. I'm betting she attended the same church Alex did. It's probably how they met. There's still a lot of questions to be answered before I close this case. It's going to take time to track down that information."

"Well, I've got plenty of that."

She made it sound like a bad thing. Something to endure. It countered the notion that she was adjusting and getting back to her normal way of living. And it made him certain he'd done the right thing by contacting Carmen Delgado.

"So how about spending some of it with me?" he responded lightly.

She couldn't have looked more surprised if he'd leaned over and bitten her on the nose. "What?"

"Spend the day with me. I've been working nonstop for a week. Now that Hanes has been found, I'm entitled to some time off."

"I don't think that's a good idea."

Neither did he, exactly, but something was compelling him. He couldn't stand the thought of her *enduring* life. She was too vibrant and special to settle for such bullshit. "Because of the kiss we shared?"

She turned away, as if that would somehow protect her from his questions. "That and the things you said... afterwards."

Yeah. *Those* things. He remembered quite clearly what he'd said.

We're going to find the man who threatened you, and we're going to catch Lindsay's killer, regardless of whether they're the same person or not. And when we do, you won't be a witness anymore. You won't be part of the job. You'll just be a woman who's attracted to me as much as I am to her.

They'd both known what he'd meant to happen next. That they'd take up where they'd left off with that kiss. While that couldn't happen, he could do one last thing for Natalie and hope it put her in a better place when he finally headed back to SIG.

"I meant what I said at the time, but frankly…"
Again, he hesitated, trying to find the right words to
explain why she couldn't count on him for anything
long-term.

"Frankly, you decided that you really don't want to
be saddled with a blind woman. Honestly, I get it."

Unable to help himself, he leaned forward and took
her hands in his. To his surprise, she let him, so he
pushed his luck and traced his forefinger along the
edges of her fingers, noting how she trembled slightly.
"It's not you, Natalie," he explained softly. "It's not
even your blindness. I was married for a long time,
and it wasn't a particularly happy experience. Most of
the blame for that is mine. I have to think about a lot of
people's needs as a cop. I can't do that and consider a
wife's needs to. And before you make a smart-ass comment about not having proposed to me—"

He deliberately paused while she closed her mouth
and released the outraged breath she'd taken.

"—I can't consider a girlfriend's needs, either."

"Wow. You're really sure of yourself, aren't you?
Why do you assume I'd even want a relationship with
you?"

He shrugged. "Let's just say I know people. It's a
necessary part of my job. We've established we're attracted to each other. We're both single. The natural
conclusion seems to be that we do something about it.
Can you honestly tell me you've ever approached sex
in a casual way?"

Her face heated at the mere mention of sex, proving

his point. "No, I can't. But clearly that's the way you prefer it nowadays."

"It's better if I'm just on my own. You don't want a selfish bastard like me to be part of your life anyway, believe me."

She snorted. "Of course I don't. No worries. I have my own stuff to deal with. I need to get a handle on who I am now and what my life is going to be like."

"Right."

"Right."

She slowly pulled her hands out of his grip. Reluctantly, he released her. It was on the tip of his tongue to recall his words. Ask her to give whatever it was between them a chance, but that was just crazy. He forced the words back. She deserved more than that, blind or not.

Desperately, he clapped his hands and rubbed them together. "Good, so now that that's settled, let me get you out of here. As lovely as Liz is, you can't even see her to enjoy the view. Let's get some fresh air. Unless you're scared, that is?"

She tilted her chin up and looked so cute he barely stopped himself from leaning over and kissing her. "That's not going to work with me. I told you I'm not going out."

Hell, she was being more difficult than he'd anticipated. "Why?"

"Why are you pushing this?"

"Because I like you. I'd like to get to know you better, even if it would be platonically. And—"

"And?"

"And…there's someone I'd like you to meet."

"Someone?"

"A woman. A blind woman."

Her expression hardened, any softness or animation she'd let slip out before ruthlessly reined in. It reminded him of how she'd reacted when he'd threatened to label her mentally incompetent. At least now he knew why. He'd taken what Melissa had told him and run with it. He'd learned Natalie had been put in foster care at the age of fifteen when her mother was institutionalized. No wonder she'd freaked.

Gently, he said, "Look, you haven't talked to anyone who's blind, have you? If you do, it might help you see that you don't have to live in extremes—either locked inside yourself or tossing all caution to the wind. Other people live wonderful lives despite their blindness."

A laugh, bitter and hard, burst out of her. "Oh, so you're an expert now? Wow, this woman must have *really* made a big impression on you." Disdain twisted her features. "Tell me, Agent McKenzie, if I have this right. While you were supposed to be finding the man who'd killed Lindsay and almost killed me, too, you decided to do what? Seek out another blind woman to get your jollies? Did you kiss her, too? Or did you do more than that?"

THE WORDS HAD ESCAPED her mouth even before she'd formed the intent to say them. Horrified, she turned around, wanting to shut him out physically even though the move didn't change what she saw in the slightest.

"Um, sorry to interrupt…"

At Liz's voice, she jolted. "Would you stop sneaking up on me!" she snapped.

Their combined silence hailed down on her.

What's happening to me, she thought. I'm out of control. Just like *her*.

"I'm leaving. I need to check in at work," Liz finally said. "When you're ready for me to come back, just give me a call, okay?"

Natalie heard the woman's footsteps retreating, and guilt made her call out, "Liz, wait."

But her front door opening and closing was her answer.

She crossed her arms over her chest and hugged herself. "Please tell her I'm sorry. I—I don't know what's wrong with me this morning."

She hadn't heard him approach, but he laid his hands gently on her shoulders, immediately infusing her with heat that made her body tremble with the need to lean back against him.

"Turn around."

"No," she whispered.

"Damn it. Turn around and look at me."

"I can't see you!" she cried.

"Yes, you can. You see me. You see me better than most."

He whirled her around. His touch—a far cry from the tentative and fearful way most people touched her—

caused her desire to skyrocket. Automatically, she flattened her palms against his chest to push him away. He needed to leave her alone, or she was going to do something terrible, like throw herself into his arms and beg him to kiss her again and this time never let her go.

"I just want to help. I know we don't know each other well. Hell, we just met. But from what I do know, I think you're amazing. Stronger than you think. I hoped that talking to this woman would help you come to terms—"

Belatedly, she shoved at him, but he didn't move. His strength and vitality angered her, and she slapped at him with her palms. "With what? My blindness? News flash! I'll never come to terms with it."

"I know you think that now, but you've already done so much to—"

"You don't get it, do you?" she screamed. She began beating at his chest with her fists. "I don't want to be blind! I don't want to be disabled for the rest of my life! Dependent on others. Having to trust strangers. Never knowing, truly, where I'm going or where I've been. I don't want any of that."

He gripped her wrists and shook her. His voice rose, losing some of its usual control. "What do you want?"

It was crazy for him to ask her. Crazy for her to answer. But she did anyway. Suddenly, all her natural defenses fell apart, and she blurted out her deepest desires, not only to him, but to the entire world. "I want what I can't have! Not just to be alive, but to live. Adventure. Beauty. Pleasure. Sex. Sex with you. Only I can't have that, can I? I can't have any of it!"

She stilled, her head hanging, her breaths shooting in and out of her like a locomotive. Why had she said that? Why had she said any of it? Now he would—

"Yes, you can."

She jerked, still caught in his firm grip. But he wasn't hurting her. His thumbs rubbed soft circles along her inner wrists, touching her the way he had when he'd traced her hands with his finger. "What? But you said—"

"I can't give you a relationship, not one that will last. But pleasure?" He leaned his forehead gently against hers, so that his scent drifted around her. Hypnotizing her. "If that's what you really want, I can definitely give you that. More pleasure than you can handle."

CHAPTER TWENTY-FIVE

MAC WAS GETTING used to reading her. Not so much her eyes, but the other ways she revealed emotion. The way she tightened her mouth when she was pissed, or let it fall slightly open when she allowed herself to relax. And she blushed easily—when she was embarrassed or angry, yes, but especially when she was turned on. The redder she got, the more she wanted him. She was a pretty pale pink right now, and he wanted to push her harder. Higher. Until her face was cherry-red, screaming out her desire for him.

But she pressed her lips together and once again tried to pull her wrists from his hands. "Don't you dare feel sorry for me. I don't need a pity fuck."

What the hell? Was that what she really thought? He dragged one of her hands down and pressed it against the straining length of his erection. "Neither do I. You may not have your sight, Natalie, but you sure as hell know what this means. And it's been like this ever since I met you. Whenever I think about you. Before I knew you were blind. Afterwards. Now."

She pulled her hand away. "You—you must have some kind of fetish—"

"Didn't you hear me? *Before* I knew you were blind.

And the woman I wanted to introduce you to? She's friends with Jase's sister. Blind. Plenty attractive. Single. And I wasn't tempted to kiss or do anything 'more,' as you called it, in the slightest."

Her brows crinkled as she took that in.

"I'm no charity worker, so don't get the wrong idea. I can give you pleasure, but you know what? I'd expect a whole lot in return. And I have no doubt you can give it to me."

She moistened her lips, her little pink tongue darting out and leaving a slick shine behind. Mac groaned, barely stopping himself from going after her tongue like a search dog with a scent.

"Look, this is crazy," she said. "I—I'm sorry for saying what I did. For everything I've said. You were right before. Neither one of us needs this right now."

"That's true. Everything I said was reasonable. We don't need it. But I want it. And I think I'm changing my mind about whether you should take it. Because I *want* you to take all of me, Natalie. Every hard inch."

It just slipped out. He wasn't trying to be vulgar. But at his words, her breath hitched, her eyelashes fluttered, and her face turned the exact color he'd been hoping for—cherry-red.

Of course.

She couldn't see him that well, but she could hear him. And she obviously liked it when he talked dirty to her.

The realization made the final shreds of his professional demeanor drop away. He was no longer a cop, and she was no longer a witness. There was no debating whether he wanted to complicate his life or whether she was too vulnerable for a sexual relationship. He was just a man who desperately wanted this woman. Wanted to show her with every part of his body that she wasn't just beautiful, but as passionate, unique and multifaceted as the pictures she used to take.

She needed to feel like a woman again, and he needed to be the man to give her that.

He tugged her closer and leaned down until he was whispering in her ear.

"Let me tell you what it would be like. Just tell you. Can I do that?"

He waited several beats, but she didn't respond. He took that as a yes. "Here's what's going to happen first. I'm going to kiss you. Touch you. Make sure you're so wet that when I slide into you, you're going to feel stuffed full, but also like a part of you that was missing has suddenly found its way home. Then I'm going to lay back and let you be the sexy, warrior woman that you are."

She shivered, and he ran the backs of his fingers down her arms, feeling the goose bumps that had formed on them. His own muscles were tight as he imagined what he was describing.

"You're going to ride me to your pleasure while I play with your breasts and suck your nipples. Then, when you've rested a bit, you're going to suck my cock, and I'm going to come inside your mouth."

She moaned, and her hands moved to grip his biceps.

He closed his eyes, enjoying the strength of her grip. He kissed the side of her neck, just under her ear, tongued and sucked the tender skin there. Shifting slightly, he caressed the sides of her breasts. She leaned closer, resting her forehead on his chest so he could feel her breaths through his shirt.

"Then I'm going to take you, but this time, I'm going to do the riding. With you on your back, legs spread wide, your feet on my shoulders. I'm going to pound into you while I stare into those pretty eyes of yours and I'm not going to stop until you come again. And finally—"

She raised one hand to his mouth as if to quiet him, but her touch was light. Sensuous rather than restraining. He licked between her fingers. "That's right. You read my mind. I'm going to bury my face in your heat and lick you. Until you're wetter than you've ever been in your whole life, and begging me to take you again." He cupped her breasts, kneading their heavy weight and pinching her nipples through her tee while he sucked at her fingers.

She withdrew her hand and pulled back slightly. He moved his own hands to rest them lightly on her hips and cleared his throat. "That's how it'd be. For starters."

They both stood still, their breaths soughing in and out. He waited for her to say something, but she didn't and he hesitated, not sure whether to push even more. He didn't want to misread her. Hell, if she decided to report him, he could kiss his career goodbye. Dropping his hands, he prepared to move away.

And gasped when she lowered her hand and once more cupped him with her palm. She squeezed him tentatively. Then harder before rubbing him.

Her face was flaming red, all right, her eyes shining with heat. And if he wasn't mistaken, she had the slightest smile on her face.

"What if it's you that ends up begging me to take you?"

His smile split his face. "Give it your best shot, baby."

MAC'S CHALLENGE hung in the air while he grew even harder against her palm.

When she didn't move, he said, "Believe me, it'll be the easiest challenge you've ever won, Natalie." Taking her hand away from his erection, he kissed the center, then pulled her toward him at the same time as he reclined back on the sofa. She perched on the cushion next to him, her bravado fleeing her.

"I'm going to put my hands behind my head. I won't move them, not until you tell me your ready. You can do whatever you want to me, Natalie. However little. However much. No matter what you do, I guarantee I'll love it."

She licked her lips, and she was sure he could see her indecision all over her face. She wanted to touch him. Explore his body. Discover his taste and texture and whether they changed the more aroused he became. But bottom line, she was afraid. What if her fumbling turned him off? If he changed his mind?

"I can't."

"Why?" No anger. No pressure. Just mild curiosity. At least, that's how his voice sounded.

"You just think you want this."

"No—"

"I'm a curiosity. Play with the blind girl before you leave town." The thought caused her eyes to sting, and she blinked rapidly. "But you'll compare me to the other women you've been with, and you'll find me lacking, I know you will."

He sat up and cupped her face. "That's impossible. No woman has turned me on the way you do. All you have to do is touch me and you'll give me more pleasure than any other woman has. Now, come on. It's just us. No one sneaking into your home. No one tricking you into a car. No weirdo—okay, none except for me—sitting next to you on a bench. Just me. You were brave all those times. You can be brave now, too."

"You're not weird. You're incredible." She spoke honestly, and she didn't regret it. He was, quite simply, a good person. A dedicated cop. Not perfect, but with a pure heart—or as pure as any mortal's could be.

"I like to think so. But my ego's been taking a bruising since I met you. It needs some reassurance."

She saw his shadow move and felt the sofa dip under her. He'd lain back down.

His descriptions of what they'd do together flew through her mind, arousing her but also intimidating her. "What kind of reassurance?"

"A kiss might help. For starters. I've been fantasizing about that kiss we shared for days."

"Me, too." Her quiet admission slipped out.

"Then come here," he whispered.

She could no longer resist. She hadn't just been fantasizing about their kiss; she'd been obsessing about it. How incredible it had felt. How wonderful he had tasted. As soon as her lips touched his, she knew it hadn't been her imagination.

As it had been the first time, their lips met with a delicate caress that quickly became more. She opened her mouth to the invasion of his tongue, and then, not content to let him take the lead, she wielded her own tongue to explore the sweet, dark recesses of his mouth. He moaned and angled his head for a better fit.

Something primal took over her body. Her fingers dropped to his chest, unbuttoning buttons so fast a few of them popped off, but she didn't stop. She caressed each patch of warm, muscular skin as it was bared, then followed with her mouth while her hand worked at his pants.

He hissed when she shoved down his zipper, then raised his hips so she could tug off his pants and his underwear in one smooth motion. She ran her hands from his feet upwards, feeling the light sprinkle of hair on his calves and the sheer power of his thighs. The sensations registered quickly, almost too quick for her mind to keep up with her hands, but she wanted to soak it all in, now, before this dream ended and she woke, alone and disoriented in her bed.

"This isn't a dream, baby," he growled. "It's real. Feel how real."

She must have spoken out loud, but she didn't have time to worry about it before he guided her fingers to his erection and wrapped them around it. He was so big. Hard and smooth. Thick with veins that pulsed along his shaft and a tip that was already wet.

She didn't worry about trying to imagine what he looked like through her touch, only about pleasing him and being pleased in the process. It didn't matter what he looked like.

This was Mac. That was all that mattered.

She pumped him in her fist several times, relishing his cries for mercy, then dipped her head, rooting for him with her mouth.

She wanted to taste him. And she did. He was an explosion of salty/sweet nirvana on her tongue. What an aphrodisiac must taste like, wholly satisfying even as it fed her hunger for more. She swirled her tongue around the head of him and cupped his balls, noting how he jerked in her mouth and lost enough control that he tangled his hands in her hair.

She pulled back. "No hands," she reminded him. Teasing him. Imagining a scowl overcoming his face, like a little boy who'd been told he couldn't have dessert until he finished his dinner.

His fingers tightened, and for a second she wondered if he'd ignore her. But with what seemed like supreme effort, he let go of her and choked out, "Sorry."

"No need to be," she said before lowering her mouth again. She showed him how forgiving she could be by taking as much of him as she could, then pulling back.

Taking him, then pulling back. Again and again until he was indeed begging, just as she'd teased he would.

"Now you. Take off your clothes. Please."

She didn't even hesitate. She wanted to feel him against her. Skin on skin. The way he'd talked dirty to her earlier, the promises he'd made, echoed in her ears. She peeled off her clothes and climbed on top of him, ready to take him inside her and ride him just as he'd predicted.

"Wait. I want to touch you."

She hesitated. She was already reeling from pleasure and wasn't sure if she could handle more.

"Please. I'm begging you."

After a brief moment's pause, she nodded.

She waited, but instead of cupping her breasts as she expected, he sat up and cupped her face. Kissed her again. This time slowly. Deeply. As if he wanted to savor the moment. He stroked her hair, her ears, the side of her neck, and then finally he cupped her breasts. "You're so beautiful," he said.

She arched into his hands, *feeling* beautiful. He pinched her nipples, tugging gently, then firmly, then gently again. Each time, she gasped. Shifted her hips until she'd aligned her core with his and ground down.

He grabbed her hips and arched upwards, rubbing directly against her clitoris. Shards of ecstasy cut through her, almost painful in their intensity. He did it again. And again. And then he slipped his hand between her legs and found her with his thumb.

She'd thought the pleasure was unbearable before. When he focused that small pad of flesh on her own and slicked circles around it, then flicked it directly, she literally thought she was going to die from the pleasure. Before she knew what was happening, her hips were moving in time to his caresses, and the pleasure was climbing higher and higher and higher. Until she was on the edge of something huge and about to fall in.

Into a huge, dark abyss with no lifeline to guide her back.

"Stop. Please, stop," she said, her urgency unmistakable.

His hand stilled, and she heard him struggling for breath. "Why stop? You were about to come."

She shook her head frantically. "I—I don't want to come."

"Bullshit," he said, his voice hardening. "You said you wanted pleasure. Sex."

"I did. I do. I want that and you've given it to me. I want you to come, but I—I can't. I mean, I don't want to."

"Too bad. I don't operate that way."

She sensed him leaning up to kiss her, and she turned her head and held him off. "I'm telling you I don't need it. I don't want it."

"You want it. You're just scared. Deal with it."

"I can't, don't you understand? I can't lose control!"

"Sex is all about losing control, Natalie. Giving it to your partner. You wanted me. You're going to have me. All of me."

He patted her clit again, then slowly pushed a thick finger inside her. It stretched her and almost short-circuited her brain.

"Don't be afraid. You need this. You know you do. And I'm right here with you. You know I won't let anything bad happen to you." He inserted another finger inside her, and then another, stretching her to the point of pain but not quite, until her hips were following his movements, trying to keep him inside her whenever he pulled back. "You gonna trust me?"

She surrendered. She should have known better than to try and control this. Control him. As his fingers continued to move, he swiftly brought her back to that place, just on the edge of a tempting precipice. In the distance beckoned pure pleasure, shimmery and hot, with a pinch of the forgetfulness she longed for. "Okay, okay. You win. Just…wait. I want to lie down. On my stomach."

Again, his fingers stilled. "Why?"

Because I don't want you to look into my face. In my eyes.

He'd said that's what he wanted, but she couldn't bear the thought of him doing that and seeing nothing but his own reflection. Seeing how empty she was even as he made her feel the most incredible pleasure. So she lied. "I like it like that. From behind. It's the best way to make me come."

"But—"

"I want it like that, Mac. Give me what I want or this ends now."

SHE MEANT IT. He could tell by the stiffness of her body and the tone of her voice. Around his fingers, her sweet heat was drenching him, pulsing and clinging in a way that belied her words. But he'd pushed her so much. Wanted only to give to her. So if being taken from behind was what she wanted…

Slowly, he withdrew his fingers, eased her off him, and pulled her up.

"Wha—"

"We need room. A bed."

He led her to her bedroom. It was neat and plain, just like the rest of the house. Nothing like the complex and sensual woman who lived there. He settled her on to the bed, kissed her, then flipped her onto her stomach. She buried her face in the sheets, and it was then he fully understood.

She was hiding from him. From what they were doing and what they were giving each other. More than physical pleasure, but connection. Intimacy.

He almost called her on it and made her turn to face him but told himself to go easy. She had far too many issues to deal with now, and he wasn't promising to stay and help her with them. Quite the opposite. The fact that she'd let herself go this far was huge. He needed to reward her for it and give her the pleasure he'd promised her.

With precise deliberation, he leaned over her and placed a soft sucking kiss beneath her ear. Then he sprinkled kisses down her body, taking care to give equal attention to every part of her. Beneath his ministrations, her body moved restlessly and her soft moans of pleasure drove him to the edge of madness.

Far too soon, he couldn't take it anymore. Moving to

a kneeling position, he pulled her up on her knees and nudged them apart. He ran a finger through her cleft, causing her to jerk. "My God, you're so sweet here. So tender and pink and pretty."

"Mac," she moaned. "Please. Do it. I want to feel you inside me."

Her impatience unleashed his own. He pressed against her, slipping inside her enveloping heat, the feeling better than anything he'd ever experienced. His head tilted back, and he closed his eyes before remembering.

"Shit," he said, gritting his teeth. "Protection. I forgot protection."

Beneath him, she tensed.

"It's okay," he said. "I've got something in my wallet, but I need to—"

"No."

No? His mind rebelled. She couldn't change her mind now. It would kill him. But if she didn't want—

"I mean, you don't need protection."

He shuddered at the implication of her words. The fantasy of all of him being enveloped by all of her. A white-hot inferno that would make him lose what little was left of his mind. But he did have a little left, enough to say, "Natalie, your life is complicated enough as it is. We can't take a chance like that. I'm clean, but—"

"I'm clean, too. And I can't get pregnant. Literally. I made sure of that a long time ago, Mac."

The revelation slammed into him like a wall of bricks. He knew immediately why she would have done so. A mother who'd passed on a genetic eye disease. A mother who'd passed on the genes and as a result the possibility of mental insanity. She would never take the chance of passing along either to her own child.

There was no sorrow in her words, only truth, but he felt sorrow for her anyway. She was a warm, wonderful woman whom he instinctively knew would have made an equally wonderful mother.

Mac rubbed her back in slow, soothing circles. "Baby, let's slow things down. Talk—"

"No, no. No talking. Sex. Pleasure. That's what I want, remember? That's what you promised me." She didn't give him the chance to argue with her. Taking him completely off guard, she pushed back against him until half of him was buried inside her.

He shouted at the sudden rise in sensation, the small of his back tingling with the need to pull out and thrust back into her completely, hard. But he forced himself to remain still. To go no further until he gave her a chance to get used to what she'd already taken. When she tried to push back farther, to take more of him, he gripped her hips tight, immobilizing her.

She struggled against him. "Please. Do it."

"Easy. Give me a second."

She countered by squeezing him internally, her muscles sucking at him like a mouth. He lost it.

He thrust completely inside her and froze. In that moment, he was the one who was blind. Lost to anything around him except her and the way she made him feel. And the way he was determined to make her feel.

Taking his time, he eased slowly out of her, then quickly punched back in.

Her wail of ecstasy was his reward.

He did it again. Then again. Urging her to squeeze him as she had before. Telling her in explicit terms that no one had ever made him feel this good. That she was a goddess. The best he'd ever had. At some point, he wasn't even sure he was understandable since his voice had turned all growly and mingled with deep, harsh moans and sobbing breaths.

She was right there with him, not speaking, but pushing back against him again and again, demanding everything he was giving her and more.

Then she reached back and grabbed his ass. Dug her nails into his skin. That small, voluntary need for connection despite her inability to see him and his inability to see her face undid him. The pressure in his balls built and built and then exploded in a flood inside her. Over and over again, he ejaculated. At the same time, she cried out and held him in a grip so tight he could barely thrust anymore.

When the pleasure ebbed and he could see again, but just barely, he stayed poised on his hands and knees over her, shaking, trying desperately not to collapse her underneath his weight. With supreme effort, he moved to the side, still partially inside her, wrapped his arms around her waist, and buried his face in her neck.

CHAPTER TWENTY-SIX

"WHAT IS IT? Is it Allison?" Clemmons rushed into Reverend Morrison's office, panting. He'd sped the whole way back to Sacramento and run from the parking lot into the familiar church building in which he'd dedicated years of his life.

Morrison had left him a message on his phone indicating he needed to get to the church as soon as possible. It was an emergency. A life or death situation. But when he'd tried calling him back, he hadn't answered.

No one at the church had. And no one had picked up the line when he'd tried to call Allison.

When he'd pulled into the back parking lot, he'd seen traces of the police security tape, and his heart had clenched in horror. His first thought had been that the police had discovered what they'd done. But if that was the case, Morrison wouldn't be standing in front of him. Which increased the chances something had happened to Allison.

Instead of answering, Morrison simply looked at him.

"What's wrong? Is Allison okay?"

"She's fine," Morrison said. "She's with Shannon. Your brother, however, is dead."

Just like that. So calmly. With no expression on his face.

Clemmons stumbled and staggered to a chair. Sat down. "How?"

"He overdosed on heroin. And rather than do it in some back alley like a regular criminal, he decided to do it in his car in the church parking lot. Which brought the police here. Not something I'm happy about, as you can imagine."

"I—I'm sorry," he said lamely, not knowing what else to say.

He *was* sorry. For everything. For Alex. He hadn't known him well, not long at all, but they'd been brothers. Clemmons had wanted to help him. Grief was a hollow ache inside him, one edged with regret and guilt. But at least Allison was okay.

"Unfortunately, Alex left a job incomplete. We're going to need you to finish it."

He stared blankly at the other man. "Wh-what job?"

When he explained, Clemmons actually laughed. But the reverend didn't.

He was a very handsome man. Tall and elegant, with no outward manifestation of the devil that was clearly inside him.

"You're serious," Clemmons said, his tone echoing the disbelief he was feeling. "You truly expect me to do what you're asking. To hurt—no, kill—an innocent woman because she might have seen something she shouldn't have?"

"Your brother was quite certain she'd seen something she shouldn't have. He came to me after he saw her photos run in the paper."

"The pictures were obviously nothing to worry about. It was his action, the action you urged him to commit, that brought the police into this."

"Actually, it was the action that *you* urged him to commit that brought the police into this. You asked him to dispose of Lindsay's body, and, because he didn't do a good enough job, because he took her necklace when he shouldn't have, the police learned her true identity and became involved. The detective who questioned me earlier today made that quite clear."

"He was fishing. Throwing out bait. You said the photos Alex recovered are benign. The fact that we haven't been arrested already proves it. Alex was wrong. Wrong to approach you about the pictures in the first place." *He should have come to me. I was his brother.* The one who wanted to save him. Yet the one, in the end, who'd pulled him back into the same darkness he'd been trying so hard to escape.

Looking back, he wasn't exactly sure how it had happened. One day his conscience had been clear. The next day, he'd been helping cover up Morrison's affair with a minor, one of Clemmons's students, a young runaway named Lauren. And then everything had truly gone crazy. Lauren had challenged Morrison. Then she'd made the fatal mistake of challenging Shannon. Enraged, Shannon had slapped her. Lauren had fallen back, hitting her head against a corner of the brick hearth. The wound had bled like crazy and Clemmons had known it was fatal.

Shannon had obviously thought the same thing.

He'd had to make an agonizing choice. He knew if he didn't do it, Shannon would. He, at least, had medical training.

So he'd cut Lauren's baby out of her to save him.

He'd thought there was no other alternative, but maybe he'd been wrong after all. He'd certainly been wrong to drag Alex into the mess by asking him to cover up his crimes. Still, he tried to focus on stopping the madness Morrison seemed hell-bent on continuing.

"They haven't arrested us yet because they obviously don't have proof that anyone but Alex was involved. Yet," Morrison emphasized, "the detective told me they have an eyewitness. Someone who saw Alex and Lindsay together in Plainville. I was with Lindsay the entire time. If they know they were together, then they know I was there, too. The photographer must be the eyewitness the police have. She knows something."

"But her pictures—"

"I don't care what her pictures show or don't show. If she saw me with Lindsay, that'll be enough. They won't stop until they nail me to the cross."

"We can tell them Alex was obsessed with Lindsay. Or that your visit to Plainville to see Lindsay was innocent, but Alex got the wrong idea and killed her out of jealousy. Or maybe he killed her to protect you, because he didn't want the congregation getting the wrong idea—"

"Listen to me, you fool," Morrison hissed. "Those are all arguments that a defense attorney will make to a jury, but they won't stop the police from questioning me further. Or arresting me even if they don't think they can convict me. Even if they eventually buy that Alex killed Lindsay, how is that kind of police attention going to look to my father-in-law? To the congregation? My reputation will be destroyed. That is not acceptable. Least of all now. You make the photographer disappear and all the questioning stops. Even with their suspicions, they won't have proof. Not without her."

Clemmons heard the unspoken addendum to his statement. Not acceptable when Morrison was so close to replacing his father-in-law as the church's national leader. "I'm not—not a murderer," Clemmons said, despite the voice inside his head telling him that a murderer was exactly what he was. "I'm not going to kill a woman to cover up what's happened. What if you're wrong about her being the eyewitness?"

"Then I'm wrong and we'll adjust accordingly."

"And how many people do you plan on killing until you're satisfied you got the right one? Think, Reverend. Alex's death is a sign. This has to stop. We need to tell the police the truth."

"And throw away everything I've worked for? My church? The power that's just within my reach? That is not going to happen."

The fear was almost debilitating, but Clemmons forced himself—too little, too late—to stand up to Morrison's insanity. "Are you threatening me?"

"I don't need to threaten you. You're an intelligent man, Clemmons. Unlike your long-lost brother, you were born with the control and the nature to get you where you need to go. It was you who came to us about wanting to take over the congregation once we vacated it. You have ambition."

He shook his head fiercely. "Not this much ambition."

"Ambition enough to cut a baby from its mother's womb."

The words made a host of bloody images erupt in his mind. "That wasn't ambition. It was necessity. After what you and your wife did to her, she was going to die. I had to cut the baby out of her to save him."

"You don't know that. She might have lived. But you knew if she had, we would have lost the baby. All our plans would have gone up in smoke, and that included your own plans to take over when we were gone."

Was that really what had motivated him? He didn't know. Not anymore. As much as he prayed for reassurance, it didn't come. But resolve did. "I can't kill for you. I'm telling you, there's no need."

"I won't leave things to chance. I want her dead."

"Or what? You'll go to the police? I don't think so."

"No, but I will go to Allison. What do you think will happen then? Do you think she'll stay with you, have your baby, let her children go anywhere near you once she knows what you're capable of?"

"And what if *she* goes to the police?"

"Allison might leave you, but she won't want that

scandal for herself or her children. Regardless, we're willing to take our chances. I'm beginning to learn that some risk-taking is necessary. Even preferable." Morrison grinned, his expression one of slipping sanity. "You must have felt it when you took Lindsay's baby. The power you wielded over life—to save it or destroy it. I'm giving you the opportunity to feel that again. If you leave it to me, I guarantee it'll be much less pleasant for everyone involved. Natalie Jones, yes, but also you. You *and* your family."

CHAPTER TWENTY-SEVEN

FOR ONCE, NATALIE WOKE to darkness with no fear. No dread. No thoughts of what her future would be like, if only she could keep her vision. Instead, she lay still and greedily stretched every one of her remaining sensations in order to savor the here and now.

She heard Mac speaking on the phone, his voice low, as if he didn't want to wake her. Automatically she sat up, wanting to see him naked. Admire the body that had so thoroughly satisfied hers. But then she remembered. And though she still didn't feel dread, her joy was tempered nonetheless.

She smelled his wonderful scent just before the mattress dipped. His hand curved around her belly, stroked her soft skin, then trailed upward to gently cup one breast. When he spoke, the addition of his decadent voice to the mix seemed only natural.

"What are you thinking?" he murmured.

She smiled. "I'm thinking we only got to one of the four things you predicted."

"One and a half, remember?"

"I'm not likely to forget something so…immense."

He burst into laughter and hugged her closer. "You want to live a little more before we go for round two?"

"What do you have in mind?"

"Ice cream?"

"What? Really?"

"I'm serious. I'm starving, and after what just happened, the only food that will come anywhere close to satisfying me is ice cream. Got any?"

"No."

His body fell back as he groaned, clearly feigning crushing disappointment. She giggled, the youthful sound almost foreign to her ears. "I could, however, scrounge up some chocolate. If you promise not to reveal the location of my super secret stash to anyone."

"Done. As long as I'm given free rein to raid said stash whenever I'm here."

She stiffened at his words. Chances were, he wouldn't be here very many times, if ever, after today.

He caressed her hair. "Natalie—"

She swung her legs over the side of the bed and stood. Wobbled slightly. Naked, she walked slowly to the trunk that rested against one wall. He shifted, likely sitting up, and she felt his eyes on her. For once, despite having to take it slowly, she moved without inhibition. She bent to lift the trunk's lid, laughing when he growled, then felt inside until plastic crinkled. When she withdrew her hand, she held a bag of assorted chocolates.

"My favorite mix. Snickers, Twix and Reeses. Think you can handle it?"

"I handled you, didn't I?"

"I think we handled each other," she countered.

"Come over here and let me handle you again."

Again she giggled. He ripped open the bag, promptly devouring several pieces and hand-feeding her a Twix. The chocolate and caramel dissolved on her tongue, but when he kissed her, then smacked his lips and said, "Yum," she knew it wasn't the candy he was referring to. With a sigh, she settled against him again while he played with her hair. His hand dropped to her breast, then her stomach. Lightly he traced the faint scar below her belly button.

"So you got your tubes tied?"

She stiffened and tried to pull away, but he wouldn't let her.

"I'm not judging. I'm just—I just want to know more about you."

It took a minute before she could answer. But she'd already surrendered her body. Why not this, too? "I couldn't chance passing along a genetic defect. Not when anticipating its onslaught caused me so much... trouble."

"Your scar's barely visible. You must've had the procedure a long time ago."

"I'd just turned twenty-five."

She'd already been told she had a 50/50 chance of losing her vision. Eight years before. It had taken her that long to work up the courage.

"Do you ever regret it?" he asked, as if reading her mind.

"I regret having to make the decision, but I don't regret the decision." She smoothed her hand over his hair. "I like your voice," she said softly.

Bending down, he kissed her. "I was wondering if you'd noticed."

He laughed. "It's on your butt cheek. You better believe I noticed." Natalie's smile widened.

"What is it?" Mac asked.

"Just a design I liked," she murmured.

"A design, huh? I need to take a closer look." He shifted so he was kneeling beside her. At the same time, he turned her onto her stomach while she giggled, the action coming easier and easier to her. "Hey—"

Her laugh skittered away as he lightly caressed the small pattern of scrolls and flowers on her butt. His breathing had quickened, and against her thigh, he grew harder. Longer. He kneed her thighs part, and she forgot the tattoo. Forgot everything but the knowledge that he was going to take her again.

He rubbed the head of his dick suggestively against her tattoo. He teased her by slipping it into the core of her desire just the slightest bit and then withdrawing. "I want to be inside you," he growled. "Today. Tomorrow. Al—"

He stopped, as if only just realizing he was talking about the future. Her heart leaped into her throat, and tears filled her eyes. Her past was her torment, but so was her future. She'd be a burden to anyone who shared her life, and he already shouldered too much as it was. There was no getting around that.

"Mac—"

He smoothed a hand over her back. "Don't think about it. Just think of me. Think of us. Here. Now."

She planted her face in the bedsheets—an offer she hoped he couldn't resist.

They both groaned as he pressed into her again, and her muscles involuntarily clenched, simultaneously trying to keep him out and draw him in. Inch by inch she took him, until he was so far inside her she didn't know where he ended and she began. When she thought he was in as far as he could go, he pushed deeper, proving her wrong. She moaned as she took in all of him. Everything he was.

He curled his body over hers, kissing her ear and then her mouth when she turned toward him. Then he reached under her, tweaking her clit while he moved, rubbing his fingers inside her nether lips.

She gripped the bed. A low, keening cry came out of her. He was so big, making her feel safe. Making her feel cherished.

He stilled. "Are you okay? Am I hurting you?"

She shook her head frantically, pushing her hips back toward him. "No. God, no! I love—I love it."

He stilled instantly and withdrew from her.

She bit her lip. *Fool. Why did you use that word? Why don't you ever learn?*

Turning her onto her back with exquisite care, Mac shushed her and slipped back into her. Cupping her face in his hands, he whispered, "I love this, too. I love how damn amazing you feel. I love how brave you are."

He brushed a soft kiss against her lips. Once. Twice.

She relaxed against him, leaning into his kisses, addicted.

Afterwards, when he'd wrung every trace of pleasure from her body, Natalie smoothed her palm across Mac's chest, trying to memorize the feel of his hard muscles, soft hair and smooth skin, imprinting everything in her mind: his warmth, his scent, the feel of his abdomen clenching when her fingers teased the area just above his groin. He shifted slightly, and her hand dropped away.

She cleared her throat and sat up, hugging her knees to her chest. His hand caressed her calf. "Was that Jase on the phone earlier?"

"No, it was the detective who found Hanes."

"It isn't over yet, is it?" she asked.

His hand paused. "No."

"It would be too easy that way. So what are you thinking?"

He hesitated, obviously not used to sharing his thoughts about cases, at least not with someone who wasn't also a cop.

"It's okay. I understand why you can't tell me. Forget I—"

"I think something's going on with a church called Crystal Haven. Something Alex was involved with, yes, but we believe he may not be the only perpetrator involved with Lindsay's murder."

"What makes you say that? The fact that his brother works there? Do you think he had something to do with Lindsay's death?"

"I'm not sure. He's got a clean history, but I suspect Alex went to the church to talk to his brother. The fact that he ended up OD'ing before he could do so might be an accident or might not."

"You think he was murdered."

"Again, I don't know." Yet. That word was implicit in what he didn't say. "Or maybe he had a guilty conscience and killed himself in front of the church because he thought it was symbolic somehow. Either way, there's all kinds of red flags going up about the church. The detective who found Hanes said the church doesn't have a security surveillance system, which made me curious. It's a big building. The congregation is extremely wealthy. And it's had its fair share of burglaries and other types of trouble. And still they haven't gotten a surveillance system? Why not, unless they're hiding something and don't want to be monitored that closely? Plus, I've watched some of the sermon videos, and the church's leader, seemed a little too interested in the young girls in his church. Call it instinct from years of experience, but I could tell there was something not quite right about him."

"Could that be your religious bias sneaking in?"

"I don't think I have a religious bias, not when it comes to my work."

"You think you're that good at keeping personal and professional apart?"

"Obviously I'm not."

She understood immediately what he meant. "Meaning it was a mistake to sleep with me?"

"Mistake or not, it wasn't the professional thing to do."

"Well, we've already established this was just about sex, not commitment. I haven't forgotten."

"It was more than that, but that doesn't change what I can or can't give you. And it doesn't change the fact I've got to keep my head in the game when it comes to this investigation."

"But you're keeping the investigation open based on speculation. Maybe I can—"

"It's more than just speculation. The detective found Hanes's cell phone under the passenger seat. He traced several calls to numbers of the church staff."

"But he belonged to the church, so that doesn't necessarily mean anything."

"No, but it's possible for us to determine where a call has been made based on the cellular transmission pinging off service towers. On the night he assaulted you, he called someone at the church from this neighborhood. That's a connection I'm not willing to ignore. Someone in that church knew what he was doing."

"Who?"

"Again, I don't know. The numbers in his outgoing call log were all registered to the church, no private name given. Now we're going to have to make the connection the old-fashioned way. Jase had an appointment to talk to the reverend at the church earlier today. I haven't heard back from him yet, but I'm going to have my shot at the reverend, too."

"But now he's been put on notice that you suspect him."

"Sure. That doesn't bug me. Cops question suspects whether it puts them on notice or not." The mattress dipped as he shifted and rose. She barely stopped herself from reaching out and pulling him back down, but she couldn't stop an idea from taking form. Maybe she wasn't as useless as she thought. Maybe she could help Mac with his investigation after all.

"Wouldn't it help if you could get information from a private source?" she asked. "An everyday citizen?"

"What are you talking about?"

She ignored the frown in his voice as excitement pumped through her. "I can help you! I can pretend I'm looking for a new church and—"

"No."

"I can read people. It's what made me so good at my job." *When I could see.* Those were the words that formed between them, silent but as loud as a cannon shot.

"If they're in league with Alex, then they're the ones that were trying to kill you," he pointed out. She heard the sound of fabric sliding into place. A zipper closing. He was getting dressed, and she was still naked. Unlike before, when she'd retrieved the chocolate from her trunk, her nudity suddenly bothered her. She felt around for a sheet to cover herself as Mac continued speaking.

"And you think I'm going to let you walk in there with a target on your back? That I'd let any citizen do that?"

The excitement that had heated her blood suddenly

dissipated, leaving her cold and unsure. "I don't need your permission to attend a church service."

"Don't make this a power game, Natalie. You won't like how it turns out."

"You're the one who's making this about power!" she protested. Anger flickered just out of reach, and she grasped for it, pulling it closer and wrapping it around her like body armor. "It must make you feel great. Getting to be the big, bad cop that gets to push everyday citizens around."

"You forget that right now you're under police protection. Liz is going to be coming back here." His voice was calm. Detached. It only served to highlight how out of control she felt. No, not just *felt*—how out of control she truly *was*.

No, she didn't want Liz back in the house. Especially not after what she and Mac had done together. "I don't need protection. I'm blind, not helpless."

"This has nothing to do with you being blind," he said, some of his detachment slipping.

Because he knows he's lying, she thought. "This has *everything* to do with me being blind."

"You know, you're right. To you everything is about your blindness."

She jerked back as if he'd slapped her. "What the hell does that mean?"

"Don't ask unless you really want the answer."

"Tell me."

The bed shifted as he sat beside her and gently grasped her arms. "You make everything about you being blind. Where you live. Who you see. What you do. Which is, by the way, nothing. Unless you're taking unnecessary risks to prove that your blindness isn't an issue. Then you go from hermit to daredevil in under sixty seconds. You take risks out of pride and hide from life out of fear."

Violently, she pulled away and scooted to the other side of the bed. "That's not true." She gave him her back and placed her feet on the floor. But she didn't stand. Didn't want him to see her stumbling around for a place to hide.

"Prove it."

Automatically, she raised her chin at the challenge in his voice. "How?"

"By doing the reasonable thing and leaving the investigative work to the professionals."

Her mouth twisted. "To the *sighted* professionals, you mean."

"I'm not even dignifying that with a response."

"You just did," she shot back.

"And you're acting as crazy as your mother!"

She reeled back, her face going deathly pale. Before she knew it, she was on her feet, the sheet falling away from her as she took two steps forward, arms outstretched so her palms found the wall. Closing her eyes, she leaned her forehead against it. Hadn't she just been happy? Hadn't being in his arms made her feel whole? Why, then, was she suddenly breaking apart? "What do you know about my mother?" she whispered.

He was by her side now. "I'm sorry. I shouldn't have said that."

"No, you shouldn't have. But that doesn't answer my question."

He remained silent.

"Melissa?" Her feelings of betrayal were evident in her voice.

"Don't be mad at her. She mentioned your mother, but she didn't tell me about her mental illness. I found that out on my own."

When she remained silent, he touched her arm, dropping his hand when she flinched back. "Your mother's history is irrelevant to who you are. It's irrelevant to how I feel about you, Natalie. Melissa was just trying to be a good friend. Telling me what she knew so she could protect you."

"Protect me from who? Alex Hanes? When it was really you I needed protection from all along?"

"I understand why you're saying that now. But I care about you, Natalie, and—"

His phone rang. "It's Jase. I have to get this."

When she sensed him turn away, she bent, gathered the fallen sheet and wrapped it protectively around her. She remained standing, however, her right shoulder pressed against the wall.

"What's up, Jase?…I'm not surprised at all that she attended the church. You got a hit?" She heard him scramble for something and begin to make notes. "A cabin in Redding belonging to Lester Phillips. He's the reverend's father-in-law?…Good work. I'll gather a team of officers from the local station while you work on the warrant....Yeah, it'll be a tough sell, but I've got additional facts you can include." He proceeded to update Jase on everything he'd told Natalie. "You've got enough to work with. Convince the judge. Nice job."

He closed his phone, and she could feel him looking at her.

"We've got a lead. Something that connects the church to Redding and possibly to Lindsay's murder. I'm sorry, but I've got to go."

He didn't say anything else, but he didn't leave either.

She remained where she was, trying to look dignified despite feeling pathetically defeated. "Did Melissa tell you about Duncan, too? About how he left me when I lost my vision? About how I couldn't get off with him in bed? Did she tell you that? Is that what today was about? A pity fuck, after all."

"No and no. Today was about passion. Don't turn it into something ugly."

"If ugly is the absence of beauty, then everything I see is ugly, isn't it?"

"Natalie, don't be this way. We can talk—"

"I don't want to talk and you don't have time to anyway. Go."

"We'll talk later. I'll just call Liz—"

"I told you. I don't want Liz. I don't want anyone. I'm rejecting police protection. I have that right."

"Damn it, don't try and punish me by endangering yourself. Don't make me feel guilty for just doing my job. Don't be like my ex-wife—"

"I get it. First my crazy mother, now your needy ex-wife." She laughed bitterly. "You obviously think very highly of me. I bet you can't wait to be on your way. Well, you don't need to make excuses. Maybe I'll see you around someday. Not."

"Natalie, don't do this, damn it. Don't endanger yourself—"

"I'll be careful. I won't let anyone inside. In fact, I'll stay right here, all by my lonesome. Just the way I prefer it."

CHAPTER TWENTY-EIGHT

NORTHERN CALIFORNIA HAD been hit by an unexpected storm. Clemmons imagined the tears fell from the eyes of a God who'd witnessed far too much sin to hold back any longer. Despair was a heavy weight that led Clemmons straight to his empty home office. With despair, however, also came resolve.

Morrison had underestimated both Clemmons's faith and his love for his family. Obviously Clemmons had made mistakes. Let his ambition guide him instead of his morality. But he wasn't going to let Morrison lead him into the depths of hell any farther.

Though suicide was a sin, murder was a far bigger one.

He'd take his chances that God would be merciful. But either way, he couldn't—wouldn't—kill Natalie Jones or anyone else to save his own skin. Unfortunately, however, his actions would hurt the ones he loved most.

His shoulders shook with silent sobs. His wife. His children. The little girl he'd never get to hold. He'd betrayed them all. Was going to betray them yet again by taking his own life. But he didn't know what else to do. He couldn't ask them to live with his shame. This way,

Morrison would have no reason to tell Allison what had happened. She'd be devastated from losing him, confused, but *someday* she'd be able to move on. She'd have her faith to console and strengthen her. At least she wouldn't think of him as a monster.

Hands trembling, he removed the gun he kept in his drawer. The one he'd bought the day after he'd returned from Plainville with Morrison. He'd suspected then that his life might be in danger, but he'd quickly grown complacent. Fallen for Morrison's act once again.

Pressing the barrel under his chin, he squeezed his eyes shut. His hands shook so badly that the metal raked his skin, but he tried to block out the pain.

He bit his lip until he tasted blood. Then, with a tortured groan, he lowered the gun.

Tears stung his eyes but refused to fall.

Coward. Coward. Coward.

With shaky hands, he tightened his grip again. This time, he was going to do it.

"Clemmons."

He frowned. He swore he'd heard Allison. That he could even smell her. But that was impossible. He'd convinced her to take the kids and visit her parents in San Diego. He'd driven her and the boys to the airport himself.

"Clemmons."

Clemmons jumped and turned, his muscles taut. Those same muscles seized and trembled when he saw her, her beautiful hair floating loose around her. He swallowed hard. He loved it when she wore her hair down for him, especially in bed.

Quickly he shoved the gun back into the drawer, thankful that she hadn't seen it. "What are you doing here, Allison? Where are the kids?"

Instead of answering him, she simply stepped inside his office, closed the door, then bowed her head. She placed a hand on the wall as if to steady herself. Clemmons frowned and took several steps closer to her. The skin that had glowed so healthily this morning now seemed sallow, and dark circles nestled under her eyes. Panic quickened his heart. Was she sick? Or had Morrison already—

He crossed the room and cupped her chin, tilting her face up and forcing her to look at him. Tears filled her eyes, making him want to howl. No, he thought. "What's wrong?"

She pulled away, walked slowly to his desk chair and sat down, leaning her head back as if she didn't have the strength to remain upright.

He followed her and knelt on the floor next to her. "Are you sick? Tell me what's wrong."

"My husband has left me."

When he didn't say anything, just continued to gaze at her in disbelief, she raised her head. Raised a trembling hand to smooth back his hair. "You don't think I've sensed it? How distracted and troubled you've been? I kept hoping you'd confide in me. That you'd come back to me. But you didn't. And this morning, when you pushed us away so suddenly, I knew it was happening. You're leaving us, aren't you? You've found someone else?"

It took him a minute to understand what she was saying. He shook his head. "No!" He carried her hands to his mouth and kissed them repeatedly. Reverently. "How can you think that? You're the only one, Allison. I've never been tempted, not once, to stray from you."

Pulling her hands out of his grip, she cupped his face and stared into his eyes. She frowned. "I—I believe you. I do. But then what's going on? What's taken you away from us? Why did you want us out of the way?"

He closed his eyes and rubbed his face against her gentle hands, soaking her in. He didn't deserve this, didn't deserve her, but he drew strength from her touch nonetheless, even as he anticipated the way she'd pull away once she knew. "I've done a horrible thing, Ally," he choked out. "Horrible *things*. I've tainted everything I believe in, everything we've built together. How can I even look at you?"

"By remembering how much I love you," she said softly. "By remembering how much *God* loves you."

He shook his head. "I can still see her blood on my hands…Lauren's…"

She sucked in a breath and the hands pressed against his face trembled. But her voice remained steady. Calm. "Lauren. The girl from the church. The one whose body the police found. What happened?"

Blinking, he opened his eyes. "Aren't you going to ask if I killed her?"

Her eyes were steady on his. "Did you?"

"I—I—no. She was dying. I'm sure of it. But the baby—her baby—"

She narrowed her eyes, a sudden flash of understanding flaring in them. "Tell me."

He felt something break inside him, imperceptibly loosening his voice and his muscles from their atrophied state. He flexed his fingers as he felt blood rushing inside him. Strengthening him. Breathing feelings into him that he hadn't felt in two months.

Strength. Courage. Hope.

He'd been wrong. She wasn't going to turn from him. No matter what happened, she would stand by his side. She would be his salvation.

All he had to do was face what he'd done and try to make it right.

MORRISON WATCHED rain fall onto his windshield. The light patter on the glass irritated him. Made his head pound.

His skin felt stretched tight like dried leather. The rain outside offered no solace from the heat burning him from the inside and out. He took one hand off the wheel and scratched at his arm, raking his flesh until blood welled. He pinched his skin over and over, imagining he was being drenched by the raindrops outside, knowing his expensive suits would hide the telltale marks.

With each jolt of pain, he imagined hurting *her*. It made him breathe more easily.

She was his problem, one he'd have to deal with soon. And he'd have to do it himself.

Despite Morrison's threats, Clemmons wasn't going to do what was needed. He'd been horrified by the idea of Morrison telling Allison what he'd done, but he hadn't been swayed. Morrison had seen it in his eyes. Although he was ambitious, his ambition wasn't about fame, power or money, but about making a difference by spreading God's love. He'd struggle with what to do, but ultimately that same love would stymie him.

Morrison knew this. Because despite what his wife thought of him, he wasn't a fool. He'd gotten where he had because he knew people. Granted, Shannon's family ties had sped the process along, but she'd be nothing without him.

She'd be nothing.

She wouldn't even be a mother.

But was she satisfied? Had she started giving him the respect he deserved?

No. She continued to harangue him. Mock him.

She took no responsibility for the fact that Morrison had to turn to other women, younger girls, in order to experience any semblance of softness and affection. She characterized it as *his* weakness. His failing.

Yet he knew the truth. They were his reward. His reward for putting up with such a heinous bitch for a wife. Until he could get rid of her.

He momentarily let go of the wheel to press both hands against his head, trying to drive the thought away. He'd loved Lauren—Lindsay. He truly had. She was sweet. And most of all, she'd *loved* him. She would have been a good wife. A good mother. Or so he'd thought.

In the end, she'd harbored the same stubbornness that Shannon had. She'd thought she could dictate to him. Dictate what was going to happen with his son.

His son. Not hers. Not Shannon's. *His*.

He hadn't wanted her hurt. He certainly hadn't wanted her dead. But afterward, when he'd watched Lauren dying, the blood seeping out of her, he'd imagined she was Shannon.

A sense of pleasure and power unlike anything he'd ever felt—not even when he'd forced himself into his wife's body—had filled him.

And he'd been biding his time ever since. Because he still needed her. But someday… Someday…

A blare of a horn from a passing car jerked his attention back to the road. He'd veered to the shoulder, and he jerked the wheel, gasping when the car fishtailed out of control. He braked hard, and the car's engine trembled in protest.

He took in several calming breaths before pulling carefully back onto the road.

He couldn't rid himself of Shannon yet, but he could deal with the photographer—the police's eyewitness. When he did, Shannon would be pleased. She'd feel comfortable again, lost once more to her flock and to mothering Matthew.

But someday Morrison would find another wife, one who was softer. Gentler. Like Lauren. Or Trisha. Or

Michelle. Or any of the other girls he'd pleasured and blessed over the years.

And someday soon he'd be blessed with the life he truly wanted. One without Shannon.

CHAPTER TWENTY-NINE

MAC AND SEVERAL OFFICERS from Redding PD had to leave their cars on the side of the road and walk a mile through a dense grove of trees before reaching Lester Phillips's remote fishing cabin. The inside was innocuous. Clean. Very little furniture. White walls. Not exactly where one would expect a host of violent crimes to be committed.

But they had been committed.

He found the bloodstain almost immediately. Someone had tried cleaning it out of the carpet with bleach, but it was still there, right next to the brick hearth. And by the size of the stain, the victim's wounds—*Lindsay's* wounds—had been massive.

Lights flashed as one of the detectives took a picture of it.

Mac put on some latex gloves and walked to the neat stack of videos next to an ancient VCR and a modern-looking, though dusty, DVD player.

Old movies. *Casablanca.* A couple of Doris Day films. Then one in particular caught his eye. He picked up the well-worn paper case.

Singing in the Rain.

It was the song that Hanes had hummed in the cab.

This was where he'd been staying, at least until he'd returned to Crystal Haven.

Next to the videotapes were several DVD disks, unlabeled.

He slipped one into the DVD player, turned on the TV and switched it to the right channel. It was a recording of Lindsay, her hair dark, similar to the way it had been in Natalie's photographs. She was pretending to give a tour of the cabin.

"It's nice, don't you think? All the comforts of home." She rolled her eyes. "Not! But what's a girl in love supposed to do?" She shrugged, then continued to walk through the cabin, describing each room as she passed it.

"Hey, Mac. I found something."

Keeping the DVD running, Mac turned and walked toward the back of the house. A young detective named Heath Parker jerked his head toward a small bedroom. A twin-size bed covered with a worn quilt, a stuffed bear perched against the pillow. A couple of loose dresses hanging in the closet, none of them, he noted, the white dress Lindsay had worn to the farmers' market. "What did you find?"

The words stuck in his throat as he spied the book on the night table. *What to Expect When You're Expecting.* His gaze skipped to the corner of the room where a small cradle was half covered with several blankets. He shifted them aside so he could look into the cradle; inside were a couple of neatly folded baby outfits. Small. Blue.

"—baby boy."

The words were spoken in a feminine voice that drifted into the bedroom from the living room. From the DVD player Mac had left on.

With a feeling of dread, Mac stepped in front of the playing TV. This portion of the video had obviously been taken several months after Lindsay had given her little tour. Her hair was still black but longer. And although it might not have been noticeable at first glance because of her small stature, Lindsay was pregnant. She leaned back, thrusting her stomach out and pressing her dress against its roundness. She was smiling, but her eyes were slightly sad as she described how her baby boy was going to live with his father "Morris" while Lindsay went to college. Someday, she said, they'd all be a family.

Morris. Reverend Morrison. *M.* The father of Lindsay's baby. A baby no one had known about. Had he died with her? Because he hadn't been buried with her. If that was the case, they would have found its fragile bones right along with hers.

Briefly he wondered why the pathologist hadn't discovered the fact that Lindsay had been pregnant. The only explanation was that the killer had taken the baby, dead or alive, separating Lindsay from any of its genetic material—didn't the placenta carry the DNA of both the mother and her fetus?—before burying her. Even so, wouldn't Lindsay's bones have revealed something? Wouldn't she have been wider through the hips, from having delivered the baby? But that was assuming Lindsay had given birth to the baby naturally. It was entirely possible, he realized, given the state of the bones they'd found, that any trace DNA had been corrupted. And if the baby had been cut from Lindsay's body—

He shivered, trying not to picture a small, shallow grave somewhere outside.

For now, he had to believe Lindsay's baby was alive.

So where was he?

BONNIE STOPPED THE CAR and turned to Natalie, who sat in the passenger seat. "Are you sure you don't want me to come in with you? I don't mind."

"No, thank you. But I really appreciate the ride."

"You know which mobile home your friend lives in?"

"The light blue one, about halfway down the lane. He—he always had an American flag out front."

"I see it."

Natalie sighed with relief. Chances were Pete still lived there. "So you'll pick me up in thirty minutes?"

"Sure thing."

"Thanks again for doing this. I'm just—just not ready to ride in a cab again."

"No worries, Natalie. I'm proud of you for having the courage to get out again at all." She heard the slight note of criticism in Bonnie's voice, indicating she actually felt the exact opposite. Natalie ignored it and stepped out of the car with her cane. She stood there and listened to Bonnie drive off.

The sudden rain that had started a few hours ago had let up a little; it was only a light drizzle now. Still, she shivered in the cold. She tried to draw on her memories of what the mobile park looked like. She'd walked the adjacent neighborhood numerous times. Should have been able to picture the houses that lined the street just outside the mobile park entrance. But her memory was sluggish, even more so than her vision.

She didn't have that much time before Bonnie came back. Plus, it was going to start raining harder. She needed to ask Pete her questions right away.

The only trouble was she was tired, so tired. Suddenly making the effort to walk to Pete's trailer seemed too much for her. She'd love to fall asleep to the sound of the rain. For a second, she imagined doing just that. But her imagination quickly betrayed her, tormenting her with memories of being in Mac's arms again.

Up until they'd fought, she hadn't felt tired at all. In fact, she'd felt more alive than she had in a long time. The weeks prior to meeting him had been comfortable, predictable and boring. Ever since he'd come crashing through her door, things had been sheer madness. Would she ever be able to find a happy medium between the two extremes?

She listened to the wind's lonely howl. The world faded in and out, keeping time with her slow, shuddering breaths. Once again, she felt utterly alone. With no warning, she was transported back to that musty old closet, and all her childish fears of boogeymen and monsters welled up inside her.

The neighborhood houses she'd tried to picture finally formed in her mind, but instead of appearing comfortingly familiar, they were now ominous. Windows became demonic eyes, staring at her with malicious intent. Manicured lawns and trees were sinister hands, reaching out to grab her. Arched doorways were transformed into gaping, sharp-toothed mouths, ready to swallow her whole.

If she died right now, no one would know. If she screamed, no one would hear. In some ways, wouldn't that be better? Even if Mac was right about someone in the church being after her, they wouldn't chase after a dead woman. Perhaps with Lindsay gone and Alex Hanes dead, too, things would stop there. Mac could move on to another case....

Stop it! She wanted to slap herself. What was wrong with her? Despite the fact Mac thought she was foolish and had a death wish, it wasn't true. She didn't want to die.

What she wanted was to put all this behind her. Help Mac close his case. Learn the truth. Get on with her life.

It would be a life without Mac, but it would be a good life nonetheless.

She started moving forward, struggling to put one foot in front of the other, carefully making her way over the uneven, pebbled terrain, hoping she was actually getting closer to Pete's front door.

"Why are you crying, pretty Natalie?"

Natalie gasped. She hadn't even realized she was crying, but she was. "Pete?"

"That's right. I remember you, pretty lady. You always stopped by to say hello and drop some bills into my basket. So kind."

She recognized his voice. Pictured him as she'd last seen him. Bewhiskered face and dingy tattered clothes. She felt a simultaneous urge to hug him and run away.

"Come on in so we can talk."

Natalie nodded and smiled weakly. She let him lead her inside his home and to a chair. When she sat down, he placed a throw around her shoulders.

"Why are you here, Natalie? Why are you upset?"

She opened her mouth, then shut it again, not quite sure where to begin. Finally she settled for the truth. "I'm here on a wild-goose chase. The last time I saw you, it was at the farmers' market. About two months ago. You said something to someone. Something I remembered. And it might be important."

"What did I say?"

"You called someone a hypocrite. A charlatan. You said someone was blinding a woman and that she shouldn't give him what he wanted."

"Ah, now I remember."

"You do! That's good. I half thought I was imagining it. Was it someone you know?"

"No. No one I ever met."

"Then why did you say those things?"

He didn't respond. Instead, he sighed and shifted. "I've got some wine here. You want some?" He brushed past her, and it was only then she smelled the alcohol on him. "It'll warm you up."

She hesitated. She was cold. Freezing. She nodded.

"Here you go."

She reached her hand out. He handed her a glass. She took a long sip, then another because it indeed made her warmer.

"I remember the couple you're talking about. But she didn't listen to me, did she? She gave him what he wanted. I knew she would. By her own choice or not, she gave him her baby."

Baby? Pete had obviously been drinking before she'd shown up.

He began to sing a lullaby. Something about singing until a loved one felt safe, closed his eyes and slept well. Slept tight.

She sighed. Yep, he was drunk. But he had nice voice. And the words of the song were lovely.

She took another sip of wine. Closed her eyes. Listened as he continued to sing.

"I'll stroke your hair as you sleep," he crooned. "You won't be alone...."

Natalie was almost falling asleep herself. She imagined a baby falling under the spell of Pete's voice. Lindsay's baby.

"She was pregnant?" she muttered softly.

But even as she asked the question, her memory flashed with a blurry picture of a petite, dark-haired girl and a tall silver-haired man at her side. There was something about the girl's posture that had bugged her. Something about the way she'd placed her hand on her stomach. What was it? What...

It came to her.

It hadn't been a flat stomach, but it hadn't been huge either. Natalie hadn't readily recognized her as pregnant. But the way she'd stood was how Natalie had often seen pregnant women standing. The way they unconsciously protected the baby in their belly.

Her mind clicked through the possibilities. Mac thought the reverend might have had a thing for young girls. Unspoken was his suspicion that he might have been having an affair with Lindsay. What if he had found out she was pregnant? What if he'd needed to hide that fact? What if he'd been the one to hire Alex Hanes to kill her?

She didn't know whether it was true or not, but she believed her vision of Lindsay was a memory, not her imagination. If it was true, Lindsay's pregnancy was a clue Mac should know about. It was a clue she could give him.

"Thank you, Pete. I have to make a call."

His singing abruptly stopped. "Of course. Don't be afraid, pretty Natalie. Everything's going to be just fine."

His words brought a well of tears to her eyes. Unlike the last time he'd said them, she didn't believe him, but the words still offered a hint of comfort.

She waited until Bonnie picked her up and took her home before she called Mac.

He answered on the first ring.

"What is it, Natalie?"

He sounded aloof. Curt. She almost regretted calling him, but she forced herself to continue. "I remembered something, Mac. Something about Lindsay. I—I think she was pregnant."

There was an odd, tense silence on the other line before he finally spoke. "What makes you think that?"

She told him about Pete. How she'd tracked him down. What he'd said.

She waited for his voice to soften. For him to show some sign of appreciation.

"You went to a lot of trouble for nothing, Natalie. I know Lindsay was pregnant."

"What— When—"

"It doesn't matter when," he snapped. "And you shouldn't sound so surprised. It's *my* job to find these things out. I asked you to leave the investigating to the professionals, but you just can't do it, can you? Are you still at the trailer park?"

His tone, his disdain, his anger hit her in the face and brought her back to reality—her reality—so fast that she actually staggered. She shook her head, only belatedly realizing that he couldn't see her. "I—I'm sorry. I won't bother you again."

"Natalie, wait—"

Mac cursed when Natalie severed the connection. Several of the officers who were still processing the fishing cabin looked at him curiously.

Fuck! What had he been thinking?

He'd regretted what he'd said as soon as the words had left his mouth.

She'd just been trying to help, but all he could think

about was how she'd visited some stranger in an isolated trailer park—after he'd already warned her she
still might be in danger—because she couldn't accept
her blindness or the fact that, like it or not, it made her
more vulnerable to those who wanted to hurt her.

He was right to have turned down her help. Blind or
not, she was an untrained citizen who didn't have any
business trying to track down criminal elements.

Still, he should have handled the situation better.
He knew she had issues about her blindness. That she
didn't want to be thought of as "less than" because of
it. He should have been more patient with her. More
understanding. Instead, he'd driven her away when he
didn't want to drive her away at all.

There, he'd admitted it to himself.

As much as he'd been denying a future with her, he
couldn't imagine one without her, and he didn't even
want to.

He could also admit that perhaps it was *him* who was
a bit too obsessed with her blindness. That while she
shouldn't be taking all the risks that she did, some of
the risks she took were worth it. After all, she'd actually
discovered a vital piece of information about Lindsay,
something he'd only just discovered himself.

Yes, she was needy. Or rather, she had needs. Needs
that he could try to fulfill but might not be able to. But
did he really want to turn away from her without even
trying? He didn't, and that's what made her different
than Nancy.

He hadn't wanted to try with Nancy. Not really.

He wanted to try with Natalie.

The question was whether she'd even want him to.

"Clemmons—"

Mac's head snapped up when the male voice erupted from the television and the DVD that was still playing.

The person taking the video had turned the camera around so his face was reflected on the screen. It was Alex Hanes. "—is a great father. He has twin boys of his own. He says your little boy will grow up with them. In the church's family. They'll be his brothers and you won't have to worry about him. Brothers take care of each other. Brothers have a special bond…."

Shit. There it was. Everything they needed, right on tape. Morrison. Hanes. Clemmons. They'd known about Lindsay's baby. That meant Morrison and Clemmons probably knew where the baby was now. Pushing away his regret about Natalie, he called Jase.

"She was pregnant, Jase."

"Mac—"

"She had a baby. A little boy. The reverend's."

"Mac, I know."

"What?" First Natalie, and now Jase? "How do you know?"

"Because Alex Hanes's brother, Arthur Clemmons, and his wife contacted me a few minutes ago. He's told us everything. How the reverend got her pregnant. How his wife pretended she was pregnant so she could pass Lindsay's child off as her own. How Lindsay died."

"Did they kill the baby, too?" Once again he imagined having to look for a small burial site in the nearby woods. He wasn't sure he could stomach it right now.

"No. The baby's fine. Well, as fine as it can be, given it's with a crazy woman."

Automatically he though of Natalie's mother. "What crazy woman?"

"Shannon Morrison. The reverend's wife. She's passing the baby off as her own just like they'd planned. It wasn't in the plan to kill Lindsay, but that's what happened, and Clemmons cut the baby from her body himself. To save it, he says."

Fetal abduction. He'd dealt with it before. One woman had even used a set of car keys to steal another woman's child. "Where is Mrs. Morrison?"

"She should be at home. What do you want me to do?"

Mac was two hours away from Sacramento. It would take that long to get a warrant. "Get the paperwork started. Call a judge and let him know it's coming. Let's get a warrant and get that baby away from her. What about the reverend?"

"Clemmons called him. He isn't answering. Have you talked to Natalie?"

Hearing her name so suddenly threw him. "She just called me."

"So she's okay?"

"What's wrong, Jase?"

"Morrison wanted Clemmons to kill Natalie. He thinks she's an eyewitness and can tag Morrison with Lindsay at the farmers' market."

"Why does he think that?"

"You said to shake him up. I implied we had an eye-witness when I talked to him. I never mentioned Nata-lie's name but—"

"Shit," Mac whispered. "Call Liz at Plainville PD Have them get a car to her house immediately. I'm on my way there. Once you have the warrant, arrest Shan-non Morrison. And put out an APB for the reverend."

"I fucked up, Mac."

Mac heard the anguish in Jase's voice and thought, *So did I.* "No, you didn't. We shake them up. Some-times we show our hand. We let them know we're on to them. Then they make stupid mistakes. You couldn't have known…. But that doesn't matter now. What mat-ters now is making sure Natalie's safe."

That's *all* that mattered.

CHAPTER THIRTY

LYING ON HER living-room sofa, Natalie hugged her knees to her chest and rested her head against them. Tremors racked her body as she tried to ignore the ringing of her phone and the knocks on her front door.

It was so unfair. She didn't want to be alone. She wanted to reach out to someone. Wanted to talk to someone about how confused she was—by the passion she and Mac had shared, and by her own desperate needs to alternately pull him closer and drive him away from her. But she had no one to talk to. She'd tried to talk to Mac, and he'd pushed her away. The only other person she might have confided in had betrayed her.

Melissa, the woman who even now was knocking on her door.

"Natalie, I know you're there. Please let me in so we can talk."

The other woman's voice was filled with urgency and guilt. Instinctively, Natalie wanted to forgive and comfort her, but something held her back. An icy shell surrounded her, numbing her pain, luring her with the promise of control and autonomy.

"Natalie, enough is enough. It's raining out here. Let me in!"

Her friend's words sliced through her cool resolve. *She* had had enough? Angrily, Natalie surged to her feet and moved to the door. When she bumped against it, she slapped the wood with her palm. "Leave. Leave and tell the police more of my secrets, Melissa. I'm sure you got a big laugh telling Mac all about them."

"He thought I might be involved with someone who wanted to hurt you. I was scared. And he said the more he knew about you, the more it would help keep you safe."

"So he what? Forced you to talk?" she practically sneered.

Melissa was silent for several beats before she softly said, "No, no. He didn't. I'm sorry."

Natalie curled the palm resting against the door into a fist and steeled herself against the despair in Melissa's voice. "That's not good enough. Not anymore."

"I—I didn't tell him everything. I just wanted him to know what was important."

"You told him enough. You told him about Duncan."

"He said ex-boyfriends were often the first suspects that had to be eliminated. I was just thinking about your safety."

"Just like when you left me standing out on the curb, right? Do me a favor. Leave the concern for my safety to the only person who really cares. Myself."

"You're being ridiculous—"

"You need to worry about your own life, Melissa. Your own problems. In case you don't know it, you've got plenty."

"What does that mean?"

"It means your boyfriend is a lazy mooch and you're nothing but an average photographer, so if you hope to continue supporting him, you need to look into a career change. Fast."

The words weren't out of her mouth before she regretted them. Her stomach actually rolled with nausea as she imagined her friend's hurt expression. What was happening to her? Her own mother had struck out at others out of pain, and she was doing the same thing.

"Melissa—"

"Well, looks like I've been the blind one. I'll just leave you to continue hiding here, away from everyone, so you don't have to risk anyone else disappointing you. So long, Natalie."

She remained frozen. Willed herself to remain that way. But she couldn't stand it. "Melissa, wait," she called. She fumbled with the locks and had just pulled the door open when she heard the screech of tires.

Someone screamed, the sound high-pitched and filled with fear.

There was a sickening thud before the scream cut off.

More squealing tires.

She stumbled outside, only to slip on the wet pavement. "Melissa? Melissa!"

But there was no answer. Until she heard the sound of opening doors and running feet. "Natalie? What— Oh, no! Edward! Edward, call the police."

"Is she okay? Melissa—" She crawled forward, thinking only of getting to her friend.

Someone crouched next to her and caught her arm. "Natalie, wait. Don't go in the street."

"Who are you?"

"Maureen. I live next door, remember? My husband is checking on your friend now."

Natalie gripped Maureen's shirt. "What happened? I heard tires screeching. An accident—"

Maureen clasped Natalie's hands in hers, her grip firm but comforting. "Some guy barreled around the corner. Headed straight for her. He didn't stop, just kept going."

Automatically, Natalie turned her hands until her fingers were interlocked with Maureen's. "Is she okay? Tell me!"

"I don't know. He hit her hard. She looks bad. I'm sorry."

MAC DROVE TOWARD Plainville with his siren blaring and his foot jammed down on the accelerator. He kept calling Natalie, but she wasn't answering.

She's okay, he told himself. She was just pissed off at him. Ignoring his calls. Why wouldn't she be? She'd tried to help him, and he'd lashed out at her. Hurt her just like her mother. Duncan Oliver. Melissa.

God knows, he hadn't meant to hurt her.

His cell phone rang. "Natalie?"

"It's Liz."

"Liz. Where is she?"

"On the way to the hospital."

Horror squeezed the air out of his lungs. A hospital?

So Morrison had gotten to her. She was hurt. Maybe even dead. "Morrison—"

"No. She's okay, but Melissa isn't. We just answered a call of a hit-and-run outside her house. It was raining. I'm betting the driver mistook Melissa for Natalie. I'm at the scene now—"

"Why the hell aren't you with Natalie?"

"She left in the ambulance with Melissa before I got here."

"Send an officer to the hospital. Make sure she's kept under guard."

"I've already made that request. But we've had a bad night. All our officers are out on active calls."

"Damn it, I don't care. Get in touch with the on-call officer."

"He's already out. I'll head over there right now. I'm only about fifteen minutes away. I'll wait with her while Melissa's being treated."

Fifteen minutes. Too long. "Is Melissa going to be okay?"

"I don't know. From what the neighbors say, she was hurt pretty bad."

Mac slammed the steering wheel with his palm. "Get to her, Liz. Please. Keep her safe for me."

"I'll try. I promise."

As she sat in the E.R. waiting room of Plainville General Hospital, Natalie tried to call forth the numbness that had always brought her comfort in the past.

It didn't come.

She felt every slice of pain. Every tremor of hurt. Her heart pounded erratically against her chest, seeming both hollow and heavy.

She grieved for her loss. For her inability to protect herself. For her inability to forget. But at the same time, she knew why numbing herself was no longer an option.

This was where hiding had gotten her. Where it had gotten Melissa.

She couldn't hide anymore.

"You're going to be okay, Melissa," she whispered, not caring who heard her or that Melissa wasn't even there. "You're going to be okay and I'm going to help Mac find the person who did this to you."

She *would* help him, whether he wanted her help or not.

She didn't care if he thought she was crazy or if she angered him further. Her friend had been hurt because of her, and she was going to get her justice. No matter what it took.

The longer she sat there, the more determined she became. Her grief and pain faded, and she welcomed their transformation into anger. She barely noticed the antiseptic smells and bustling sounds that had haunted her nightmares in the past. She was filled with resolve.

It must be a small fraction of what allowed Mac to do his job so well. The knowledge that the closer he got to finding clues, the closer he got to avenging someone important. Not necessarily important to him personally, the way Melissa was important to her, but that was the most amazing part. That he didn't even have to *know* the people he was helping to dedicate his life to them.

Maybe you should call him. Return his calls. But she'd left her cell phone at the house. Besides, she knew what would happen if she called Mac. He'd want to tuck her away. Keep her safe. From someone who, like Alex Hanes, allowed holy words to justify committing unholy acts.

Whoever had hit Melissa had meant to hurt her. It had been dark and rainy, so it would have been easy to mistake them for one another. Which meant it was her fault. If only she'd opened the door instead of pushing Melissa away....

Mac had accused her of letting her pride get in the way of common sense, and perhaps she'd reacted badly because on some level he'd spoken the truth. But common sense had never really been a big part of her life even when she'd had full sight. Playing it safe had never been her style. If anything, she'd lost her nerve only when she'd lost her vision. It was back now, carrying her away on a whirlwind of emotion that she surrendered to completely. The horror of Melissa's scream still echoed in her ears, urging her on. Giving her purpose.

She stood but then froze, realizing that she didn't even have her cane with her.

Her laugh was filled with both bitterness and defeat.

Just what did she think she was going to do?

Take a cab to Sacramento, knock on the church door, and what?

The reality of her helplessness showered down on her.

It was at that moment that she finally got it.

This was what Mac had been trying to tell her. It didn't matter that she was blind. Even if she was fully sighted, it would be foolish for her to confront a man who could run down an innocent woman in cold blood.

She'd spent so much of her life thumbing her nose at destiny and death that in some ways she'd begun to think of herself as superhuman. Blind or not, she was just a human being. One who wasn't trained to bring down criminals the way Mac was.

He was right; she'd had no business interfering with his investigation.

Leave things to the professionals.

That's really all she could do.

But perhaps…

Perhaps she could still do something for her friend. Something that might be just as important.

"Excuse me," she said. She was seated next to the check-in window, where she'd given the nurse information about Melissa.

"Yes?"

"Does the hospital have a chapel?"

"It's across the street at the old hospital building. There's nothing but medical offices there now. They're all closed, but the chapel should be open."

"Do you think there's someone who can take me there?"

"It might take a few minutes but I'll find someone."

Twenty minutes later, a nurse led Natalie across the street to the chapel. The moment she entered, the room filled her with a sense of peace she hadn't experienced in a long time. The air was cool. The quiet stillness like a comforting embrace. There was still no color, but she could envision candles flickering and stained glass pictures hanging on the wall.

She heard hushed voices as several people entered the chapel behind them. A baby babbled loudly, and a woman shushed it in Spanish. She felt several bodies brush past her.

"I'll go check on your friend and be back in a bit?" the nurse asked.

"Thank you. That would be great," Natalie replied. The woman left. Natalie felt her way to a pew and sat down. Somewhere to her left, voices whispered. The baby laughed, and the exuberant sound made her smile. Folding her hands on the back of the pew in front of her, Natalie lowered her head.

Please, she prayed. *Please let Melissa be all right. Please keep Mac safe, too.*

Almost immediately she realized the inherent conflict in her prayer. Mac had a job to do, and it was a dangerous one. To stop a killer, he had to be willing to place himself at risk. She knew she couldn't change that about him. He was a cop every bit as much as she was a photographer. He wouldn't be complete otherwise.

Yet because she cared for him, she wanted him safe, too. She wanted to be his safe haven when his work was done and when he could simply be the man rather than the cop.

It was what he wanted for her, as well. That's why he'd gotten so angry, so *scared,* when she'd talked about infiltrating the church. He knew she wasn't trained for that kind of thing. In the end, whether she was sighted or not was irrelevant.

You see me. You see me better than most, he'd said.

And she did.

But the same was true for him.

He'd seen *her.* How scared and angry and lonely she'd been. How she'd feared being like her mother, lost to mental illness as well as darkness. Yet he'd seen her strength and her beauty, too.

Giving her the chance to do the same.

Whether she lost the rest of her vision or not, whether she and Mac worked things out between them or not, *she* was going to be okay.

She wasn't her mother. Yes, she'd let her escalating blindness mess with her head, but she hadn't *lost* her head. She'd made mistakes but hadn't become a victim to the point that she'd hurt others. She never would.

Natalie could no longer hear the baby or its family. She squinted but saw no trace of them. She'd been so preoccupied she hadn't noticed when they left or if anyone else had come in.

The nurse had said she'd be back, but Natalie didn't want to wait. Mac had been calling her and even though she didn't have her cell phone, there had to be a public phone around here somewhere. She wanted to let him know about Melissa. Tell him she was okay. And that she finally understood what he'd been trying to tell her.

She stood. "Hello?" she called. "Is anyone here?"

"I'm here, miss," a soft male voice answered. "Do you need anything?"

She turned toward the voice. "I need to use a phone. Have you seen one?"

"I believe there's one a few halls down."

"Can you help me get there? I'm blind."

Funny how she didn't even hesitate to say the words.

She heard nothing but breathing as the man considered her request. He probably felt awkward, uncertain how to react to a blind person asking him for help. Impatient, she almost told him to forget it, but then...

"Of course," he finally said. "Here. Take my arm."

MAC WAS CLOSE. He'd be in Plainville in the next fifteen minutes. Since he still hadn't heard from her, he called Liz. "Do you have her?"

"I just got here. I'm going to find her right now."

"I'll stay on the line," Mac said.

He heard Liz talking to the nurse on duty.

"Natalie Jones...the patient's friend. She's blind. Well, where is she?" Static came on the line as Liz juggled the phone. "She's here. She just went to the chapel. It's across the street."

"Get to her, Liz."

"I'm running. But—hang on!"

Mac heard silence interrupted by periodic bumps, static and the sound of Liz's breathing. A soft curse.

"Liz, what is it?" Mac snapped.

"I just got an update from dispatch. Morrison's here."

Liz's words stopped Mac's heart, but she kept talking.

"We checked the hospital parking lot. His car's here. The same car seen leaving the hit-and-run."

THE MAN WHO GUIDED her was charming. Too charming. He wanted to chat when all Natalie wanted was to get to a phone and call Mac.

"Are you sure you know where we're going?"

"I saw the phone down this way. It'll just take me a minute to find it."

"You don't work here?"

"No, I'm visiting a friend at the hospital. You?"

She pictured Melissa, fighting for her life in surgery. Waking and wondering what was going on. Feeling frightened that she was alone. She'd head back to the E.R. as soon as she called Mac. "The same."

"Will your friend be okay?"

"I—I don't know. She was run over."

The man tsked. "An accident?"

"Deliberate."

"By whom?"

"I don't know. But I have my suspicions. The worst kind of coward. A pathetic excuse for a man."

The man jerked to a stop. "That's not something a lady should say. Women should respect men. They are superior."

Natalie's laugh was as automatic as breathing. He

was joking, right? "Do you know that most serial killers are white males?"

"No. I didn't know that. But men are worth more than women. Leviticus 27:1-7."

The phrase made her frown. It sounded like something Alex Hanes might have said.

"Ah. That got your attention, did it? You're blind, but now you see?"

She wrenched her arm away from him and backed away. "Who are you?"

"I'm a messenger from God, just like Alex was. The God who wants to meet you, face-to-face, Natalie Jones. But Alex wasn't smart enough or ruthless enough to get the job done. I am."

"You're with that church. You're the minister Mac told me about. You ran down Melissa."

"Reverend," he said gently. "And I don't know who Mac is. I assume he's one of the cops working on Lindsay's case?"

"Did you kill her? Did you kill her baby? Or did you just hire Alex to kill her, being the coward that you are?"

He sucked in a breath. "So you do remember seeing her. That's how you know about the baby. But I didn't kill him. Of course I didn't. I'd never kill my own son. Not when I could give him to my barren wife and in turn get everything from her and her father that they've been withholding."

She continued to back up. She had no idea where she

was, but the nurse had said there was nothing but medical offices here now. Closed medical offices.

Leaving her isolated and alone with a madman.

But she'd automatically been keeping track of their walk. They'd walked about 250 feet from the entrance to the chapel. He'd taken three turns—a left and two rights.

She whirled and ran, keeping one hand against the wall.

He laughed harshly. "Where do you think you're going?"

Several times she slammed into an obstacle, but she kept moving. He was right behind her, his footsteps heavy and ominous. She pushed herself faster and made several turns, elated when she no longer heard him behind her.

After rounding another corner, she paused for breath.

He wasn't laughing now. "Come here and let's end this, my dear."

She jerked into motion again. His voice was clear but some distance away. He sounded tired. His breathing labored.

Not wanting to give away her location, she bit back her retort but feared he heard her heavy weaving steps anyway. She pushed herself to continue running in the same direction until she finally hit a dead end. Frantically she felt along the wall until she came to a door. She tried pulling it open, but it was locked. Same for the door that was right next to it. A whimper escaped her.

She heard him again. Closing in. She kept moving.

Kept patting the wall. Kept trying to open any door she came to. She could practically feel him breathing down her neck when she finally found a door that gave way when she turned the knob. She fell into the room, took a few running steps and immediately crashed into a low, hard surface.

She jumped when several items fell to the floor. The noise was going to bring him right to her, she thought. For a moment she wanted to crouch down. Cover her ears and hide in a corner the way she had when her mother had locked her in the closet. But she knew the man after her would be even more merciless than her mother had been.

So she wouldn't hide.

She stuck out her hands and felt in front of her. There was a smooth surface. A table. Maybe a desk. She felt along the edges. There was a phone. A cup with pens and pencils that she'd knocked over. A stapler. She gasped when something cold and sharp pricked her fingers. She picked up the item and carefully ran her fingers across it. A pair of scissors.

She wielded it in front of her, facing what she thought was the door to the hallway. Shadows flickered as the door opened, and he stepped through.

"I was going to make this fast and painless," he gritted out between heavy breaths, "but you've made me angry, Natalie. You really thought you could get away from me? Even though you're blind? You females are all alike. You and Lindsay and Shannon. You need to learn your place in this world. On your knees."

A sound crashed behind her, and she jerked. He'd thrown something, deliberately wanting to shake her.

"Are you familiar with the book of Matthew, Natalie? I'm particularly fond of verse 18:9. Shall I quote it for you?"

"How about you just go to hell instead?" She slashed out with the scissor blades even though she really had no idea how close he was. "Stay away from me."

"Verse 18:9 says that 'if thine eye offend thee, pluck it out, and cast it from thee: it is better for thee to enter into life with one eye, rather than having two eyes to be cast into hell fire.' God took your vision because you offended Him, Natalie. Now you've offended me, and I'm going to take your life."

He threw something hard into the corner of the room again, then something else. Each time, she jerked. Helplessness washed through her, quickly increasing her terror. All the air in the room suddenly disappeared, and she struggled to breathe.

God, not now. She couldn't have a panic attack. She needed to be strong. She needed to be ready.

She forced herself to take deep breaths. Recalled the peace she'd felt while she sat in the chapel. *Don't be afraid. Everything's going to be just fine.*

Along with the memory of Pete's words came the faint sound of a siren.

It could just be another ambulance.

But somehow she knew it was the police.

Somehow she knew she wasn't alone.

She wasn't the only person she could rely on any

longer. If the police were here, Mac wouldn't be too far behind. Mac would come for her. Somehow Mac would know where she was, and he would save her.

She yelped as cruel fingers clamped on her wrist and twisted the scissors out of her hand. He yanked on her arm, sending her flying. She hit the edge of something hard, more objects falling around her, then fell to the ground herself.

"You've caused me nothing but trouble," he said from above her. As soon as the words left his mouth, he kicked her in the ribs, hard enough to make her scream. "Even more trouble than my wife, and that's saying a lot."

After her initial scream, Natalie breathed through the pain and remained silent. But still, she kept track of where he was, noting from his voice the way he walked around her.

"A pity I couldn't make sure your friend was dead, but it wouldn't have been smart to hang around. She wasn't really who I was after anyway. I'm sure you know that now."

She couldn't hold back her scream of fury. "You bastard!" she yelled, struggling to get up, but he simply kicked her again. She crumpled, and he was on her, trying to drag her away. Her hands scrambled to find purchase, to stop him from taking her wherever he was taking her. There were objects all over the floor. She tried to grab hold of something, but he was moving so fast....

Feeling his breath close to her ear, she squirmed, trying to knock him in the head with her own. He slowed down but stayed out of reach, laughing at her struggles. "The police stopped by to talk to me. Arrogant pricks. I wish they could see this."

"Let them see what a maniac you are? Believe me, they already know."

For an answer, he kicked her again. This time in the face.

Natalie heard the bones in her nose break and felt the warm spray of blood that covered her cheeks and lips. She choked, trying to fight off the sudden rush of dizziness. She collapsed onto the floor and closed her fingers around something hard. She had no idea what it was.

He kicked her again, but she barely felt it this time. "After you, I'll work on the cops next. I never knew it was quite so simple. My wife always told me to be more ruthless. She was so right."

Pain radiated from inside her, making the blows he'd landed seem feeble by comparison. Mac was smart, but she didn't even want to think about this psychopath going after him.

He crouched next to her again, grabbing her hair and pulling her head up until her neck muscles screamed in agony. "It was all under duress. The devil made me do it. Only it was my devil of a wife. You're just like her, you know. So hard. You think you can do everything. That you don't need a man. But you do. All women need a man."

She raised her arm, tried to hit him with whatever it was that she held, but he deflected the blow. The item slipped out of her grasp. "Bitch!" He thumped her head against the floor. When he released her hair, only a whimper escaped her. She couldn't move. She could barely hear him.

"Well, I've spent enough time here. I need to get this over with. I'll put you out of your misery now." He kissed her cheek softly, and his warm breath puffed against her. She let out an involuntary gasp but then immediately bit her lip hard, refusing to make another sound.

She slowly blinked her eyes open, trying to focus on him. To get a clear sense of his shape. She couldn't. She couldn't see anything, but she could feel the blood covering her face. Getting into her eyes. "See anything?" he taunted.

"Yeah," she snapped, unable to help herself. "I see a giant coward."

He slapped her hard. She made one final attempt. Threw her arms wide, sweeping the floor, grabbing anything that came in her path and slashing out at him with it.

He screamed just as she heard someone call her name.

"Natalie!"

It was Mac.

She heard crashing sounds. Felt a heavy weight on top of her. Screamed and thrashed. Heard a gun go off.

Then her heart was pounding so fast it was all she could hear. Her lungs were being squeezed so tight that it was all she could feel. She struggled to stay conscious. To hear him say her name once more.

"Natalie. Baby."

There it was.

Faintly she was aware of him cradling her against him. She couldn't see him. Had never been able to see him. Would never be able to see him smile, but oh, how she wanted to. "I knew you would come," she said. "Got to—got to stop meeting…this way…"

CHAPTER THIRTY-ONE

NATALIE APPEARED TO lose consciousness. Mac had only a few seconds to hold her before some EMTs, led by Liz, came careening into the room. They took her gently from his arms, ignoring the prone body of Reverend Carter Morrison altogether.

He never took his eyes off her, but his tears made keeping her in focus difficult. God, the bastard had hurt her. Her jaw looked as if it had been fractured, and her eyes were swollen shut.

The EMTs put her on a gurney and wheeled her toward the E.R. across the street while he ran alongside her. He fumbled for her hand, sighing with relief when she weakly squeezed his fingers. He knew how afraid she must be. How much she hated hospitals. How much she hated feeling helpless and out of control. "Natalie. You're okay. I'm here, baby. I'm right here."

She didn't squeeze his hand again. Didn't move at all. Still, he sensed she heard him.

A small whimper escaped her, and she tried to speak but couldn't.

"Shh. It's okay. You're going to be okay."

"Mac..." His name was as thready as smoke, but he heard her. Barely.

"I'm here, Natalie. I'm not leaving."

"Mac…" She stopped when she was hit by a round of coughing. A liquid gurgling rattled in her chest, and Mac looked at the doctor who was now pulling the gurney with the EMTs. The doctor stared back at him grimly.

"Natalie, don't try to talk. The doctor's here. He's going to take care of you."

Natalie shook her head. "No. Mac…need to tell you…"

He leaned closer as her voice faded out. "What? What Natalie?"

Someone shoved Mac back. "Back off, Detective. She might have internal bleeding and maxillofacial trauma, with possible fractures to her eye socket and skull. We're going to need to do a C.T. scan and possible surgery to lift any fractured skull bones off her brain."

Mac held on to Natalie's hand as long as possible until they pushed the gurney through a set of sliding glass doors. One of the EMTs and a nurse blocked his way. "Stay here, Detective. We'll come out as soon as we know something."

Mac watched as the gurney was navigated around the corner. He looked down at his hand and at her blood that stained him.

MAC SAT IN THE HOSPITAL lobby long after the solemn-faced doctor walked away. The SIG team had arrived to lend their support, but he didn't talk to any of them as images of Natalie clicked through his mind. The day they'd first met. The first time he'd kissed her. The way she'd looked and felt and sounded when they'd made love. But most of all, how she'd called him to tell him that Lindsay had been pregnant—how she'd been trying to *help* him—and how he'd pushed her away. Because he'd cared for her—hell, he'd fallen in love with her, a woman who seemed hell-bent on endangering herself to prove she was still normal—and that had scared the shit out of him.

Grief and guilt pounded at him with equal force. He'd delivered bad news to families before. Had become somewhat inured to their suffering. In truth, he'd always viewed grief as an obstacle to overcome, maneuvering around it until a victim's family had finally given him the information he'd needed. It had always been about solving the case after that. Yes, that included bringing the victim justice and the family closure, but he'd never truly focused on those as his ultimate goal. Always in the back of his mind had been his success record, and the fact that he didn't want to let a criminal get the better of him.

Someone knelt in front of him, cradling his face. His vision slowly focused on Carrie Ward. For a moment, her mouth moved silently until sound penetrated his brain.

"Mac...she's going to be okay. The doctor said so himself."

Mac's hands shook as he grabbed her wrists and gently pushed them away. He didn't deserve her comfort. "Her eyes. The doctor said she suffered head trauma.

That the bastard kicked her in the face. He doesn't know how it will affect her vision—"

"You don't know if it's permanent. She's lost her vision before and it came back."

"And what are the chances of that happening again? Damn it, she could have been killed!"

The knowledge had shocked him. Made him realize how much color and vibrancy she'd added to his life in such a short time. It had all become about the job for him. He'd told himself that being relieved to be out of his marriage with Nancy proved he was meant to be alone. That he'd be happier that way. But that hadn't been it at all. Nancy had simply been the wrong woman for him. He'd finally realized that when he'd met Natalie, but only after he'd almost lost her.

"But she didn't, Mac. She fought him and she survived because she didn't want to leave you!"

He stared at Carrie, not sure where this was coming from. A glance at Jase confirmed the other man's discomfort. He'd obviously told Carrie how much Natalie had come to mean to him. He wasn't angry. He didn't care who knew how he felt about Natalie, even if those feelings cost him his job. But he remembered the way she'd sounded when he'd rejected her. Both times. After they'd made love and after she'd called him. He wasn't counting on her wanting to see him again, especially after today.

His mouth twisted at his unfortunate choice of words.

"Excuse me."

Carrie moved aside as one of the surgical nurses

asked, "Does Ms. Jones live by herself? It will be a while before she's ready to be released, but I need to know who to contact when the time comes."

"Me," he choked out, and passed the nurse his card. "You can call me. If I'm not here. But I'm going to be here," he added lamely.

The nurse smiled. "She's lucky to have you."

Was she? Mac thought as the woman walked away. He doubted she'd see it that way, whether or not her vision had worsened. Would that be the final straw? Would she even want to go on? How could she, after everything she'd suffered?

But she *did* want to go on, he reminded himself.

Natalie had fought for her life. First in her own home and again across the street. That knowledge had him suddenly reconsidering Carrie's words.

She'd fought for her life. And what was he going to do about it? Let her face her recovery alone, just like that prick Duncan Oliver had done? Hell, no. She might not love him, might not want to have anything to do with him, but that was going to be her choice. He wouldn't abandon her when she needed him, and he was going to do his damnedest to make sure leaving him wasn't the choice she ultimately made.

He stood and touched Carrie's shoulder. "Thanks, Carrie. I'm going to see her now. Even though she'd not awake and probably won't be for a while, I—I need to see her."

With a final glance at Jase, who gave him a nod of support, Mac left.

As Mac walked away from her, Jase put his hand on Carrie's shoulder. To his surprise, she leaned back against him. She kept her eyes on Mac, but when she spoke, her voice wasn't quite steady.

"He's going to be okay."

Jase nodded. "Thanks in part to you. I could see the guilt eating at him. What did you say to him?"

He'd looked more than guilty. He'd looked dead. Literally. As if the very soul of him had been sucked out and nothing but a shell remained. It had been a wonder the guy had even been capable of standing.

When he'd stood and looked at Carrie, however, something had changed. Something encouraging had lit his eyes. A fire of resolve and determination and strength that told Jase his friend was going to be okay. And that he was going to make sure Natalie would be okay, as well.

"I—I just told him she fought for her life. Fought to stay with him." Finally realizing she was leaning against him, Carrie straightened. She quickly swiped away a tear, as if she was embarrassed someone would see it.

"So, looks like the Monroe girl's case is closed. You've got cause to celebrate. Which one of your women are you going to call first?" She smiled weakly at him, yet he saw her words, mild-sounding as she tried to make them, for what they were. Her attempt to push him away yet again.

What surprised him was his sudden urge not to let her do it.

"Come here, Carrie."

Her eyes widened before he pulled her into his arms.

She held herself stiff at first, then slowly relaxed into him. Even though it made him feel like a bastard, he couldn't help the way his body hardened at the feel of her against him. Still, holding her wasn't about desire. It was about wanting to be her friend. Offer her comfort. Give her a little of himself just the way she was giving him a little of her.

Far too soon, she pulled back. Smiled at him.

And he couldn't help himself. That smile took all his genuine and well-meaning intentions to comfort her and transformed them into something dark and intense.

He leaned down and kissed her.

CHAPTER THIRTY-TWO

WHEN NATALIE WOKE and was strong enough to actually stay awake, she immediately sensed Mac beside her. She couldn't see him. She couldn't see anything at all. Not even shadows. But she could hear him breathing. She could smell his wonderful scent. And those two things gave her the strength to speak even though part of her wanted to curl up and hide from the horror of what had happened.

She remembered everything. Melissa being run over. Morrison chasing her. Him taunting her and kicking her.

"It's okay, Natalie. I'm here." He took her hand.

She nodded. "I know." She wanted to tell him how much that meant to her. How glad she was to be alive. But she didn't know if she had that right yet. "Melissa?"

"She's doing well. She's in stable condition. She's asked about you, too, and I promised you'd see her as soon as you were well enough."

Her relief was instantaneous.

Mac raised her hand to his lips. Kissed her fingers. "I'm so sorry. So sorry, baby."

"Sorry for what?"

"For everything. How I pushed you away. How I

reacted when you told me Lindsay was pregnant. For Melissa. For not being here for you."

"Shh. I forgive you for the first two, if you forgive me for the things I said, too. The others aren't your fault."

She sensed he didn't believe her, but she wasn't surprised. That was Mac, her stubborn good-hearted cop, wanting to take the weight of the world on his shoulders. "What happened to the reverend?"

"He's dead."

She remembered slashing out at him with something. "Did I—"

"No. You fought back, but I shot him."

Despite everything, part of her was glad she hadn't killed him. The other part of her wished Mac hadn't needed to do so either. "And—and his wife? He said he'd given Lindsay's baby to her." To his barren, troublemaking, devil of a wife, more precisely. The man's hatred for his spouse had been palpable. And even though Lindsay's baby had also been Morrison's Natalie couldn't bring herself to think of the baby that way. He'd been *Lindsay's* baby boy, and Morrison had stolen him from her just as much as his wife had.

"She's in jail. She put up quite a fight. Right or wrong, there's no doubt that she loves the baby. I think some part of her truly thinks she's his mother. He's in foster care right now, but Lindsay's family is making arrangements to see him."

"That's good." She yawned—her eyelids were getting heavier. She was so tired, but she remembered there was something she'd tried to tell him. "Mac, you were right about me being reckless. I understand that now. I wanted to be normal so badly. To prove I was the same person despite losing my vision."

"You are the same person. You're a *better* person."

She smiled. "I love you for saying that, but let's not get carried away."

"Do you?"

"What?"

"Do you love me? Can you?"

Her first instinct was to resist answering the blunt question. The last time they'd talked, before they'd made love, he'd made it clear that a relationship was the last thing he wanted. But she wasn't going to lie to him. She felt how she felt. Whatever that meant, she wasn't hiding from it anymore.

"I love you."

He laid his face against hers. "I love you, too, Natalie."

His response didn't surprise her. Neither did his kiss or the moisture she felt against her face. "Well, of course you do. Why wouldn't you? I'm pretty awesome."

She laughed, but he didn't. He just kissed her again. "That you are."

They didn't speak for several minutes. She was content to simply be with him and had even started to fall asleep when he spoke.

"Your eyes… They're still swollen shut, but even once they heal, the doctor isn't sure that you'll have any vision left. Not after what he did."

She nodded, not surprised. "It doesn't matter."

"How can you say that?"

"Because you're here and I see you, Mac. I see all of you. That's all that matters."

CHAPTER THIRTY-THREE

FULLY DRESSED, Mac and Natalie lay on their sides in her big bed. He stared at her, into her beautiful eyes still framed by bruises, evidence of the pain and fear Carter Morrison had put both of them through. Natalie didn't try to hide or turn away. Instead, she let him look. At the same time she caressed his face, using her hands to see everything he was and more.

"Tell me," he whispered. He planted a kiss at one corner of her mouth and then the other, savoring the pillowy softness. She moaned, a deep, needy vibration drawn from the very depths of her, urging him to sprinkle kisses down her slender throat before burying his face in the tender crook of her neck. He inhaled her fragrance, letting it wash over him.

God, he ached. In his skin. In his bones. In every organ of his body, a hollow, painful throbbing that would only be soothed by burying himself in her sweet depths. It had been weeks since he'd had her. Weeks that her body and soul had needed to heal. But in those weeks he'd stayed with her. Learned her. Loved her.

Now he couldn't imagine his life without her.

It still scared him. Made him wonder what he'd do if he ever lost her. But then her hands caressed his hair, then his face again, their touch whisper-soft. She stared blankly but with unerring accuracy into his eyes and gave him the words he needed.

"I love you."

NATALIE'S SENSES were extra sharp. As soon as the words left her mouth, Mac's body tensed. A deep growl rushed from his throat. She braced herself but was still unprepared when his mouth urgently rocked over hers. His tongue didn't ask for entry, it simply took it, breaching her lips with a hard thrust before parrying with her own. Her insides swirled at the warmth and promise he was offering. She opened her mouth, nipping his lower lip with her teeth.

He groaned and she stopped. "I'm sorry—"

"Don't be. Ever." His hands frantically grasped her face and tilted it back. She opened her mouth wider and sank her fingers into his hair. He moaned, seeming overcome by her kisses. A thrill traveled through her. Clinging to his shirt, she dragged her mouth across his jaw.

He pulled back slightly. "You make me lose control." He stroked her hair with a shaky hand. "But this is our first time since… I can be gentle. I can be slow."

She shook her head. She didn't want him to be gentle. Didn't want him to remember that horrible night and the way she'd almost left him. She'd fought against the darkness to be with him, and she'd won. She wasn't fragile. Right now, she felt more powerful than she ever had. And she wanted all of him. "I don't want—"

"Shh. I won't hurt you." He brought his lips back to hers, gossamer soft. "I can't." This time, she took his gentleness for what it was. What he obviously needed to show her. It was like a new beginning. He'd hurt her in the past but wanted her to know she could trust him. She felt his passion in her bones. He licked at her mouth, teasing her with an erotic dance of give-and-take until she was on the verge of screaming. Was he taking care with her, she thought wildly, or deliberately teasing her into a frenzy? He delved deeper with his tongue and she pulled at his shoulders and moaned.

He laughed, a dark, delighted sound, before nipping at her chin. "I can't believe I found you," he said.

The intensity of his words threaded through her like a lifeline. She touched his lips with her fingertips, and her body clenched and dampened. She felt ready to explode, but not yet. She wanted to make this last. To slow things down a little, she tried teasing him. "I'm not too crazy for you?"

In response, he moved over her, between her legs, his erection firm against her core. "Am I too crazy for you?"

An ache she'd never felt filled her. "You're just the right amount of crazy for me." The frustrating barrier of clothing made her insides twist. The longer they stayed like this, the more she doubted she'd ever actually feel her naked body against his. Taste the salt on his skin. Feel him inside her. And she wanted that. It had been too long since she'd held him inside her.

He ratcheted up her impatience when he latched on

to one nipple through her clothing. The hot, firm pressure of his mouth had her biting her lip to stifle her cries of pleasure. Her lids drooped as the heat gathered at her core, in her nipples, where he'd exchanged one peak for the other, and at the base of her neck—in every erogenous zone in her body. She wasn't good enough to fake control.

He unbuttoned her shirt, kissing each bare spot he revealed along the way. "Are you sure about this?"

She nodded, dizzy with her need to have him. Even as she soaked in the pleasure, even as she hugged him tighter and stroked his back and shoulders, she felt an incredible sense of peace. Of rightness. This was all she'd ever wanted. It was more.

"Tell me what you're feeling. Are you scared?"

Swallowing, she stroked his jaw. "A little," she finally confessed.

"Talk to me. Tell me why you're scared."

"I—I'm afraid this is just another dream. I'm afraid to reach out and take what I want. When I have in the past, it's always come back to hurt me. And you don't know how lonely I've been—" Despite her resolve to enjoy this moment, her voice broke. "I'm scared something terrible will happen. What if I'm not strong enough? What if I end up breaking like my mother? What if you regret being with me?"

"Never," he promised. "No matter what happens after this, we'll have each other. I will never regret it. Your arms make me feel whole. Hell, your kiss makes me feel stronger than I've ever felt before."

"You said you didn't want another needy woman," she murmured, only half teasing him.

He froze, kissed her jaw, then lowered his forehead to hers. "You're the least needy woman I know."

A smile tickled the corner of her mouth. "Not true. I need you. You fill a hole inside me I didn't even know was there."

"You don't *need* me. But I'll settle for you wanting me."

"I do. I want you so much. I always will." Suddenly she couldn't stop herself anymore. She sought out his mouth and arched her hips to meet him. He groaned, a sound that filled her with delight. She obviously made him as desperate as he made her.

Cupping her breast, he plumped her flesh, then slipped his finger inside the lace to nuzzle her nipple. She writhed under him, the weight of him like a warm blanket against her. Lifting her head, she sought his mouth again. He shook his head. "Uh-uh."

She jolted. Uh-uh? What the hell— He moved his body down hers, trailing kisses over her arched neck. Over her bra. Over her nipple.

She moaned, pulling at his clothes and fumbling with his buttons. Before she could undo two of them, he'd released the front clasp of her bra and peeled the cups back. His big hands covered her completely, stroking downward to the top of her pants before moving back up to her breasts again. He repeated the soft, long strokes as if he was caressing something miraculous.

"You are so gorgeous." He picked up her hand and

brought it to the hard bulge inside his pants. "I'll die if you don't touch me, Natalie."

They both gasped when she curled her fingers around him. Gently, she stroked him, relishing the way he groaned and arched into her touch. In that moment, she believed him. Felt that with every touch she made him stronger. With her other hand, she tried to undo the rest of his shirt buttons. She fumbled for several moments but finally it was done. "Help me take this off."

She let her hands wander over his chest. He wanted her. He needed her. His body shook with need for her. For a second, regret filled her. She wanted more. She wanted to see all of him. To bare him to her in the same way she was baring her heart and soul to him. But her regret flickered out as her impatience took over.

She unbuttoned his pants and slid the zipper down. "Greedy," he rasped, then hissed when she slipped her hand inside.

She swallowed at the warm weight of him, but then smiled. "Very greedy. I've been waiting over a month for this."

"I wanted you when I first saw your picture, Natalie. It scared the shit out of me. But I'm not scared anymore."

Joy coursed through her even though she knew it was a lie. They both knew it. Outside this room, there was plenty to be scared of. His job. Her disability. It made them more vulnerable to the forces in the world, but they were also more powerful because they had each

other. Here and now, they could shut the door and relish that power.

"I'm not scared either."

In seconds, she was naked, but he still had his pants
on. So much for power. She didn't care. Mac took her
hands and pinned them to the bed next to her head.
She felt drugged, but in a good way. Free to enjoy this
pleasure. "Oh, my God. You're gorgeous all over, but
this—" Holding her wrists with one hand, he raked his
other hand softly through the dark triangle of hair between her legs. "This is paradise."

Heat flushed her cheeks and traveled downward,
staining her pale skin. She strained against his hold,
wiggling back and forth so even her breasts jiggled.
She knew instantly his eyes were on her. Like a bee
drawn to honey, his mouth lowered, kissing the tight
nipple before licking it and sucking it into the warmth
of his mouth.

Natalie hissed, every nerve in her body tingling.
"Oh, God, Mac."

He raised his head and blew on her wet nipple. She
arched up, wanting him to take her other bare breast.
"Please. Oh, please."

He cupped the breast he'd just kissed, rolling the nipple between his thumb and forefinger while he brought
his mouth to her other breast. His free hand trailed down
her side, pulling her leg up and around his waist while
his hips ground into her.

"Maybe you should try this without clothes," she said

coyly. If he didn't take his pants off, she was going to rip them off of him.

"Patience, baby." He released her nipple with a lingering swipe of his tongue and then trailed kisses up her neck to her ear. He flicked her lobe with his tongue before biting down gently. Then he dropped his hand back to "paradise." "You're incredible. I want to taste all of you."

She couldn't think of anything she wanted more than Mac's face pressed into the damp warmth between her legs. She slowly relaxed her thighs, pulling a groan of anticipation from him. He lowered his mouth back to hers as he inserted his hand between them, letting his palm skim her belly, her hip, her thigh. Finally, his fingers searched through her sensitive folds until he found her clit. He kissed his way down her body, slowly, torturously licking and kissing her breasts, then her belly, her hip. He blew on her tender flesh, making her squirm. "I'm very gentle when exploring holy territory," he murmured. With excruciating patience, he pushed her thighs apart and settled between them. "Gentle, but extremely thorough." His fingers separated her as he licked up her cleft with a firm, gentle stroke before swirling around her clit. She arched against him, letting him delve deeper.

She grasped his hair tighter, pushing against him, but he wouldn't be rushed. He licked and kissed, alternating between soft and hard until she was mewling with frustration. Then he worked a finger inside her. Her hips bucked, his fingers and tongue dragging against her swollen nerves. He pushed her further and further until she lost control. Her body shook, a tremor building within her until it burst into an explosion.

Helpless to move, she could do nothing but catch her breath. Then she suddenly realized he'd been doing all the work. She wanted to push him back and caress him from head to toe, appreciating every hard muscle and plane of flesh along the way. She rose up and reached out, but he shook his head.

"Later," he said, taking her hands and once more pinning them to her sides.

"But I want—"

With one thrust, he was inside her. No hesitation. No fumbling. Just a smooth, deep connection that robbed her of breath and brought tears to her eyes.

Finally. Finally he was hers again.

His chest heaved, his eyes closed. "I'm sorry, baby. I wanted to make you come some more. I wanted to make you come so hard. But I don't think I can wait."

She arched again, a silent message of wanting. Of invitation. And that's all it took.

With a hoarse shout, he let go. Began pumping into her in a hard driving rhythm. Incredibly, she felt herself hurtling toward orgasm once more.

Determined to take him with her, she wrapped her arm around his neck and pulled herself up toward him. His hips jerked. Quickened. She felt him expand inside her and squeezed her inner muscles tight, hugging him to her, bringing them as close together as possible. His

moan started low in his throat, growing until it burst
out with a low cry.

He grabbed her hips, arching her into him, heightening her pleasure until with one more powerful thrust,
they came together. And as they did, they each pulled
back their heads, and she let him see her for all she was.

A woman. A normal woman who happened to be
blind.

A normal woman who was his.

MAC DIDN'T MOVE. He couldn't. He was blown away by
the tremors still coursing through his body, almost as if
he was caught in an unstoppable orgasm. He arched into
her, moaning as the pleasure peaked again. This had
never happened before. He was still hard. She squeezed
him with her thighs as if she would never let him go.
His eyes rolled to the back of his head.

He kept pumping. Slow and steady. Her mouth
opened on a silent moan, and he caressed her face. He
didn't want this time to end. He could tell by her expression, by her touch, neither did she.

He stared into her eyes until his vision blurred. His
muscles tightened. His body shook. But he held on, not
wanting to go over the edge by himself. Now that he'd
felt her come against him, he wanted to savor the sensation again and again.

He went slow, so she had no choice but to feel everything. The smooth tickle of his hair against her thighs
and stomach. The subtle texture of his facial stubble
against her wet folds. And his dick. Filling her up, hit-

ting that one precious spot inside her that made her moan louder.

He was inside her. A part of her. Locked forever in her heart. She'd never be able to rid herself of him now, even if she wanted to.

He stopped his thrusts and gently pushed her thighs out and back until her legs were folded in on her. She gasped and grabbed his forearms. "Mac!"

"I want to look." He withdrew almost completely from her, then slowly sank back in. "We look so good together, Natalie." Their moans mingled together. Out and then in. Out and in. He repeated several thrusts with the same slow drag, gritting his teeth against the pleasure threatening to make his head explode.

Her nails dug into her arms just before she fell back. Her legs quivered. He moved harder. Tore his eyes away from their joined bodies to watch her face. With a high cry, she came again. His thrusts grew faster and faster until he was pounding into her.

With a rough bark of passion, he emptied himself into her slick warmth.

His breath bellowed in and out of his chest, and he lowered his forehead on hers. All he could think was… Natalie. She was his.

He felt reborn. Saved. The sins and regrets of the past shattered.

He tightened his arms around her and pulled out, amazed he was still hard. But he ignored his body's hunger for more and sank into her, letting out a shaky sigh when she threaded her fingers through his hair. Drowsily, he closed his eyes.

"I love you so much. I want to stay here forever," he whispered. "I've never wanted anyone more than I want you."

Her hand stilled. "I know exactly how you feel."

They kissed, their mouths mating with a gentle thoroughness that filled him with contentment. His eyelids grew heavy. He felt something shift inside him, clicking into place as if all these years a piece of him had been broken, and he hadn't even known it.

Natalie fixed it. With her strength. With her gentleness. With her unwavering goodness.

She made him strong enough to do anything.

She made him brave enough to turn away from fear and death and simply…love.

* * * * *

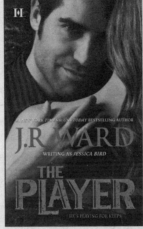

PAMELA CALLOW

When a body is found on the outskirts of Halifax, rumors run wild about the victim's identity. But tattoo artist Kenzie Sloane knows *exactly* who she is. They share a tattoo...and a decade-old secret.

Lawyer Kate Lange remembers Kenzie Sloane. The former wild child was part of the same crowd that attracted her little sister, Imogen, before her death. Now Kenzie needs Kate's help. And Kate needs answers.

But there are others who know about the tattoo and its history. And one of them is watching Kenzie's every move, waiting for the perfect moment to fulfill a dark promise that had been inked in her skin.

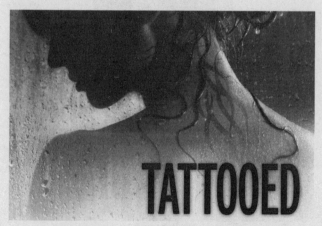

TATTOOED

Available wherever books are sold.

MIRA | HARLEQUIN®

www.Harlequin.com

MPC1302R

REQUEST YOUR FREE BOOKS!

2 FREE NOVELS
FROM THE SUSPENSE COLLECTION
PLUS 2 FREE GIFTS!

YES! Please send me 2 FREE novels from the Suspense Collection and my 2 FREE gifts (gifts are worth about $10). After receiving them, if I don't wish to receive any more books, I can return the shipping statement marked "cancel." If I don't cancel, I will receive 4 brand-new novels every month and be billed just $5.99 per book in the U.S. or $6.49 per book in Canada. That's a saving of at least 25% off the cover price. It's quite a bargain! Shipping and handling is just 50¢ per book in the U.S. and 75¢ per book in Canada.* I understand that accepting the 2 free books and gifts places me under no obligation to buy anything. I can always return a shipment and cancel at any time. Even if I never buy another book, the two free books and gifts are mine to keep forever.

191/391 MDN FEME

Name	(PLEASE PRINT)

Address	Apt. #

City	State/Prov.	Zip/Postal Code

Signature (if under 18, a parent or guardian must sign)

Mail to the **Reader Service:**
IN U.S.A.: P.O. Box 1867, Buffalo, NY 14240-1867
IN CANADA: P.O. Box 609, Fort Erie, Ontario L2A 5X3

Not valid for current subscribers to the Suspense Collection
or the Romance/Suspense Collection.

Want to try two free books from another line?
Call 1-800-873-8635 or visit www.ReaderService.com.

* Terms and prices subject to change without notice. Prices do not include applicable taxes. Sales tax applicable in N.Y. Canadian residents will be charged applicable taxes. Offer not valid in Quebec. This offer is limited to one order per household. All orders subject to credit approval. Credit or debit balances in a customer's account(s) may be offset by any other outstanding balance owed by or to the customer. Please allow 4 to 6 weeks for delivery. Offer available while quantities last.

Your Privacy—The Reader Service is committed to protecting your privacy. Our Privacy Policy is available online at www.ReaderService.com or upon request from the Reader Service.

We make a portion of our mailing list available to reputable third parties that offer products we believe may interest you. If you prefer that we not exchange your name with third parties, or if you wish to clarify or modify your communication preferences, please visit us at www.ReaderService.com/consumerschoice or write to us at Reader Service Preference Service, P.O. Box 9062, Buffalo, NY 14269. Include your complete name and address.

Coming home may be more dangerous than she thinks....

A new story of tradition, love and danger from

MARTA PERRY

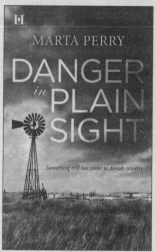

Libby Morgan never wanted to return to Lancaster County. She'd made her own life in the city as a news photographer, leaving the slow pace of Amish country behind. She'd left love behind, too, when she fled the old-fashioned ways of Adam Byler. But when a friend in trouble beckons, Libby knows she has no choice but to return. What she doesn't know is that something sinister awaits her....

DANGER *in* PLAIN SIGHT

Coming in June 2012!